# BELLE'S DILEMMA

## JO DONAHUE

Belle's Dilemma
Jo Donahue

This book is a work of fiction. Any references to real places, the characters, events, and scenes are either products of the author's imagination or are used fictitiously.

Copyright © 2021

Paperback ISBN: 979-8-5203699-2-9
Ebook ISBN: 978-1-7375473-0-3

*To my family, who never lost faith in me, my parents Doretha and Woodrow Donahue, and my children Ron, Kelly, and John Grummer, and Ikaika Apuna. May they always be as happy as they made me.*

*To Chuck Mann, for making me want to prove him wrong.*

# CHAPTER 1

Watching the pheasant leave the ground, Belle Stoval took careful aim and squeezed the trigger slowly. A wave of excitement came over her as she watched a flurry of feathers fall to the ground. Belle ran to pick up her prize, adding the pheasant to the others shot that morning. Gathering her things, she headed back down the dirt path to town. Stopping at the edge of the woods, Belle stared at the familiar scene. The small church with the tall steeple provided a sense of comfort.

Belle stopped at the gate of the wooden clapboard home of her friend Mary. As she passed through the gate, she noticed the well-cared for flower beds and window boxes welcoming her. Rapping twice, then opening the door, Belle heard the cook beyond the hall humming outside in the back. Taking the pheasants into Mary's kitchen, she sat them in a tub at the end of a work counter.

"Sally," looking out the kitchen door, "are you here?"

As Belle looked around, she saw Sally had started a kettle of soup, and the smells were delicious, reminding her she had not eaten since breakfast. The window curtains were tied with blue ribbons. At that moment, a large woman with an apron over her full blue-flowered dress came through the back kitchen door.

"Miss Belle!" she exclaimed as she walked to the tub. "What did you bring us today?" Sally looked into the tub. "Those are nice-looking birds. I expect I should get them cleaned before you change your mind. You are getting better and better with that gun." Rolling her eyes, she continued. "Better than the boys around here."

Taking the pheasants out of the tub, Sally went outside to an old, weathered bench and started heating water on the open fire pit to clean the birds, humming as she went.

"Tell Mary to come over when she gets home," Belle said, smiling. "I want to talk to her about the big dance on Saturday. I have got to get cleaned up before Aunt Hester gets home. You know how she is about my hunting."

Laughing, Sally watched Belle walk away towards town.

"If Miss Harriet Hester saw that girl in her brother's clothes again, I am sure she would have a lot to say." Laughing gently, the elderly cook continued cleaning the birds for their dinner.

Belle hurried home to change her clothes and start dinner before Aunt Hester came home from her shop. She had just finished the vegetables when Hester opened the front door.

"Belle, are you home?" She took a deep breath. "Something smells wonderful. What are you cooking?"

"It's almost ready, Aunt Hester." Belle stirred the pan. "We have the leftover ham with some Johnny cakes. Oh, I also picked some beets out of the garden. To top it off, I made a toffee cake to go with our tea." Wiping her hands on her apron, Belle started setting the table. "I hope you don't mind. I invited Mary over to talk about the dance on Saturday night."

"I hope Mary can talk you into wearing something fetching. Not that blue dress you seem to like so much." Looking towards the ceiling, Hester continued. "You will never get a man if you don't at least try a little. Mary always dresses so pretty and looks like an angel." Turning back to Belle, "I forgot, I have a shipment of trinkets for the new hats coming in tomorrow, so I have to work on the displays and the books a little this evening. You girls have fun, and don't forget to lock up before you go to bed."

Later, as Belle was cleaning the kitchen, she heard Mary at the door. Mary swept through the door in a blue-gray dress with white collars and trimmed around the sleeve.

"Belle, I got your message. Mother has a lady's church meeting this evening, so she dropped me off and will pick me up in a couple of hours. Let's look at your dresses. I am sure that I can help you gussy up something nice."

Sweeping up the staircase, with Belle close behind, Mary carried her sewing basket ready to work.

"Mary, you are always so happy about these kinds of things. I hate going to parties, dances, and all the social stuff. Especially when Aunt Hester knows this will be the magical dance where I meet 'the one.' The one dance where I will meet the man of my dreams."

Sighing, Belle walked into her room. Looking around, it was a typical girl's room—pale pink roses on the wallpaper, with white trim around the door and windows. Belle's desk sat in front of the window where the sheer curtains moved in the gentle breeze, cooling off the day's heat. Mary sat in the chair in front of the dressing table, looking at the perfume bottles, touching her hair as she looked into the mirror.

"Belle, I know you don't like this kind of thing. I have never wanted to meet men. I have Phillip. I will always love Phillip."

Smiling, Mary held her locket close to her lips.

"Mary, you have been in love with Phillip since you were

two years old, it seems. Haven't you ever once seen a man that made you forget about Phillip? Oh, I know he's steadfast, loyal, and all the other attributes of a hound dog, but is that enough?" Turning towards the window, Belle raised the edge of the curtain and looked down the street. "Just once, I wish I could meet a guy that interests me enough to make me want to like them. The boys around here are just boys. They aren't men. I swear, Mary, I just don't want to keep doing this. I miss Jeremy so much. He would understand how I feel. I think Aunt Hester just wants to get rid of me. After all, it can't be easy to be single, then have someone else to be responsible for. How do I handle this?"

Crossing the room to give her friend sympathy, Mary hugged Belle.

"Belle, you have to face it. Jeremy is a brilliant brother. Any girl would have counted herself lucky to have him as a brother, but he's gone to make his way in the world. Besides, if Jeremy were here, he would act like a brother; none of these boys could get five feet around you. Then you would meet no one. You must have patience, Belle. If I know Jeremy, he will be back home and ready to settle down," she laughed and continued. "Patience has never been your strong point." Taking Belle's hand, she led her to the wardrobe. "Now, let's see what we can do with your dresses."

Pulling out a light-yellow dress, Mary held it under the light.

"I think this will be just fine." Holding the dress up against Belle, she measured from the waist to the high neck collar. "Try this one. I have an idea." Mary had her scissors in her hand. She cut a scoop neck out of the dress's high neckline and cut the sleeves, leaving the sleeve cap near the neckline. Holding a lace trim near the scoop neck, she basted it to the front to see how it looked. Standing in front of the mirror, Belle saw the difference immediately. Belle took off the dress and gave it to Mary. She glanced out the window.

"Mary, I think I see your mother coming. Just take the dress and do whatever you want with it. You always make everything look great." Sighing, she looked down towards the floor. "I don't want to go to the dance, but I have to, I guess."

Later after Mary left, Hester called Belle into the sitting room. She began pacing as she spoke.

"Belle, your attitude is upsetting me. Ms. Jenkins said she saw you coming out of the woods in your brother's clothes again, carrying a bunch of pheasants. You know how I feel about this crazy notion you have about hunting. What are you going to do with your life? It would help if you thought of finding a husband and settling down." Hester started pacing in front of the fireplace. "No man wants a woman who dresses like him or tries to act like him. Men like women who act and dress like a woman. They want you to depend on them, take care of them. Most girls your age already met the men of their dreams. You don't want to spend your life as a spinster, do you?"

Belle rolled her eyes.

"Hester, I don't want to get married, just to get married. When the right man comes along, I will know it, and then I will take the plunge. Every time a dance happens, we go through this. Give me some room to make my decisions. It's not as if I need the money or need to decide right away. I promise I will consider your wants. Let me enjoy my life while I can."

Standing, Belle looked towards the door. Hester moved in front of her.

"You can't run away every time I bring up this subject. This dance will allow you to see different prospective suitors. At least promise me you will at least consider them." Belle passed her and went up the stairs to her room.

"It's always the same, Aunt Hester. Please let me be the one to decide, not you."

Closing the door gently, Belle gave an exasperated sigh and went to bed. As she laid deep into the featherbed, looking at the ceiling, Belle's thoughts kept her awake. *How can I make Aunt Hester realize I have to decide for myself who I live the rest of my life with, not just marry for security? I want the love I see with Mary and Phillip. They have a genuine love and see each other as partners in life. I wish Jeremy was here. He would help me show her what I need.* Gentle tears flowed down her cheeks as she fell asleep, dreaming of a man she had never seen.

As Belle came down the steps to greet Mary on Saturday night, Hester stood and looking amazed at the transformation of Belle. Mary had finished the dress, and it fit Belle beautifully. The dress was pale-yellow with dainty lace and tiny yellow rosebuds around the scoop neckline and had the same miniature roses around the bottom of sheer organza. Mary's addition to the dress's skirt made Belle's waist look small, and it swirled around her legs when she walked. The coloring enhanced Belle's lightly tanned skin, and her curly red hair shined in the lamp's light. Mary draped Belle's hair off her shoulders into a loose bun with small curls pinned close to her face. She took several matching yellow rosebuds and pinned them throughout her hair.

"Belle, I would have never known you if you hadn't come down those stairs," whispered Hester as she moved towards Belle. "Mary, you are truly a genius with a needle. The added ruffles of the petticoats make Belle look so petite and beautiful. Thank you."

Belle, not sure she wanted all this attention, turned to leave with Mary.

Hester continued. "The way Mary did your hair, well, I don't know how she tamed all those curls. You look absolutely stunning." Turning towards Mary, Hester took her hand. "Mary, thank you. You have made me happy. Keep her close until I get there. I need to stop by the store."

As the girls were walking towards the buggy, Belle felt pretty in the dress, but it also made her uneasy. She did not like being in the limelight. Belle wanted to be roaming the woods, hunting, or any place other than at this dance.

# CHAPTER 2

As they arrived at the Tunisian home where the dance was being held, lights glowed from every window. They could hear the music coming from the ballroom. The doorman took their wraps and announced them as they entered the room. The music and merriment of the guests gave air to fun and light heartiness. Mary and Belle slowly looked around the room. There were a good deal of townspeople there they already knew, but there were also strangers. The dancers passed by them in a swirl of colors as the music played a familiar waltz.

"Look, Belle." Mary pointed to a woman dressed in a long pink floral dress. "There is the hostess. We must say hello. Then we can join the others."

Two gentlemen approached them to add their names to the girls' dance cards as they left the hostess. As Belle looked across the room, her eyes landed on a tall, blonde man. He was talking to another girl, but his eyes connected with Belle as he spoke. Turning to face Mary, she ignored his stare. Stopping mid-sentence, he excused himself and walked towards Belle. Mary started grinning.

"Well, here comes the first one. Be prepared, Belle. This dance is going to be an interesting night."

Belle turned to see what Mary was talking about. Coming towards her was the tall blonde man she saw across the room. Noticeably confident of his looks, he kept his eyes focused directly on Belle until he reached her. Bowing slightly, he reached for her hand. Taking her dance card, he carefully added his name in several of the places.

"I see my first dance with you will be number three. Until then." He kissed her hand and left.

Belle and Mary looked at each other. Mary spoke first.

"Who is that man? First time I have ever seen a man kiss a woman's hand before." Turning to Belle, Mary could see a faraway look in her eyes.

"I have never seen him before, but I am sure I will get to know him before the night is through." She looked at her card. "He signed for three dances. I think that is a little forward, don't you think?" Before Mary could answer, several other men surrounded the two ladies to complete their cards.

Belle and Mary stood by the buffet table as their dance cards filled, putting small amounts of food on their plates. Taking them to the sidelines, they found chairs so they could listen to the music before the actual dance cards started. Belle and Mary watched the other girls surrounded by men while their cards filled. The blonde man marked cards and tentatively smiled at each girl. Mary, suspicious of his behavior, spoke to Belle.

"I'm not sure I would like that man. There is something about him that sets off my internal alarms."

Belle watched him as he went around the room, bowing to the girls and taking special notice of the mothers who sat around the room.

"I know what you mean, but it is not as if we are targeting him as a marriage partner. He's just a man at a dance to pass the time with. I am always careful when I notice a man is too friendly, which fits the bill. Surely women don't fall for all that charm?"

As Belle and Mary danced with various partners, Mary was sure the blonde man was interested in Belle. His eyes followed her around the dance floor, even as she danced with her other partners. When their turn came, he held her possessively, causing her to back away.

"If you don't mind," Belle said quietly, "I dislike being held that close."

Looking at her closely, he laughed and danced a little further away than before.

"I have not introduced myself. I am Tomas Cavelier, and I am from California." Looking across the room at one of her friends, he nodded in that direction. "I am staying with my cousin but heading back to California at the end of the week. I wished we had met sooner. I think you are by far the prettiest girl in the room."

Blushing, and without knowing how to answer to this, Belle remained silent.

"I'm sorry. I came on too strong for the first time we have met. Please don't judge me too harshly. I just have met no one like you before. Just relax, and we will enjoy tonight."

Without saying anymore, he danced with her until the music stopped, and it was time to change partners again. At the end of the following dance, the orchestra broke for a break. Joining Mary at the punch bowl, they filled their cups and retired to the sidelines to rest.

Not drinking, just holding the cup, Belle turned to Mary.

"Maybe I am overreacting, but Tomas comes on a little fast for a stranger. I am not used to that kind of man, no matter how good-looking. He said he was going back to California, so at least I only must be near him tonight. I wonder if he knows Jeremy?"

Tilting her head to one side, Mary looked thoughtful.

"I don't know, Belle, I heard California is extensive. If he does know Jeremy, it will surprise me."

Mary's next dancing partner came to claim her for his dance. As she left, Belle watched Mary. Her green ball gown suited her. It was narrow and long, tucked neatly under her bosom with tiny lace around the empire-type bodice. The sleeves were to her elbow, and she wore matching gloves. *She is beautiful. Too bad Phillip couldn't be here to see her.* Standing to greet her old friend George, who had the next dance, they twirled onto the floor. Belle had two more dances with Tomas, who proved to be quite charming and kept his distance. Unlike before.

"Miss Belle, you seem quiet. Is this normal for you? Most women want to talk your head off." Pulling back, Tomas looked at the beautiful girl in his arms. "How about a turn around the garden? After all, I am leaving soon. I don't know when we will have another chance."

Tilting her head upwards, "No, I don't think so. I hardly know you. Besides, I have things to do tomorrow," replied Belle demurely.

"Belle, I want to get to know you better. If I could think of an excuse, I would stay here and court you properly. Is it okay if I call on you? I think we have a future together," he whispered.

She stepped back with her hands on her hips.

"Tomas, I do not think there is a future for us. I hardly know you. Rushing me will not win me over. It won't work. I can't stop you from writing, but I am not sure I want to answer. Thank you for the dance."

Belle turned abruptly, leaving him standing on the dance floor. Watching her leave the dance floor, he rubbed his chin. *That girl has a spirit. It will be fun to tame her.*

On the way home, Mary joined Belle and Hester to talk

about the dance. Tomas did not impress Hester. Especially when she saw Belle abruptly walk off the dance floor.

"Belle, what did he say to you to make you act so rudely?" Hester inquired.

"Let's say he was not my type and leave it at that. Aunt Hester, I would like to have sworn at him, but decided he would look more like the fool he was if I just left him standing there. Definitely not on my list of favorites."

Looking carefully at Belle, Hester changed her tactics.

"The banker's son looked interested in you, Belle. You should be more kind to him. Think about the husband he would make for some lucky girl? He has a good job at the bank, money in savings, and a grand future. Some lucky girl will turn his head if you don't wise up."

Smiling at Mary, Belle just listened to Hester without saying a word. After leaving Mary at her home, Belle hurried to her room. Carefully hanging her dress up, she suddenly felt tired and was glad to go to bed. As she laid there, she appreciated the dress Mary had remade for her. Mary had a natural talent. The gown is lovely. With that thought, Belle quickly went to sleep without the thought of the blonde man.

# CHAPTER 3

The next few weeks were busy for Hester and Belle. Spring started with the first jonquils blooming, making the townswomen think about new dresses and Sunday clothes. And those thoughts led to hats. Day after day, Belle and Hester worked in the millinery shop, creating hats to match the townswomen's dresses for their Sunday best. Two local girls were planning their weddings in the middle of those orders, which meant hats for the wedding party. Even though the work was tedious, Belle thought it was fun. She watched Hester and learned how to make roses and rosettes, and how to shape the various hat forms. Fashioning hats was one job that Belle loved best. However, her most favorite part of the job was watching the women's faces when they tried the hats and discovered how to enhance their dresses. Each hat perfectly matched and made the women proud. Belle and Hester often ate lightly at the end of the long day and were glad to go to bed. Belle had forgotten about the unsettling blonde man from the dance.

Tomas had tried several times to call on her, even stopping by the millinery shop. Each time, Belle told him she was too busy. Each time he left his card and a note. As Belle read the notes, she tossed them in the trash. Later, her aunt would read the notes and shake her head.

However, the banker's son had not forgotten her either, as they had known each other from school. He showed up when she went to the general store for supplies or church.

She told Mary, "It's not that he is ugly or has a wort on his nose. He's a nice guy. I am not ready to settle down, nor do I want to get married. I feel there is so much of a world out there, and I want to see some of it. I would like to find my brother, but most of all, when I am ready, I want to find a man who accepts who I am and how I am. Not to marry me and become his slave. That's not my cup of tea."

They would laugh at the thoughts of a man accepting a girl who liked to hunt, wear pants, and make hats. Where would she find a man like that?

Mary lived with her mother, three stepbrothers, and Sally, the cook, who had been with her since birth. It wasn't always a happy household, but she loved her mother and would not leave her. Mary's stepfather had died the year before, leaving her mother sad and unable to recover from his death. Mary's mother had inherited monies from her family in England, which she planned to entrust to Mary. When the boys' father had died, it astounded them that their father had not taken over Mary's mother's estate. That was the right of the man when they married. It was unheard of a woman owning anything. Over time, they became ruder and more obnoxious to Mary, until she told her mother. Understanding their views, she gave them some money and asked them to leave. Later, Mary's mother bought them a few acres on the other side of town and explained there would be no more money. They needed to learn to earn their keep.

Phillip had been Mary's boyfriend since she was in the second grade. He was tall and had light brown hair that faded to blonde in the summer sun. Every time Mary saw him, she had chill bumps and couldn't quit smiling. Watching them together, Belle could see he felt the same about Mary. As they became older, Phillip asked Mary for her hand in marriage, but with a clause.

"Mary, I want to take care of you and give you everything you need or want. So, I have something to tell you. I heard the gold rush has changed everything in California. I want to go out there and set up a general store just like Pa did here in Maryville. When I have it set up, I will send for you. I promise, for I love you and can't imagine a life without you."

A few weeks later, he said goodbye and left. It devastated Mary. However, she wrote every day and mailed the letters in one packet at the end of each week. Phillip wrote to her also, mailing the letters at the end of the week. They never failed in their faithfulness to each other.

At the end of summer, Mary's mother fell sick. Belle came to see them often, bringing soup and flowers. She prayed with Mary for her recovery. One day Sally rushed to Belle's house to have her go quickly to help Mary while she ran for the doctor. As she crossed the threshold, Belle heard Mary quietly sobbing in the bedroom.

"Mary, are you okay?" She opened the door and rushed to Mary's side, hugging Mary in her grief.

Walking to a side cupboard in the room, Mary took out a large envelope and handed it to Belle.

"I want you to take this and hide it until I ask for it. When my stepbrothers find out about my mother, I fear of what they will try to do." Hiding the envelope in her coat, she sat down to wait with Mary for the doctor's arrival. As they sat, Mary's mother held Mary's hand until she slowly let go and left them. With tears flowing down her cheeks, Mary turned to Belle with sadness. "She told me to stay with you if you will have me until I have the estate settled. She had everything planned. Oh, Belle, what am I going to do?" Belle just held her and let Mary cry, trying her best to comfort her friend, but seeing it would take more than the comfort of a friend to make things right. That evening, Belle came to stay with Mary, as Belle's house was small, and it made more sense for Mary to be with things that comforted her at a time of sorrow.

Staying with Mary through the week, Belle knew how important it was for Mary to have company. After several nights, Belle awakened suddenly to whispering and soft talking. Hearing a thump, she thought Mary must be up. Belle pulled on her robe and went down the stairs, thinking to provide company for Mary. When she reached the bottom, she saw Mary's stepbrother rummaging through the desk. Looking through the doorway, it was evident the stepbrothers were looking for something. There were books and papers laying on the floor. Picking up an umbrella out of the stand by the door, she entered the room.

"What do you think you are doing? You have no right in here! Get out! Stop at once and get out."

The three brothers stopped and looked surprised. They moved towards her menacingly, but stopped when they saw she had an umbrella in her hand.

"Do you honestly think you can handle us with an umbrella?"

They laughed and moved towards Belle.

"Well, maybe this will make you leave."

As their eyes looked upwards to the top of the stairs, they saw Mary and Sally, both with shotguns pointed at them.

Mary continued down the stairs with the gun pointed at the older brother.

"If you are looking for the estate papers or wills, I already filed them at the courthouse. The trustee has copies, so does the lawyer. You were too late. Now get your backsides out of my house."

They drifted towards the door.

"Mary, we only want what should be ours. Our dad was too easy on your mother. She should have turned her money over to him. We want our share. We'll be back, and we'll take what should be ours."

One by one, carefully backing out the door, they left.

Waiting until they heard the horses drum off, Mary and Sally ran down the stairs, hugging Belle.

"Belle, what did you think you were doing? You should have awakened us, not faced them alone! They are wicked."

Sitting on the settee, looking at the surrounding mess, Mary closed her eyes. Tears fell down her cheeks.

"Belle, I have turned everything over to the trust company. They will keep it safe. I want you to hang on to the papers I gave you until I can send for them. Aunt Della is coming tomorrow on the afternoon stage to help me settle everything. I made a lot of decisions, Belle. I think you need to know. I am so fortunate. Mother left detailed instructions to help guide me in making the tough decisions."

Rising, she held Belle's hand.

"I think I want to join Phillip. I know we planned to wait for a couple of years, but I don't want to be alone. Sally and I have talked; she will go to the farm. I must see that Sally's future is secure. I owe her so much. More than the salary she gets."

Sally walked back into the room.

"Miss Mary, I spoke with the tenant farmer. He told me

what you arranged with him. Are you sure you want me to stay here in Maryville? I could go with you."

Taking Sally's hand, Mary looked lovingly at the woman who had been with her throughout her life.

"Sally, you have grandchildren. You need to stay here so you can be with them. I have set up your retirement with the trustee. You can live here until I come back, if I come back. Just take care of it."

Mary looked around at the mess.

"Belle, surely you understand. I can't stay here, as I will have to deal with my thieving brothers all the time. Surely you understand."

Mary turned away from Belle to face Sally and looked sadly at her.

"Oh Sally, the trustee will send you a monthly payment for keeping up the house and so that you don't have to worry about living expenses. And Belle, I've decided. I am going."

Not knowing what to say, Belle led Mary back upstairs. When they reached the landing at the top, Belle looked at Mary and brushed her hair out of her eyes.

"Mary, I know this is hard. I wanted to run away when my mother died, but I also knew I had to grow up a little to know what I wanted. It has not been easy. Get some sleep, and we will talk tomorrow. Is Sally coming?"

"No, she wants to sleep downstairs with the gun. I don't think they will be back tonight, but Sally insisted. Thank you for being here."

Mary kissed Belle's cheek and turned to go into her room. As Belle watched her friend go, a plan was developing in her mind. Leaving here. Maybe that's what I need. She smiled as she returned to her room.

# CHAPTER 4

Mary's aunt Della arrived the following day from St. Louis. Greeting the girls as she stepped out of the carriage, she hugged Mary for a long time. Belle could see the tears gently flowing down both of their cheeks as they tried to comfort each other.

"My sister was proud of you, Mary. She knew that this would be rough. Now, what are those no-account step-brothers of yours up to since this has happened?" Lifting Mary's chin, "I am here to take care of that mess."

Turning, she had the driver carry her bags into the home.

"Belle, thank you for helping my niece. She is lucky to have you as a friend."

Later, sitting at the parlor desk, Mary gave her all the trust papers and documents to read.

"Aunt Della, I want you to understand. I have made some decisions that are important to me."

Watching her niece closely, she saw the determination in her eyes and the stiffness of her shoulders as she explained.

"Mary, wait a few minutes. I just got here and need a little time to read everything, and then we will talk about your future. Is that okay? Your trustee is the same one that serves both mine and your mother's estate. I want to be clear when we meet tomorrow. He will be here in the afternoon. I am sure we will have time to talk before he arrives."

Sally brought a tray of small plates of food and tea for them as Della started going through the paperwork.

"Mary, what about the papers you gave me? Now that Della is here, do you want them back?"

"No, those are the originals. Della can go over the unsigned copies."

Leaving them to work, Belle walked into town and found her Aunt Hester hard at work in the millinery shop.

"Can I help?" Looking around the shop, she could see there were several orders all ready to be made.

"That would be great. I am suddenly behind. I gathered the colors for each order together in the different bags, so just grab a bag and get started."

As Belle put the materials on her work desk, she marveled at the many colors in the bag.

"What is this occasion? There are so many colors."

Looking at the sketch, Belle started working.

"I learned a long time ago, when a woman visualizes, we can only try to take that vision and make it work."

Picking up a sketch of a multicolored hat, Belle looked at her aunt.

"However, in that case, all I can say is good luck. This lady's vision is a merry-go-round of colors."

Putting down her work on the table, Hester turned to Belle.

"I am glad you are here. I need to make a bank deposit. Can you look after things for a little while?"

As Hester left, she turned to look back at the shop. It was small, but the light tan color of the shop contrasted with the dark brown trim. It had a large glass window with displays of many types of hats. She had fancy hats for special occasions, everyday hats that were well designed but more sedated in looks. Hester had recently added a new hat line for "everyday chores," with wide brims for working in the garden and walking. She was proud of her shop and hoped someday she would become independent instead of constantly feeling stressed from borrowing money from Belle's estate. Hester had kept it a secret, Belle had an estate. She faithfully gave Belle money each month, pretending it was from working in the shop. As she entered the bank, she deposited money in the business account. A part of the deposit went into a separate account to pay back her loan. The banker met her at the door.

"Hester, how are you and Belle doing? I see you are making regular deposits, but Belle doesn't have to pay back the money; after all, it is hers."

Looking sideways and fidgeting with her bag, Hester winked at the banker.

"This is how we want to do it. I would appreciate it if you didn't discuss it with anyone. Belle wants to have money for her dowry when she gets married, so we keep her finances quiet. After all, we don't want any fortune hunters, do we?"

Smiling nervously, hating to lie, she left the bank. Hurrying back to the shop, she didn't want Belle to suspect anything. As she reached the shop, she could see Belle working hard on the decorations from her sketch. *Only a little while longer before I can put back the money in her account before she is aware.*

Three men sat around a fire near a river outside of Maryville. As he poured a cup of coffee from the pot resting on the coals of the fire, Marcus's hand shook. The rough-looking men had been on the cattle trail for several days. They were hot and dusty from driving cows. One man looked towards the man standing.

"Marcus, I don't think this is a good plan. Mary is stubborn. Ever since Phillip left, all she talks about is when they get married. Besides, she is never without Belle or Sally. Now that Aunt Della is here, we will have a hard time catching her alone. That housekeeper is scary. I saw her and that Della person going in and out of the bank several times yesterday. How is our plan going to work?"

Setting his cup on the ground, Marcus looked at his two brothers.

"You are sniveling cowards! Of course it will work. Once I convince Mary to marry me, she will realize she has a real man, not the goody-two-shoes Phillip. After all, Phillip is a long way from here."

He looked into the fire.

"She can't be with her guards forever. We just need to stick to the plan and keep a close watch on her. We need to set up a surveillance, and the minute one of you sees her trunk leave the house, we can set the plan into action. I feel that her first action will be to try to go to this Phillip guy."

The youngest looking of the three men, Charley, stood up and stretched. He was a thin, wiry guy, dusty, with a thick, messy beard. Spitting on the ground, he turned to look at his brothers.

"I think we need to forget about this plan. Mary offered us some land, and she gave us money to buy some cows. It would be better to take it and build our own lives, not worry about Mary. Somehow this plan doesn't seem right."

Marcus, quickly rising, punched him in the face. Charley stepped back, holding his bloodied nose.

Marcus continued, "I am in control here, and don't forget it. I want all the money, not a handout. It should have been ours, and I am going to make sure we have it. If you want out, then you leave with nothing. Take your choice."

The third brother, Bob, stepped between the two.

"The plan is no good without all of us. Pa was weak around Mary's mother. I never understood it. However, we have a plan, and we will all go with it. No more fighting. Mary must pay the price for her mother being selfish, and we will take what should be rightfully ours."

Walking towards his horse, he mounted and looked at his brothers.

"I will take the first watch. Settle your differences and then get busy. We have work to do."

Entering town, Bob settled down under a tree in the park down from Mary's house. From his angle, he could see the house and the activity of the front door. Staking his horse so it could eat the surrounding grass, he settled down, watching.

After a long day in the millinery shop, Belle went home and changed her clothes. On her way over to Mary's, she decided to take a shortcut. She saw the brother in the park but decided not to let him know she saw him. Slowing her steps, Belle strolled down the path. Stopping at the gate to smell the flowers over the fence, she glanced back, then stopped to pick a few of the flowers to take into the house. Knocking on the door, she entered when Sally opened it.

"Shush, don't look surprised or past me. One of Mary's brothers is watching the house."

Hugging Belle for a show, then smiling and taking the flowers, they entered the house and closed the door.

As Belle and Sally entered the kitchen, Della and Mary were sitting at the table.

"Belle, so good to see you. Sit down. I will pour you some tea." Looking closely, "What's wrong? You look worried."

Sitting the flowers on the edge of the sink, she turned.

"I just saw one of your brothers at the edge of the park, monitoring the house, Mary. They are watching for you. It can only mean trouble."

Mary put the flowers in a vase.

"Belle, you always worry too much. What can they do?"

"If they start any problems, they will have problems." Della shook her finger towards Belle. "Mary has been sharing her ideas, and I agree. Mary needs to be with Phillip. Other than us, Mary has no one else here." Putting her hands on her hips, Della looked at them smiling. "At first, Mary was going to send Sally to live at the farm, but I think it would be better for Sally and me to stay here. I have a small amount of monthly monies, so Mary would not have to spend hers. We just need to figure out a safe way for her to get to California."

Belle interrupted.

"Aunt Hester would have a fit for sure, but I will go with her. It would give me a chance to travel, look for that wayward brother of mine, and have an adventure. You know how Aunt Hester is. I will live and die here, married to someone I don't love and who doesn't understand me." Standing with her hands clenching on her lap, Belle began again, "I hate deceiving Aunt Hester, but I don't want to stay here and have men thrown at me to marry. I want to find my own."

Laughing, Della put her arms around Belle's shoulders.

"You are going to upset Hester, little girl. I have known her for years; Hester will not take this lightly." She shook her head. "I would have to figure out how to get two women out-of-town unseen."

Slowly, after a long afternoon of tea, biscuits, and honey, the women hatched a plan of their own. Holding her cup close to her chest, Belle looked at both Della and Mary.

"I know you think it isn't a good idea, but I have to go with Mary. Do not look at me like that! Aunt Hester does not need me anymore. I secretly think she wants me to get married so she can have her life back." Looking back at the two women, Belle looked determined. "I want to travel. If I get married, it will be to someone who can love me for me." Mary looked shocked. "Then it will be with who I want. You should understand, Mary, you are marrying the love of your life." Turning back to Della, "It solves the problem of Mary traveling alone."

Letting out an exasperated sigh, Della looked long and hard at Belle.

"Have you told Hester about your plan?"

"No, not about leaving, but I have about her constantly trying to pair me with some man, but she won't listen. One week it is 'that nice banker's son,' the next week is 'old man Watkins' who owns the hotel." She screwed up her face. "Honestly, who would want to marry a man twice her age? I'm eighteen. I am old enough to be on my own. I know, I know, women can't be on their own without a man."

Della patted Belle's shoulders and rolled her eyes upward after seeing Mary smile. Della looked from one girl to the other.

"Belle, this is a hard decision, not to be made lightly. It's a rough trip, and you need to understand that a woman's life is different in the West. I'm not sure you will be any happier out there than you are here."

Sighing and looking at the floor, Belle stood up.

"Della, Mary, you have no conception of how my life has

been since losing my family, then Jeremy leaving. I was already planning on an escape before all this happened with Mary. Mary has been my best friend for a long time. This trip is a chance I need to take. If it doesn't work out, what have I lost?"

Laughing at her seriousness, Belle looked at Della.

"Della, I have it worked out. I will dress in my hunting clothes. You know, Jeremy's old clothes. And I will be Mary's escort. They will leave her alone if they think she has a man to protect her."

Belle crossed the room, looking smugly at Della.

Suddenly Della choked, spewing her tea. Embarrassed, they passed the towel around.

"Do you honestly think you can pull that off? You no more look like a boy than I do." She picked up her fiery red curls. "What will you do with this stuff? They will take one look at you and know this is a farce. Surely, Belle, you can come up with a better idea."

Turning towards Mary she said, "Mary, I don't know if I can support this idea. Hester would have a fit. Your Uncle George's son, Brett Sanders, is visiting California. Why don't I have him travel with you girls? Then we would not have to go through this farce. Belle, surely you can see what I mean? Brett is stopping to visit with me tomorrow. Surely watching over you two would not be too much of a bother for him. He has three sisters; two ladies should be easy for him. Besides, he is traveling there anyway. I am concerned, Belle, about you leaving Hester with no notice. You need to make sure you have thought this through."

Walking to the window, Belle looked towards the park.

"Now a different brother is sitting there. He's just behind the tree, see his feet sticking out? Mary, this is not a safe time for you. We will have to plan it right to get you past them. I just don't like it. They are planning something."

Opening the curtain slightly, Mary looked out.

"It is Marcus. He is the worst one! You are right. They are up to something."

Pulling them away from the window, Della grabbed her bag and marched out the front door. Walking with purpose, Della confronted Marcus. Shaking her finger at him, Della suddenly stepped backward. Marcus did not take her gestures lightly. Rising, he made a threatening move toward Della. Abruptly, she turned and stomped towards downtown. Within minutes she was back with the marshal. Still watching from the window, they could not hear anything. Marcus slowly and angrily rose from behind the tree. Not phasing the marshal at all, Marcus was led to the marshal's office in town.

Slamming the door as she entered, Della was flustered and red in the face.

"It will serve him right talking to me as if I was some saloon floozy. The marshal will make him spend the night in jail for threatening to assault a woman in broad daylight—no telling when the others will come to find him. We need to get our plan into action. I sent a telegram to my nephew Brett, but I don't think we can wait much longer."

Belle hurried out the door to her home. She took out a trunk, packed several pairs of clothing, her mother's jewelry, and changed into her brother's clothes she had washed several days before. Putting her trunk into the handcart, she wheeled it to Mary's house. Entering the house, Belle met her near the back door.

"I put the cart in the barn so they can't see it. They are still watching in the front."

Della and Sally re-sorted and loaded both Mary and Belle's trunks on the buggy.

"We will take them to the stagecoach station and ask them to hold them for the morning stage. It won't look so suspicious when we leave the house. They know I am just visiting and will think I am leaving if they are paying attention."

Turning, Mary started laughing.

"Belle, there is no way anyone would think you were a boy. Let us see what we can do to make the disguise more believable. Are you sure you want to do this?"

Nodding her head yes, Belle watched as Mary snipped the ends of her hair and applied pomade to the sides to control the wayward hair. She sewed ties to Belle's hat to secure it, then reinforced the pockets inside her pants to hold the money they needed for food and necessities on the trip. Watching Belle walk in the clothes, Mary shook her head.

"This just will not work. Look in the mirror while you are walking towards it. That's not how men walk."

Walking towards the mirror back and forth, Belle let out a sigh.

"I'm doing the best that I can." Changing out of the clothes, she grabbed Mary's hand. "We need to do some research."

Laughing at Belle's determination, she walked with Belle downtown. Sitting on a bench across from the saloon, they watched the men leave the saloon.

"Mary, I never paid attention to how men walked before. How do some of them ever get from one place to another?"

Pointing at a cowboy walking through the saloon doors, swaggering down the sidewalk, Belle stood and exaggerated his walk. Mary placed her hand over her mouth to cover her laugh.

Stopping, looking around, she hurried Mary into the alley.

"I don't think I can walk like these guys." She peered back at the saloon. "Look at that guy." She pointed towards a cowboy, lifting her skirts so Mary could see better. Straightening her back, tucking in her hips, bowing her legs, she walked backward and forward.

Mary bent at the waist, laughing at the picture Belle presented.

"No, Belle, like this." Raising her skirt to show her lower legs, Mary walked, shifting her hips.

Walking arm and arm, laughing at their secret walking trial, Belle and Mary walked back to Mary's home.

"Mary, I promised I would help Aunt Hester this afternoon, but I will be back early tomorrow in time to leave. Are you sure you will be okay tonight?"

Belle looked closely at Mary.

"I know this is the right thing. We will be all right."

Hugging Belle, they separated.

# CHAPTER 5

The following day, Belle was sitting at the kitchen table with her aunt.

"Aunt Hester, I know that I have been at Mary's a lot since her mother died. I hope that has been okay with you."

She watched Hester closely, trying to gauge her mood.

"Belle, it is fine. I know Mary appreciates your company, especially with her stepbrothers hanging around. I have always felt Mary was a wonderful influence. It is essential to have your friends nearby during times of sorrow. I have planned nothing for you. I need to go to St. Louis for a few days and wanted to see if you would mind spending a few days here alone? Or you could go to Mary's?"

"I will be fine. Della and Mary are close if I have problems. I will probably be over there most of the time, anyway."

After Hester left, Belle picked up her satchel and walked to Mary's house, keeping an eye open for her brothers. As Belle reached the home, Sally opened the door and ushered her into the kitchen. Della, smiling, motioned her to sit down. Handing her a stagecoach ticket to New Orleans, Della started explaining.

"After reading the paper, I booked the tickets to New Orleans. Then you can take a clipper ship to San Francisco. The papers are full of reports of war. Then there are many reports of the Comanche uprising in the West. I hope you don't mind?"

"Aunt Hester has gone to St. Louis for a few days so she won't know about my escape until next week. Della, I am sure that this is fine. I am surprised that we are not taking the stagecoach the whole way. Are the Indians really that much of a problem?"

Della frowned, looking worried.

"Belle, the stories about the Comanches are gruesome. No white person is safe when they are around. I am so glad that Brett will travel with you. Between the Indians and the threat of war, this is not a good time to be traveling."

"Aunt Della, there are posters everywhere recruiting for the army. Maybe it is a good thing we are leaving. We just won't take any chances if a war does start up. None of this is worth losing your life."

Mary spoke with a worried tone.

"I hope Phillip decides not to be a part of it. Brother against brother, father against sons, what are these people thinking of?"

Della sighed and looked down at the papers again.

"We haven't been involved in a war in some time. Pray and hope that our politicians can work out the problems before it gets started."

Belle took money out of her bag and tried to hand it to Della for her fare. Della, putting her arm around Belle's shoulders, hushed and hugged her simultaneously.

"You are going with Mary, and as a companion, I know she will be safer than trying to travel alone. My nephew telegraphed he would join the stagecoach down the road as he had a few things to catch up on before he left St. Louis."

Looking off into the distance, Della continued, "Let's see how to describe him. . . . Brett Summers is tall, good-looking, has dark hair, and a small scar across his left cheek. He hasn't seen Mary since she was little," looking at Mary, "but you may recognize him when you see him. It was so sad when his wife died a few years ago. I don't think he has been the same since. He has been quiet and kept to himself since he lost her and their baby. It was clear he loved her tremendously. However, he is strong. I'm sure that he has come to terms with the loss by now."

Belle looked at Della and laughed.

"Della, are you sure that he wants to babysit two women?" She swallowed and said, "Oh, before I forget, I've decided I am going to wear Jeremy's clothes. I know it is unconventional, but I don't want to wear hot skirts, and no one will know me, anyway. Besides, I have to carry my money. I withdrew most of my savings and needed to figure out a way to hide it. After talking with Mary, and since your nephew will not start with us, I think it would be better if people thought Mary had male protection. At least until Mr. Summers shows up, don't you think? Especially if her stepbrothers ask around."

Mary looked at Belle.

"We are starting a new life, so why shouldn't you be how you want to be. You may wear whatever. Just don't do that walk you practiced."

Both girls laughed as the picture of Belle walking drunk came to mind.

Della shook her head.

"Looks like you girls have it all figured out."

As they left the house that afternoon, there was no sign of the stepbrothers. Mary and Belle climbed the steps onto the stage, with Della and Sally standing solemnly on the sidewalk.

"Let us know when you get there. Don't worry about

Hester, Belle. I will talk to her when she gets back. Sally will watch your house."

Waving, the driver latched the door, climbed on top, and shook the reins, yelling to the horses as they drove out of Maryville. Mary and Belle smiled as they took a last look at their hometown.

Several hours later, the afternoon sun was in full force. As Mary wiped the dampness from her face, she noticed her light green dress was limp and dusty, not as lovely as it looked when they left Maryville.

"Honestly, Belle, I never thought it would be this hot riding in a stagecoach. Already, my backside is getting sore from the constant bumping and riding on this dirt trail."

"At least traveling in pants is better than wearing all those petticoats. Goodness Mary, I don't know how you stand it."

Looking around at the other passengers in the stagecoach, Belle could see they were not faring any better. Mr. Post had introduced himself when they first left Maryville. He was an older, thin man with a full head of bushy white hair, thick white eyebrows, and dressed in a tan suit with a wilted red flower in his lapel. He leaned on the edge of the window, dozing, looking uncomfortable in the heat and dust.

There were other passengers with them. The man next to Mary was a quiet guy. He sat in the corner, sleeping since they left Maryville. Occasionally they heard a snore, but mostly, all they saw was his hat bobbing. His canvas pants were dusty. He wore a plaid flannel shirt, the kind farmers wore around Maryville. His boots looked almost as worn as Belle's, but she noticed the arch of the boot was worn-out like he had ridden horses a lot.

Belle and Mary fastened the curtains across the window to tamper the dust being kicked up by the horses from the trail. Still, nothing could stop the small clouds of dust settling on everything. With her hat pulled low to cover her mess of copper curls and her tan leather jacket, Belle tried to sleep. The stagecoach rocked, bumped, twisted, and rattled. Its rhythm was unkind to the backside of the travelers.

Belle, trying to pass the time, watched the scenery out the narrow part of the window where the curtain did not completely close. The sloping hills were covered with brown and tawny grasses, both short and tall. They looked much like the hills near St. Louis. The end of summer is always the golden part of the year. Belle looked behind the stagecoach, watching the swirls of dust formed from the horses' kicking. The constant moving and the squeaking of the stagecoach springs against the rocks on the trail, soon had the four passengers dozing. Mr. Post was snoring gently, almost to the stagecoach's rhythm.

After several hours, the slowing of the stagecoach awakened Belle and Mary. Stretching, Belle pulled the curtain back. They had pulled into a way station to rest and change the horses. The driver unlatched the door of the stagecoach and assisted each of the passengers down the steps. As Belle and Mary looked around, they walked to the station itself. Sitting down in the shade, Mary took off her bonnet to let the breeze cool her hair.

"I knew this would not be easy, but there must be a better way."

Mr. Post walked shakily, with a firm grip on his cane, as he approached the girls.

"They usually have some food in these places. I suggest we see what we can get. It's been a long trip today without proper nourishment. May I assist you?" He offered his hand to Mary and turned to look at Belle. "Sonny, come on and join us. I reckon you must be hungry too."

The way station was an old building, grayed with the weather. Some of the porch railings were missing posts, but it seemed sturdy enough when Belle reached for it when climbing the steps. The porch had a few missing boards, but overall, the flooring did not move when they walked towards the door. Belle could see the windows were cloudy and could have used a good washing. As they entered the main room, it was cheerful, with several lamps lit, even though it was late evening. Mary took a deep breath.

"Mmm, the stew smells good, Belle. I didn't realize I was so hungry."

Sitting at the long rough-cut wood table, the station-master sat a steaming bowl of stew in front of each of them. He sat the butter and biscuits on the table and smiled.

"My wife Betsy churned the butter fresh this morning. In fact," he winked at the girls, "she usually does all the cooking, just lets me take the credit."

As they ate, Belle looked around the way station. The floor was worn in many places but still clean and sturdy. There were bunk beds around the outer walls, with one side having single beds. Sitting next to the fire was a man drinking a cup of coffee and reading a book. In the fire's light, Belle could see that his hair was solid black. He had a black, well-trimmed mustache and a small scar crossing over his lower lip. His skin was sunned brown, making his bright blue eyes stand out. Nudging Mary, she looked up.

"Could that be your cousin?"

Mary looked harder through the smoky room and stood up. She walked towards the man.

"Brett, is that you?"

He looked up from his reading, acknowledging her presence. Taking in the tired look on her face, her disheveled clothing, and her slight smile, he stood and hugged her.

"I thought I recognized you when you came through the door, but you have grown up more than I had pictured. Who is the boy with you?"

Turning to see who he was staring at, she remembered

Belle. Taking Brett by the hand, she led him to the table where Belle was eating.

"Brett, this is my friend Belle." She saw his face looking questioningly at her. "Belle is dressed like this as a type of protection for me. We didn't know when you would join us, so we decided we would disguise her."

Standing, smiling, Belle looked at Brett.

"Glad to meet you. I am more comfortable in these clothes than Mary is in her dress. The stagecoach is not exactly the most comfortable ride, is it?"

Looking around the room to see if anyone was listening, Brett took in the view. Belle dressed in her brother's pants, an old faded blue shirt, and a denim jacket. She had on old boots, scuffed and worn, that were too large for her. Her bright copper-colored hair was stuffed upwards into a worn tan hat and tied under her chin.

Sitting at the table, Brett couldn't think of anything to say.

"Brett, don't worry about Belle. She will change when we get to New Orleans. It's simply better and safer for people to think she is a guy right now. Have trust in what I say, okay?"

"Well, Della said it had to be secret, so I guess I will play the game."

Looking back at Mary, he couldn't help but wonder why it was important that Belle stay hidden.

"How are you holding up? I know it must have been hard. Your mother and I grew up together. What's all this stuff about your stepbrothers? What do they have to do with anything?"

Sighing, "She was a genuine lady, but like all the women of our family, she was stubborn."

Taking another bite of her stew, Mary motioned for them to step outside.

Brett, seeing how uncomfortable she was said, "Mary,

finish your food. It will be awhile before breakfast tomorrow. You will need your strength to make this trip."

Focusing on her food, Mary wondered how she would explain the past few weeks without breaking down. Belle, watching Brett with Mary, felt strange. He was handsome in a rugged sort of way. It was plain that he did not feel out of place with Mary. She saw him smile at Mary, giving her support, helping her not break down in tears. I was not expecting someone like him. He must think I am strange, dressed in men's clothes. Suddenly, I wish I were back in those horrible petticoats and suffering from the heat. It would be worth it.

That evening, sitting on the porch, Belle watched Mary bring Brett up to date. Some stories she had not heard before.

"Brett, one evening, the three brothers broke into my house and were going through everything. They were going through Mother's desk. I am not sure what they wanted. Belle confronted them with an umbrella, giving me and the cook time to aim shotguns at them. I just felt that if I didn't leave Maryville, I would not be safe. They were planning something evil. One night, they were mean and they threatened me. They said if I didn't give them their share, they would force me to give it all to them. Thankfully, Belle came at that moment with Della, and they left. However, they have been watching the house for the last few days. That is when I decided I couldn't stay there any longer. I had to leave. Belle came with me because she was having problems with her aunt. I know part of it was to have an adventure, but her aunt was seriously trying to arrange a marriage for her. So, we left. I am sure that we have not heard the last of my brothers. You don't know how glad I was to see you sitting there by the fire."

"So, how does Phillip fit into this picture?" questioned Brett. "As I remember the last time we talked, you were still starry-eyed over him. Is that still true? Is the aunt such a problem for Belle that she feels she has to run away? And, does Phillip know what is happening? Is he expecting you? Sorry for all the questions. It seems like you girls had a lot of factors to consider in deciding to run away."

Belle sat quietly, listening to the story. She noticed Mary was facing Brett, and he was holding her hand sympathetically.

"Brett, I wrote to Phillip and let him know what was happening. He should have the letter by now. We have been planning to get married since grade school. I am just moving it up a little. I am sure he will be fine. Just help me get there safely. I need help right now." She looked at her friend. "As for Belle, that is a different story. Belle's brother left her to find his way in the world, so it has been just Belle and her aunt Hester. Hester is pushing her to get married. I don't know if Hester's tired of having her around or thinks it would be better for Belle to marry and grow up. Belle is my dearest friend." She lowered her head as tears fell. "Without her, I would never have tried to go to California. So, we are a team. I know we are two young girls to you, but we need you right now. Please say that you will take us to California?"

"Mary, I will help you get there." He looked and gave a wink towards Belle, "And the little boy that seems to tag along, too. So, let's go in and get some sleep. Tomorrow will be a long day."

Holding out his hand, he assisted Mary to a standing position. Motioning to Belle, "Let's get some sleep, son."

Turning, he walked into the station's main room.

Belle rose slowly. Putting her hands on her hips, she strolled into the station. His words stung, and she didn't understand her feelings. *Why should that bother me?* Belle watched Brett as he led Mary to the single bed by the wall. As she prepared for bed, Brett took the lower bunk next to Mary. He pointed to the upper bunk.

"Well, son." He smiled at her discomfort. "You take the top so that I can watch you both."

As she tried to climb up to the top bunk, her foot slipped several times. Brett laughed as he boosted her up. As she bumped her head on the ceiling, she laid down, thinking of several unladylike words she would have liked to say. After tossing for a while, finally, Belle fell asleep. Her dreams were wild, causing her to wake up several times, but finally, she fell into a deep sleep.

The following day, Belle awakened to the heavenly smell of fresh coffee and biscuits. Stretching, she noticed Mary and Brett were already sitting at the table. Standing in front of the washstand, Belle washed her face, then brushed her hair back into a bun on the top of her head. Pulling her old hat firmly on her head, she sat down to eat. The stagecoach driver stood up.

"You need to fill your canteens and bring a couple of those biscuits with you because it is a long way to the next way station."

Belle washed her hands and walked out onto the porch. She ate the broken eggs and biscuits and then stuffed her bag with food and water. Sitting on the bench, she overheard the driver talking to the guard.

"Be sure you have your guns loaded. I heard the outlaws are causing a lot of trouble on this route. We need to be prepared."

Belle went back into the way station and checked her pistol and rifle to ensure she had loaded them, hiding the pistol back in her bag. As she turned, she saw Brett was staring at her.

"Do you know how to use that gun?"

"I spent many hours hunting with my brother. I not only

know how to use it but have a good aim with the rifle as well. So, don't worry about me. Just keep Mary safe."

She walked rapidly towards the stagecoach. Two other men joined them as they climbed the steps onto the stage. The driver closed the outer door latch, and they were off. This day was like the day before. The stagecoach followed a dirt trail, kicking up dust and causing the air to be stifling. Mary had left her petticoats off, so she was more relaxed, and each had a handkerchief covering their mouths and noses. Mr. Post sat in the corner, often coughing from the dust and holding the thick curtain on the window next to him tightly closed. The two new passengers seemed bored and continuously complained about the rough ride. Brett didn't seem to mind as much. He sat back on the seat and peered through the slot on the side of the curtain.

# CHAPTER 6

The panel above Brett's head suddenly slid open as the driver hollered down.

"Hang on, looks like we have a little company coming up fast and on the right. If you have a gun, get it ready for action. They look mean."

With that, the stagecoach picked up speed, tossing the passengers around on the seats. Mr. Post grabbed his cane to support himself against the seat.

Brett watched the riders coming fast and hard. Each of the outlaws had bandannas across their faces. Shouts rang out, urging their horses to go faster. Then the shooting began. Watching them approach the stagecoach, Brett aimed and shot as soon as they came within view. The other two passengers pushed Mary aside and leaned close to the window to shoot.

Suddenly, Belle heard the driver yell, "They hit me!"

The guard slid down on the seat to help control the horses as they ran fast down the trail.

"Someone needs to get on top to help," shouted Belle.

None of the other passengers seemed to hear her.

Reaching outside the door, trying to unlock the lever, Belle found it stuck fast. As she looked out the sliding panel, she saw the driver and the guard trying hard to manage the horses. Looking back at Brett, she knew it had to be her to go up top. Brett was too large to make it through the window.

Hanging off the stagecoach side, Belle tried to find a handhold to climb to the top. Grabbing the luggage rack, she pulled herself up, bracing her foot on the window. Feeling her foot slip several times, she finally pulled hard enough that she was able to shimmy up to the top. Laying flat on the top of the racing stagecoach, feeling her heart pounding, Belle glanced at the driver. She saw him bent forward, but he still held the reins tight. The guard was also still holding the reins, trying to help the driver manage the runaway horses.

Shots whizzed over her head as she ducked closer to the top of the stagecoach. Raising her rifle, bracing it against the rim of the handhold, she fired. The shooters grew closer. Scared by the gunfire, the horses were frightened, wild-eyed, and running at full speed. Looking downward, she saw Mary lean out the window.

"Here's your saddlebag. I think I recognized one of them. They may be my stepbrothers. Just scare them, don't hurt them," Mary pleaded.

Belle reached over the edge of the stagecoach feeling wildly for the saddlebag. Thank goodness she was wearing her brother's pants and not having to mess with a bunch of petticoats.

As the stagecoach swerved back and forth, Belle repeatedly tried to grab the saddlebag. Finally grasping it, she pulled it upwards and laid down flat against the top of the coach. She felt every bump of the road and held on for dear life. Even loading the rifle was difficult with all the bouncing and swerving of the stagecoach. Hooking her foot around the luggage rail to brace herself, Belle raised the gun and started firing. *These guys are shooting for real. The only way I will be able to scare them off is if I hit one of them.* Quickly using up her cartridges, reaching in her bag, she realized she was almost out of ammunition. The Henry would hold fifteen rounds, and she only had thirty left. Still bracing herself, with her foot under the rod of the luggage rack, Belle reached for the last of her ammunition. Loading as fast as she could, Belle shot wildly towards the fast-riding men. Gunfire rang from inside of the coach, which hit one of the horsemen. Suddenly, as quickly as they arrived, the riders faded off to the left into a rocky area.

Holding onto the luggage rack, she slowly inched her way towards the driver. The coach seemed to hit every rock in the road. Still holding on for dear life, Belle reached the driver. The guard was not moving. As she got closer to him, she saw the blood slowly staining his shirt. Sliding forward into the seat beside the driver, she reached out to the reins. Grabbing the reins from the driver's hands, she pulled hard. She saw the horses arch their necks backward, then strain left and right. The driver cautioned her to loosen up a little.

"Give them time to slow down. If you pull too hard, it scares them. They will either get hurt or turn the stagecoach over."

Loosening up on the reins, the horses gradually slowed to a slow trot, then stopped. Panting and foaming with the heat of the run, the horses stamped their feet.

Wiping her forehead with the back of her arm, Belle chastised herself. *What was I thinking? Why did I think that I could do something like this? Have I lost my mind?* Looking over at the driver, she could now see that he was injured as well. The guard still was not moving. The wild-eyed horses continued stamping the ground, pulling tight on the reins. *What will happen next?* Belle thought as she climbed down, nearly sliding off the top of the coach. Reaching for the edge of the window, she lowered herself to the stagecoach steps. As she yanked on the latch, Belle was able to open the door.

Upset and eager to get out of the stagecoach, two passengers pushed Belle, causing her to lose her balance, slide from the steps, and fall to the ground. Mary and Mr. Post, following the other two passengers, rushed past her to help the driver. The men slowly lowered the guard down from the stage, ignoring Belle down in the dust. As Brett exited the stagecoach, he extended a hand to Belle as she stood and dusted herself off. Embarrassed as she looked at the others, Belle turned away from the group.

Mary immediately took over caring for the driver's wounds. First, she cleaned the wound with their drinking water, and then using whiskey from one of the other passenger's bags, she cleansed the wound against infection. Gritting his teeth, the driver yelled loudly as the alcohol hit the injury. Tearing off strips of her petticoat, Mary wrapped the skin carefully. There was no hope for the guard. He laid still on the ground where they placed him. Brett and the other male passengers used a shovel to dig a grave for his body. Leaving the driver to the other passengers, Belle walked over to the horses. Shaking her head, she turned her head away from the group. The burying of the guard left her feeling unsure. *What about his family, his friends? It would be terrible to be buried along a trail somewhere without a proper burial. The code out here is different from living in the city.* She felt a little queasy from watching Mary work with the bloody wound.

Watching Belle unhook the horses from their yoke and then the wagon tongue, Brett walked over to Belle to help lead the horses to the shallow stream. The horses were wet with sweat and still foaming from the hard run. Leading them into the water, Belle let them drink slowly. She led them in and out of the water several times to slow their drinking. After they had drunk, Belle walked them into waist-high water, splashing the water from the stream over them to help them cool down.

She was not expecting them to lie down and roll in the water. The first jerk on the line caused her to lose her footing when they laid down, falling headfirst into the shallow water. Sputtering when coming up for air, she laughed and let the horses enjoy the water. After drinking their fill, she led them to the grass alongside the river and hobbled their feet. Leaving the horses to eat the tall grasses, Belle limped over to a clump of bushes surrounding some large boulders. Dusting off a large boulder, Belle sat in the dappled sunlight on the boulder, slumped over, wet, tired, hurting, and feeling short of air.

Brett, still wet from the stream, sat on a rock not far from her, laying his shirt on the next boulder to dry. As she slowly recovered, she tried not to think of her situation.

*Whatever possessed her to believe, she wanted to leave her home to do this?* At this moment, she realized that she missed her life as it was before. Sure, Aunt Hester was a pain, but at least she never had to worry about Hester trying to shoot her. The predictable daily chores, the millinery shop's work, that life was so different from what she was doing now.

Laying there, Belle wished she could take her shirt off as Brett had. The sun was so hot and made her feel almost as miserable physically as she did mentally. Belle's brother's clothes were large for her. Now wet, they flattened against her chest, outlining her shape. She covered herself and hoped no one noticed. Realizing her hair was damp and the curls were starting to squirm out of the braids, she shoved the wet hat back on her head. Looking at Brett, she couldn't help but notice the muscular shape that his clothes had hidden. His looks had started to grow on her the more time they spent with him. The dark hair, curled when damp, gave him a softer look. As she remembered his laugh when she fell in, she realized he was not quite as stern as she thought.

Mr. Post came over to her.

"Son, you did well. Your parents would have been proud of your behavior today."

Tired to the bone, Belle looked up at him. He was an older man and not okay. He walked shakily with a firm grip on his cane. A white mustache and a shock of white hair pomaded backward across his head completed his look. He wore a tan bowler hat that fell over his ears. His bushy white eyebrows had a habit of moving up and down as he talked. Since he joined the stagecoach back in Missouri, he had demonstrated what Belle thought to be a perfect gentleman.

No matter how Mr. Post felt, he always opened the stage-coach door and got out first, so he could help the ladies down the steps. However, often it was a question of who was helping who. He asked after their comfort many times during the ride. Watching him, Belle saw that Mr. Post was standing rigidly, hat in his hand with his white hair tossed by the breeze. The breeze shook him as if he were going to fall over.

"Thank you, sir," he said, pumping Belle's hand.

Trying to stand up, Belle surmised that this was how it would feel if she had been in a fistfight. Every bone in her body ached. She limped from her fall off the stagecoach steps. As Mr. Post turned to join the others, she lowered herself back to the rock. Weariness attacked her so quickly; she did not think she would be able to stand back up. She surmised to herself, *I guess boys get used to this kind of stuff. These activities are more challenging than I thought.*

Taking her rifle and cloth from her bag, she wiped down her rifle while kneeling. Her brother gave the Henry rifle to her when she was fifteen years old. Remembering her brother, she looked at the gun. Belle appreciated the self-cocking mechanism when firing at the men chasing them a short time ago. Sure, it was not as fancy as the new Winchester rifles, but she was glad she had it. As she cleaned the rifle, she remembered the fun they had hunting.

Interrupting her daydream, the driver came around the edge of the rock, where Belle and Brett rested.

"I'm good to drive now. We need to start moving before those scalawags regroup and come back."

Belle slowly rose to her feet, removed the hobbles from the horses, and led them back to the stagecoach. The driver and Brett wiped the horses down one last time, gave them a quick feed with their feedbags, then hitched them back to the stagecoach.

As she climbed inside the coach, Belle slumped against the wall. Mary handed her a wet cloth for her face.

Taking Belle's hands she said, "We're all so grateful to you, Sam."

Winking, she smiled as she teased Belle with a boy's name.

"You were so brave to ward off those attackers."

Blushing, Belle placed the rifle behind their seat, knowing it was ready if needed. Quietly, Belle reminded herself to stock up on ammunition at their next stop in town.

*This is not how I planned this trip to happen.* Belle bounced against the hard seat of the stagecoach. She felt every bump and jump to be a direct assault on her bum. The constant bumping, rattling, and creaking was getting on her nerves. She felt sore from her head to her feet. *I can do this.* Still, an internal voice told her she needed to sleep, rest, and sleep some more.

Pretending to be asleep, Belle studied the other passengers. Mr. Post, looking frail, kept a handkerchief over his nose and mouth to help breathe clean air. Even though they had the window coverings down most of the time, the dust kicked up by the horses caused Mr. Post to hold the cloth even closer to his mouth and nose. Belle noticed he had a croupy cough that he tried to suppress.

Brett was a bit of a mystery. He rarely said anything, preferring to lean in the corner of the stagecoach and watch the others. When sleeping, his jacket fell open, and Belle saw an imprint of a badge on his vest. He hardly ever spoke, and when he did, it was short and clipped. Sometimes, Brett appeared to doze.

Nevertheless, Belle felt the tension in the air and came to realize he was always watching and alert, no matter how comfortable he looked. Whenever he caught her looking at him, he looked amused. His hair, though dark as night, had little touches of gray around his whiskers. His clothes were finely made but appeared worn as if he had worn them for a long time. Now, after days on the stagecoach they were dusty. His boots were fine leather, scuffed around the toes, and the heels were worn. There was wearing around the arch, indicating he spent a lot of time riding horses.

Trying not to stare, Belle saw he was rugged looking, not handsome like the men she had known before but had a formidable, commanding appearance. His hair was a little too long, and he had a short-trimmed beard. Brett was lean, muscled, and tall for men she had known in Missouri.

He had a strong, firm chin and dark eyes. At times, when Brett looked at her, she felt he could see through her. Brett was tanned as if he spent much time in the sun. His holster untied at the bottom still gave him quick access, and she sensed that he knew how to get to his gun quickly and use it. He demonstrated his experience with his rifle during the previous attack. At times, Brett glanced out the window towards the back of the stagecoach, scanning the countryside. It was as if he was looking for someone that may be following.

The whole time Belle was studying Brett, Mary was

watching her. Smiling, Mary looked through the edge of the stagecoach curtain. Looking across the grasslands, Mary tried to focus on the differences; however, the countryside looked the same as back in St. Louis. As the breeze blew across the grass, small waves formed like those she had witnessed at the lake before. A small squirrel hopped on the side of a tree as they passed, fussing as the dust overcame him, and he jumped around the other side of the tree. Mary, not wanting them to notice she saw them watching each other, closed her eyes. Thinking about the day and the travel, she smiled quietly to herself. *Well, Belle seems to be interested in Brett. This scenario might be fun.*

# CHAPTER 7

Brett had seen the worried look on Mary's face when the bandits attacked. Even though the excitement and horror were not ordinary happenings for the two girls, he got the feeling something else was happening. Mary had not changed since she was a young girl. She was bright-eyed, intelligent, and still in love with Phillip. That romance had been going on for more than a decade. Looking at Belle, he felt confused. He had met Belle when she was a little girl, but it was apparent she had grown up as well. She used to follow her brother like a shadow. Jeremy, her brother, often tried to shoo her away, but the next time Jeremy looked up, there she was. *I would remember her bright red hair and freckles anywhere.* Of course, she didn't remember him. He was already grown. He had met Adele by then and was madly in love.

Remembering Adele's face, her lips, and the way that his heart seemed to melt every time he was around her just made his heart hurt now. She had died in childbirth. He had lost the love of his life and the life they had made together.

Shaking his head to bring himself back to reality, Brett lifted the curtain edge as he stared out the window. *What was on this stagecoach that the bandits would have wanted?* Looking back at the girls, Brett settled back into his seat. The scenery stayed the same day after day. Soft rolling grasslands, an open dirt trail, a cloud of dust swirling behind them, with occasional groves of trees dotting the trail. The never-ending dust kicked up by the horses permeated the coach, covering them with a fine layer, which if tried to brush off was just made worse. They traveled most of the day, with no sight of the gunmen that had attacked them that morning. As they pulled up to the way station, Brett noted the quietness, not even a locust droning. Nothing was making a noise, not even a bird singing. *Where is everyone?* Suddenly Brett became alert. He fastened the strap on the bottom of his holster and observed as they approached the way station.

Belle and Mary stirred. The girls stretched, then started to wake up. Belle noticed Brett had tightened his strap on his holster, stretched, and stepped down out of the coach. He cautioned them to stay inside until they were sure it was safe.

A lone man came out the door of the building. Wildly gesturing, he was talking loud and fast to the stagecoach driver. Not wearing a gun nor a hat, he continued to wave his hands. The stagecoach driver took off his hat and threw it to the ground. Stomping the hat on the ground, he then picked the hat back up. Punching it back into a wild shape, he hit it against his leg, dust flying, then jammed it back on his head.

Turning, the driver stomped back to the passengers with a scowl on his face. They could tell that the news was not going to be good.

"We have some bad news, folks. Yesterday, bandits attacked the way station, then ran the horses off. The way stationmaster was by himself at the time. When two other hired men returned to the way station, he sent them out to find the horses."

The driver took a deep breath.

51

"And, the bandits roughed up the manager looking for money, but he didn't have anything to give. Later that night, two of the horses had come back, but that was not enough for the entire exchange needed for the stagecoach."

So, the station's bad luck turned into a substantial delay. After many loud discussions between the driver and the way stationmaster, they resolved to let the horses rest overnight. Hopefully, the men would find the horses and bring them back, but they probably wouldn't be relaxed enough to help them. They would try to make it to the next station tomorrow morning. Grateful to be out of the coach, Belle limped slowly towards the porch of the way station. As Belle sat on the front porch, leaning on the wall next to the door, Belle's body reminded her of each sore muscle. Using her saddlebags as a pillow, she drifted into a light sleep on the quietness of the porch. She tried to shake off her feeling of impending doom as she daydreamed in the shade of the porch.

Later feeling full of the evening meal, they went to bed early. This way station was not as well equipped as the previous one, so they slept on the floor, wrapped in a blanket to ward off the nighttime chill. Belle noticed Brett slept on the porch with his rifle beside him.

Early the following day, Belle and Mary walked along a dirt trail beside the way station for exercise. They stopped to sit on a bench on a rocky rise overlooking the way station. Short of breath from the climb, Mary stretched her arms over her head.

"I am so glad the driver decided to leave late this morning. Not only does it give the horses a rest, but we needed one too."

"Mary," Belle slowly turned to her. "When the bandits were attacking, you thought they were your stepbrothers. Do you think they would try to hurt you? I know you were avoiding them after your mother died, and with good reason, but surely now that you have left, they would have accepted the situation."

Tracing the pattern of a flower stem on her skirt, Mary stopped and looked at Belle.

"Belle, I didn't tell you everything about what happened the night my mother died. Marcus was so angry when he heard the will did not mention them that he threatened me. I think they were stunned, finding all their mother's inheritance and part of their father's property went to me. I gave them their father's farm, but he wanted the money too. He just went off the deep end.

"One minute, he cursed his father for being so weak and not taking over my mother's inheritance when they married. The next minute he tried to make me sign it all over to him. However, the worst was when he grabbed my shoulders and said he would make me marry him, and he wouldn't be like his father but instead he would take it all from me. I was so scared. When he did that, I escaped and vowed I would never be alone again so he could follow through on his plan."

Placing her arm around Mary's shoulders, Belle tried to comfort her.

"Well, they better stop messing with us. I will shoot to damage their rotten hides next time."

Belle looked defiantly towards the way station in the valley.

"Just let them try something."

Belle saw the driver ringing the bell at the way station, which was the signal for them to return.

Making it down the trail, the girls were quiet, their thoughts weighing the severity of their discussion. They needed to ponder on the situation. As they reached the way station, they saw the horses already hitched to the stage-coach, so they hurried to pack their things. They had not taken much off the stagecoach, but it took a few minutes to load up. They were last to enter and saw that the seating arrangements had changed. Meanwhile, three other men had come seeking transportation to Natchez.

# CHAPTER 8

The gentleman on Belle's right was hot, sweaty, and seemed not to notice the others. Looking like he had not shaved for several days, his head bobbled as he slept. His hat pulled over his eyes, and his short nose seemed to snort with short grunts with each bump of the wheels. Mary sat across from Belle. She was beginning to show the wear of the trip. Several times, Mary pushed the man next to her to stop him from using her as a pillow while he dosed. Looking disgusted, she had moved gingerly as far to the side of the seat as she could. Tucking her pale green traveling dress around her legs, Mary leaned into the side of the bouncing stagecoach. The man beside her was like the one beside Belle. Unshaven, dusty, and young with a curly red beard, he tossed and turned in the small seat. Mr. Post sat next to the window opposite Belle. The third passenger was different. He, too, wore a beard but trimmed. He was tall, lean, dressed in pants rather than jeans, wore a jacket, and cocked his hat forward as he leaned back to sleep.

~

Brett, scanning around the stagecoach, let his eyes rest on Mary. Belle, still dressed in her brother's clothing, sat across from Mary. There was quite a difference between the two girls. Mary was a petite, blonde girl with stylish clothes even though they were rumpled and dusty from the trip. Belle, on the other hand, was different. Dressed as a boy, he couldn't understand the attraction towards her.

Belle looked the part of a young boy, but she looked like she might have lived in an alley somewhere in that outfit. Dusty and dirty, the clothes were too big for her. However, her curly red hair escaped out of her hat. The freckles across her nose gave her a sweetness that was hard to hide. Brett had not had feelings towards a woman since his wife died. A small mole on her right cheek, naturally, only enhanced her looks rather than detracted from it. She was wearing loose trousers and a brown fringed buckskin jacket that had belonged to someone else. The clothes were too big. The coat looked warm, lightweight, and hid her body's shape. She had a colt holstered to her right leg, and a rifle was sitting on the floor at her feet. She was not frail. He had seen how calm she was when facing the bandits and admired her ability to size the situation and act quickly. He also saw the toll it took on her emotions when it was over.

Belle watched Brett size her up with disconcerting looks. His eyes lingered on her rifle, lying at her feet beside her saddle-bag. At first, she felt flustered, then curious when she saw him watching her. Then she decided to ignore him and not let him know what effect he had on her.

As she looked out the window, she thought about her brother Jeremy. *Those were beautiful times. I remember spending many hours practicing my shooting so that he would spend time with me. I had his respect because of my skills, and even though we often went hunting, I did not want to kill anything. Oh, I didn't have any problems cleaning the animal or even cooking it. I just didn't want to kill it. I remember Jeremy's patience with me as I became a deadly shot.* She sighed. *Those were the fun days. These memories are forever etched in my mind, giving me comfort when I need support.* Belle watched the country roll by her window.

Belle had time to think about her situation during the long hours spent riding in the stagecoach. She noticed the men, when awake, stared endlessly at Mary. They did not give her much of a glance, looking like a scruffy boy, but they had their eye on Mary. *I do not like the looks of these men. They do not seem to be friendly or the type of men she would have ever allowed herself to be around.* Belle looked at Mr. Post and Brett. *At least they should be supportive if we need their help.*

The stagecoach continued to roll down the trail. The hours became long. The passengers were feeling the fatigue that comes with boredom and travel. The dust was a never-ending problem. The way stations, placed every twelve to fifteen miles, gave the stagecoaches a chance to feed and water the horses. The passengers took that time to either get something to eat or rest. As they approached one of the way stations, the passengers awakened and disembarked quickly. Belle and Mary welcomed each stop as they stretched and walked around, eager to escape the dust and body odors of the stagecoach. Then sitting on one of the benches outside the way station, Mary offered Belle some of the hardtack and fruit she had bought at the last station. As they ate quietly, they overheard voices inside the way station as they became louder and louder.

"I don't care what you say. It is highway robbery to charge fifty cents for a sandwich and bowl of soup. You don't even have any beer out here. What kind of place is this?"

Mary and Belle went to the door. Brett walked towards them.

"Mary, it would probably be best if you and Belle walk away from here for a little while. It sounds like there may be trouble, and I don't want you to get hurt."

Picking up her skirts, Mary led Belle off the porch and down nearer to the stagecoach. Suddenly, they heard gunfire. Running to the back of the stage, they saw one of the men as he untied a horse, then listened to the horse galloping off. Peeking around the edge of the coach, they saw Brett coming out the door.

"Don't worry," the stagecoach driver said to calm down the passengers. "Our gentleman rider just got a little overexcited. He won't run far. The horse he stole belongs to the manager here and won't let anyone but him ride him. Come on in and eat something. We will be leaving soon."

Cautiously, Belle and Mary walked back to the way station house. As they entered, they saw Mr. Post and Brett sitting at the table with a bowl of stew, acting as if nothing had happened. The manager brought more bowls of stew and some thick slices of cornbread for them to eat. Sitting down, they decided that they had better eat before something else happened.

A little later before leaving, they saw a riderless horse saunter up to the way station and go into the empty corral. The manager went to her, unsaddled, and took her bit out.

"Good Nellie, guess you showed him who's boss."

While rubbing her, he gave her an apple and watched her eat, smiling. *Somewhere there is a cowboy angry and walking.*

Belle leaned into the coach's back as the coach rocked roughly side to side. She tipped her hat forward and pretended to sleep. Mary, hunched up near the bottom of the seat across from her, looked worried. Taking off her travel bonnet due to the oppressive heat in the stagecoach, Mary had her blonde hair fixed in the latest style before leaving home. Curls piled high on her head, and others falling to her shoulders finished the illusion. Belle was amazed at Mary's fair skin and bright sky-blue eyes, which lit up when she smiled. Her face was flushed with the heat, but she was still as pretty as a porcelain doll. Her light green dress, trimmed with embroidery and lace across the bodice, slimming through the waist with skirts layered and long, looked hot and dusty. Her boots were made of white kid, with twelve tiny buttons on the side in contrast to Belle's scuffed, obviously worn cowhide working boots.

Leaning back in the stagecoach, Belle couldn't help the comparison between them. *Dressed like this, I would never be in any competition in comparison with Mary. No problem, I prefer not to be noticed. Mary will have a hard time in the West. Shame on me.* Belle shook her head. *How would I know if someone could survive in the West? I'm new to this stuff too. Since I cut off my ties at home, I must endure.* Belle looked at Mary again. *She would probably do better back east and married to some lawyer or banker.* Falling asleep, Belle vowed that she would ensure that Mary had more suitable clothes for traveling the first chance they had. Proper clothing was essential for traveling over the next few months. Fancy dresses were too hot and uncomfortable in this weather.

The scenery changed little as the stagecoach continued to Natchez. Even though Belle and Mary had never been to this area, it was very much like around their home. The area was flat in some areas, and in other areas took on a rolling hill effect. There were groves of trees that provided shade and relief from the sun. However, the dust of the trail was ever-present.

Dabbing at her forehead with her handkerchief, Mary sighed.

Looking at Belle, she wondered out loud, "It is so hot and

stuffy in here. I bet you are much cooler in those types of clothes."

She pulled at her tight corset and rearranged her many-layered skirts.

Belle stirred, looking concerned at Mary. Damping her handkerchief with the water from the canteen, Belle handed it to Mary.

"Maybe this will help," mumbled Belle as she slumped further in the seat. Pulling her hat down further, she pretended to go to sleep. Mary fanned herself with a lace fan and accepted that no one on the stage was in the mood to talk.

After an hour of rolling, bumping, and bouncing on the hard leather seat, the coach picked up speed suddenly, jarring the passengers awake. A rider on top of the stage hollered down in the window.

"It looks like we have company folks. They don't look friendly. If you have guns get ready to use them."

Moving the trunks around the top of the stagecoach to better protect the driver, the guard then positioned himself to protect the stage.

Stretching and looking out the window, Belle saw four horsemen riding fast, coming quickly up either side of the stage.

"Who are they, what do they want?" Belle shrunk down in her seat.

Clutching her skirts, Mary tried to miss the other passengers' feet but went down to the floor, so the riders could not see her. She slowly raised to peer out of the window.

Glancing out the window, Mary had a stricken face. As the riders came closer to the stagecoach, she hurried down on the floorboard of the stagecoach.

"Oh my, you have to help me!" Mary grasped Belle's arm. "Those are my stepbrothers! They are here to take me back home. You must help me, Belle. Don't let them take me, please." Mary looked at her pleadingly.

At that moment, a gunshot sounded close. Belle felt the bump from above the coach as one of the guards fell over. Brett looked at Belle.

"I know you know how to use that thing," pointing to her rifle, "I suggest that you use it now. They don't act too friendly."

He leaned over the opposite side and raised the dust cover from the window. Belle motioned Mary to stay at the bottom of the stagecoach and waited until one of the gunmen came close to the window before she shot. He looked surprised as he fell off the horse to the ground.

"Don't worry, I didn't kill him, only wounded him."

Belle tried to calm Mary.

Brett was able to hit two others, and the fourth turned away from the coach.

"Looks like they didn't think they would meet people who know how to fight, ma'am," stated Brett looking towards Mary.

As Brett spoke, the carriage started to slow down, but it was evident that the stage was weaving from side to side.

"You did good, son," stated the other passenger to Belle, "but it looks like the driver is having a hard time. I will try to help him."

He opened the door to climb up on top.

Mr. Post looked scared. He held tightly to the window, nervously looking back to see if anyone was there. The unkempt man jarred awake.

"What's going on? Did I miss anything? I dreamed I heard gunshots."

He leaned out the window, asking if he could help, as the coach slowed down.

Mary started to cry, holding onto Belle. She reminded Belle of the inheritance papers.

"My stepbrothers want to take my home and my land. If we make it to California, you can give them back. If not, then keep it and never let them have it. They worried my mother until she gave up. I can't let them take what my family worked so hard to gain."

Directing her words to Brett, "I'll tell you the story later."

He looked at Mary making her desperate plea, and Belle took the bundle.

Looking at Mary, Belle knew she was scared. Her helplessness brought out the fury in Belle. She knew Phillip would not stand a chance the minute Mary blinked her eyelashes, with her pleading eyes, dimples, and fragility.

"Does Phillip know about this?" Belle asked.

Mary looked nervously out of the stagecoach window.

"He knows a little of it and wants to help me. I haven't told him the whole story as it would make him worry about me."

Belle stuffed the papers in the inside pocket of her coat and buttoned it.

As the coach slowed to a stop, it was evident that the driver was having trouble managing the horses. She watched Brett climb up on top of the stagecoach. He threw down the reins to her. She grabbed the reins while Brett leaned across the top of the stagecoach to protect the driver. Keeping her hat tied low, Belle grabbed the reins and let the horses walk at a slow walk, hoping that this scene would not become a common thing during the trip. Belle knew that if it did, she was going to have to toughen up. Approaching another way station, Belle slowed the horses to a stop. A man ran out of the station to help with the horses. Belle climbed down off the stagecoach and held out her hand to help Mary down the steps. It was evident that Mary had been crying as tears rolled down her cheek. She looked so vulnerable at this moment.

Shoving Belle out of the way, the rudeness of the stranger was unsettling.

"I'll help the pretty lady. She needs a man's help, not a boy!"

Mary jerked her hand away from the stranger and drew back, not wanting to touch him.

"I'll be just fine if you want to move out of the way."

Brushing past Belle for the second time, he grabbed Mary's hand, pulling her out of the coach, causing her to fall forward. Mary fell forward into his waiting arms. She angrily pushed him aside, trying to get away from him. Belle started helping her and the man roughly pushed her aside.

"I said I would help the little lady."

Two hands grabbed the man's shoulders and pulled him away from Mary, knocking the man's hat off.

"Hey, what do you think you are doing?"

He turned around to face Brett.

"It should be obvious even for a bonehead like you that the little lady does not want your help," declared Brett.

As he took a swing at Brett, Brett grabbed his arm and twisted it backward, shoving him to the ground. Struggling as he turned around, the stranger was angry. Loosening his hold, Brett allowed him to get up. Glaring with murder in his eyes, the rough stranger stood. Dusting his pants off, he bent down to pick up his hat. He turned to Brett.

"We'll settle this later."

Belle, still holding Mary's arm, led her into the station. As they entered, Belle looked around. The room itself was small, dark, and worn looking. When Belle's eyes adjusted to the dark interior, she noticed four windows on the front and one window on the sidewall. Along two sides of the walls were rough beds, and tables were in the middle. Several lamps lit the room.

"Not a cheerful room, is it?" Belle said under her breath.

Mary silently nodded in agreement. As their eyes continued to adjust, she saw a way stationmaster near a stove. He was dishing something into a bowl from a large black cooking pot. He came over to the table where they had set down. Mary instantly put her head on the table. The station-master set the plates of beans down.

"It's not much, but it will hold you over until morning, ma'am. When you are finished, the lady can sleep on the bunk next to the wall. The boy can relax on the floor near her."

He threw Belle a blanket. Picking at the food, Mary finally quit trying to eat and went over to the bed. Belle followed her wistfully, looking at the bed. As Belle laid her blanket down on the clapboard floor, she thought to herself. *Well, it was my idea to pretend to be a boy, and this is what I get.* Within seconds she was fast asleep, ignoring the snoring around the room.

Belle felt very achy the following morning, the muscles in her body were overextended from sleeping on the hard wooden floor. She wondered out loud, "Will I ever get used to being beat-up and tired?"

Rising from the floor, she again wondered how she would make it through this day. Stretching and trying to loosen up did not help. Snatching a glance at Mary, she could not believe her eyes. Mary looked fresh and rested. She noticed that the corset was gone along with several of the dresses.

At breakfast, Belle and Mary both looked at their plates. Beans and biscuits. Picking up their forks, both started thinking about Sally and her excellent meals. Sally was prob-ably back in Maryville serving her aunt Della breakfast. They could almost smell the biscuits, light as a feather, served with blackberry jam. The aroma of honeyed ham, fresh butter, and eggs almost made their mouths water. Belle and Mary quickly returned to reality as their plates were placed on the table. The stationmaster held a hot pot of coffee in one hand and poured the coffee into their cups. They quickly motioned only to pour half a cup. After he moved on, both girls added water to dilute the brew down.

"Even though it is cold, it is still better than the full cup of that strong coffee he made last night," Mary said as she winced at the bitter coffee.

"Mary, when we get somewhere where we can write, I am going to write to your Miss Sally and tell her how much I appreciated all the wonderful meals she fixed for us. I don't think we appreciated her enough."

Belle kept looking at the plate of beans. Shaking her head, she put down her fork, picked up the biscuits and coffee, and went out to the bench on the porch.

Brett finished his plate and carried it over to the sink on the far side of the room. As he came back, he saw the look of disgust on Mary's face. Brett sat down beside her, taking her hand.

"Mary, things are always a little rough when you start a new life. You must eat and keep up your strength during this trip. Even if it is only a plate of beans, it is still for your strength. Now eat up. The stage will leave in a bit."

"Brett, there is something I need to tell you." Mary turned to face him. "Those men that attacked us a few days ago. I recognized them. They were my stepbrothers. They were not after anything on the stage but wanted to kidnap me. They want my mother's estate. Until I get on that ship in New Orleans, I am not safe from them. I am scared."

Brett saw the tears in her eyes and felt swelling compassion for her.

"Mary, I will do my best to protect you and Belle. We will

65

make it to New Orleans. I thought you wanted to go by ship because of the Indian uprising, but now I see you feel safer if you are where they can't reach you. I will get you to Phillip, I promise."

Drying her tears, she turned back to her beans.

"Surely, I can survive the food on this trip." Winking at Brett, she started eating.

Brett walked out to the porch. He watched Belle, moving slowly, stiffly, and walking with a limp. *I feel like a wagonload of cows ran over me,* she thought. She watched out of the corner of her eye as Brett helped Mary into the coach.

"Where is the stranger this morning?" Belle asked Brett as she looked around. "Is he coming?"

"Oh, I had a little talk last night with him concerning Miss Mary, and he decided to wait for the next coach. He won't be bothering her again," said Brett quietly.

Belle slowly climbed into the coach, dreading sitting on the thin cushion covering the seat, and was careful to sit beside Mary. There was more space on the bench seat without the other rider, but Belle wondered what happened between the two men.

Brett supported the older man as he got into the coach and then climbed in with them. A worker for the way station-master climbed up on top of the coach to help the driver. The manager gave the worker instructions about catching the next stagecoach back. Slumping against the side of the coach, Belle wished this day would be over, and they were in New Orleans. Belle, feeling uncomfortable, wondered how long it would take her bottom to toughen. Looking out the window, Belle thought to herself. *This is not how they described stagecoach traveling in the penny novels.*

# CHAPTER 9

From a distance, Natchez looked just like any other southern town. Its dirty and dusty streets quickly stirred up a cloud behind the coach as it entered the main road. Looking from the window, Mary immediately lifted the bib of her dress to cover her nose. Belle held her hat in front of her nose, peeking over the brim.

"This is nothing like I expected," cried Mary. "I thought it would be more civilized. More like the towns back home."

There were a lot of saloons and some shops along the main street. As they reached the central part of the city, the dusty roads turned to cobblestones. Not understanding that most of Natchez's gentile citizens had their plantations outside of town, Mary looked with wonder while passing through the main village. A few men and women were on the street at this early hour, but most shops were still closed. The houses on the edge of town had walled gardens around them with short gates to allow a passing person to peer in at the gardens' greenery. Magnolia trees lined the streets, in full bloom with Spanish moss trails hanging down from their limbs. The heavy scent almost overpowered the air.

In the town proper, several people were crossing the street, dodging the wagons and horses. The women in plain dresses, with little ornamentation, held their heads down into kerchiefs. They wore bonnets with large brims to protect them from the sun. Small children clung close to their mothers, trying to dodge the mudholes in the street. The horseback riders paid little attention to the people on foot. They stormed through the town, racing to get to the different stores and saloons. Some of the riders rode to the stores for supplies and tools.

As the stagecoach pulled up to the station, the driver declared, "This is the last stop for this stagecoach. Everyone will have to get out. The passengers traveling to New Orleans will need to stay at Ms. Dorothea's Boarding House overnight. The rooms are reserved. The next coach leaves tomorrow at seven o'clock in the morning sharp."

The coach's creaking as the driver disembarked was a signal that they needed to get off the stagecoach.

Looking stricken at the prospects of being at the end of the coach line, Mary leaned towards Belle and held onto her arm. Looking down the busy street, as the dust was billowing up, Belle continued to be disappointed at what she saw. She saw there were few town folks on the narrow boardwalks in front of the stores. Most men were mainly rough, dirty-looking cowmen, most of them standing around staring at the coach. One started towards them. Mr. Post walked as fast as he could with his cane towards them, hooking his arm in Mary's, and started towards the boarding house.

"I think the lady needs an escort," he said. Looking at Belle, "Come along, lad, keep up with us. Don't dally; I will be glad to help."

Watching the scene, the cowboy stopped and watched them cross the street. Suddenly, he turned and walked back.

Continuing to hold Mary's arm, Belle exclaimed, "Thank

you for being so kind, Mr. Post! I was starting to think we were going to have problems."

Mr. Post held tight to Mary's elbow.

"They are mainly good folk, but a pretty woman like you is bound to have problems. You should have an escort. The young man here is fine, but they wouldn't pay any attention to him."

Bristling at his words, Belle brought her shoulders to full height. *I bet I could handle them. Of course, I could*, she thought to herself.

"I know what you are thinking, young man, I am sure you could stop them, but it is best to walk with me. No matter how decent men can be inside, it's better not to test it." Passing a store, Belle motioned them to go on as she stopped to buy more ammunition.

At the boarding house, Mary explained to the owner that Belle was her brother, and she would feel more comfortable sharing a room because he was younger than the other men and he would not be safe among the rougher group that she had seen in the lobby. The owner, a little dubious, agreed once given an extra fee.

"I don't usually let females and males share a room, but since he is your younger brother, I understand your concern."

After looking at Belle, she saw the innocence that would likely be a problem among the other men. Shaking her head, the proprietor led them to a single room overlooking the front entrance.

"Now, mind you, your brother will have to sleep on the floor. I don't have any extra beds for him."

Then she walked back down the stairs with Mary following her to pay the bill.

Once in the boarding room, Belle noticed the pitcher of water on the stand and a mirror. Looking in the mirror, she was appalled at her appearance. Taking the washstand cloth, she poured water into the basin, and she started working on the dirt on her face. Once clean, she gave her body a once over and rinsed out her dirty clothes in the murky water. As she laid them across the window seat, she looked around. *A bed*, she thought, *so much paradise in one tiny room*. Rising, she folded back the covers, scanning the mattress for vermin. Once satisfied, she put on her clean shirt and fell asleep as fast as she hit the bed.

When Mary came back to the room, she saw Belle curled up on the side of the bed, fast asleep. Mary washed and cleaned her body as much as she could with the low water. Even though she did not have all the activity Belle had, Mary was still more tired than she had ever been. Hanging her dress over the side windowsill to dry, Mary heard Belle's soft, gentle snoring and eagerly climbed into her side of the bed. Stretching out, she was asleep in minutes.

At six the following day, Belle was awakened by a knock at the door.

"Hurry up, young man, we need to eat before we leave," yelled a rough voice through the door.

Pulling on her pants, shirt, socks, boots, and grabbing her hat, she stuffed her old clothes in the saddlebag. Belle looked in the mirror one last time. Satisfied that she still resembled a boy, she headed out the door. Entering the dining room, she noted the others were already there, including three others sitting at the same long table near Mary. The gong clanged just as Belle finished eating. Chugging down her coffee, she gathered with the others at the door. As Belle and Mary left, the dining room hostess gave each passenger a small basket with sandwiches for the trip.

Climbing on top of the stagecoach, the driver yelled towards the inn.

"Let's load up. Be sure to fill your canteens. We are

carrying a total of six passengers today heading to New Orleans."

As they reached the stage, they saw several trunks on top of the coach, including theirs. Mary counted hers to make sure that they had both of hers. Belle carried her belongings in her saddlebag and had a single trunk on the top of the stagecoach. Tossing the saddlebag towards the man on top, he fastened it to the roof of the coach. Her bullets were in the bag, and she had loaded the rifle. She did not want to be in the same situation as the day before if they had trouble.

When Belle approached the coach, she overheard Mary talking nervously to the other passengers.

"I know sitting behind the driver is the most comfortable, but I get vapors when I ride backward."

Brett motioned that he would sit in that seat, giving her the seat across from him. Belle steadied Mary as she climbed up the steps into the coach, rushing to go behind her so they could sit together. She noted Brett had taken his seat and had placed his rifle on the floorboard. Another woman and two other men made up the passengers. Mr. Post would not be traveling on and was staying in town with his daughter. There were six of them, three women and three men heading to New Orleans.

# CHAPTER 10

Brett sat next to the window directly across from Belle and Mary. Leaning towards the side of the stagecoach, he pulled his hat down and closed his eyes. Mary, refreshed from the night's sleep, looked excited for the next leg of the trip. Mary kept opening the window curtain to watch the countryside.

"Only two more days on the stagecoach, then we will be there. I can hardly wait," she exclaimed as she rearranged her skirts.

The other woman looked anxious and fidgeted with her handkerchief in her lap.

"I hope we don't see and outlaws or renegades. I heard there were plenty on this trail." The woman pulled on her handkerchief. "I do not like traveling when the land is so unsettled. I heard Baton Rouge is becoming the center for recruitment for the expected war." She looked at Mary. "Do you know anyone enlisting? All of this is so terrifying."

Turning to the side, Mary tried to calm her.

"They have said attacks on the stagecoaches rarely happen. Try to calm down. We have plenty of men to help if anything happens. What I heard last night is, there are a few guards waiting for us at the edge of town. Since we are carrying cargo for them, the stagecoach company is sending guards to protect the stagecoach. It's better to think positive rather than worry about something before it happens."

The woman leaned back into the seat but still looked around and ahead, looking for the outlaws. Brett listened to their conversation and watched them, and then pulled his hat down and ignored them.

The view through the windows opened into rolling hills, grasslands, and occasionally, they would see trees and smell the river's water that flowed between them. It was a pretty time of year. It was the end of summer and all the flowers bowed their heads as the stage continued to roll along the dirt road. Gradually the rolling hills evolved into flatter land, and the way became more comfortable to ride. The men inside the coach dozed. One even snored. Mary slept with her head falling forward. She would jerk, open her eyes, then nod off again. Then suddenly, they noticed the stage was slowing down. Mrs. Guthrie, the other woman, suddenly jerked up from her nap.

"What's going on? Are we okay?" she cried, wringing her handkerchief.

"It's time for the horses to rest. You might as well get down and stretch your legs," the driver yelled down from his perch.

When the stagecoach stopped, the horses were released from the harnesses and followed the driver down to a stream. Several of the horses waded into the water, enjoying the coolness of it. Leaving the water, the horses started sampling the grass. Mary and Belle spread their lap blanket on the ground and enjoyed the incredible calmness of the river.

The driver staked the horses by their leads, removed the bits, and let them enjoy the feast. The passengers strolled around the grassy meadow, glad to be out of the coach.

"What a nice place," spoke one of the men named Tim. "Wouldn't this be a good place for a farm?"

Sam, the other man, told him that the land was owned by a rancher good enough to let the coach travel through since, so far, the road was public domain. Looking around, Belle agreed with him.

"It would make a great home, overlooking the river, with the grasslands. But I heard the land was unbelievable in Oregon. That's our destination," said Sam. "Yes sirree, I have been promised 180 acres of farmland with water running through it. My brother went out last year, and he's already got it staked out. I dread the longship journey, but the Indians are getting so bad in the prairies that it is safer to travel by ship."

Taking a good look at the driver, Belle saw he was in the typical driver getup, a long linen dust coat with gauntlet gloves, a wide-brimmed hat, and a bright red handkerchief around his neck. At the last station, the guard assigned to them was dressed similarly, with his dark blue bandanna. After a good night's sleep, the driver didn't seem quite as cranky as the day before. Both wore the determined look of responsibility and were on the lookout. The guard sat on a tall boulder with his rifle on his lap, scanning the area as the others rested. The driver gathered the horses' reins, gave them one long last drink, and then led them back to the stagecoach. As he was hitching the horses, he warned the passengers of making sure that they fasten their belongings tight. As they loaded up, the driver informed them that the next stretch would be through some rough areas, so relax while they can. Belle and Mary looked at each other. *Why would he say that? Surely it could not be as rough as their previous days had been.*

The passengers climbed back into the stagecoach, glad for

the rest stop before moving forward. The driver checked the tie-down straps on the luggage and turned to reach the reins.

"Heya, heya!" he yelled as he shook the reins. With a swift response, the horses moved towards the trail. For hours they drove through the countryside. After seeing patches of swampy land, Belle noticed the flatlands eventually became drier and browner.

Some areas had some patches of green left, but most places started looking like fall. The sun, however, beat down on the enclosed coach.

"Guess we are heading towards the delta," Belle thought out loud. The rocking of the stage slowly caused the passengers to start nodding off. Belle tried to keep her eyes open, but she found that the call to sleep was too much. As her head bowed and rested against the side of the coach, Mary leaned her head on Belle's shoulders. The rocky, bumpy trip went on for hours it seemed. When the horses began slowing, Belle woke up instantly. Stretching, she wondered where they were.

As they neared another way station, the driver called down through the communication box.

"When we arrive, please stay in the stagecoach. Something is not right."

Brett sat straight and peered out the windows, scanning for trouble. As they neared the station, they could hear the driver blowing on his horn, as was the custom when reaching the stations to prepare the stationmaster to get ready for the passengers. They waited for an answer, but all they heard was quietness. As they reached the station, the horses stopped whinnying as they shook their heads. The stillness in the air put everyone on alert.

The driver came down from the coach, calling out, "Lim, where are you? What's going on?"

Brett, with his gun out of his holster, left the coach to assist the driver. Belle tumbled out the door.

"I'm coming too."

Belle checked her rifle, ensuring it was loaded, wishing she had her pistols out of her saddlebag. She loosened the safety, prepared for the worst. Together they walked up to the station. Brett came back out on the porch.

Looking at the stagecoach, Brett called out.

"We have troubles. The way stationmaster is dead. We will bury him quickly. There are no signs of who did it, so stretch, but stay close to the stagecoach. We may need to leave in a hurry."

Turning, he went back into the building.

Each of the passengers stepped out of the stagecoach and stretched, staring towards the building. Belle, impatient, walked towards the way station. As she approached the porch, the driver called through the opening to Belle.

"Son, look in the bar and see if there is a shovel. If so, bring it back quickly."

~

The three brothers sat quietly in the wooded area near the way station, watching the scene closely. As the passengers left the stagecoach, one of the men pointed towards the group.

"There is Brett, there is Mary. It looks like that crazy friend of hers is with her. This job is not going to be easy. How are we going to get her away from the others?"

Motioning the others further into the woods, they stopped to talk. Marcus looked haggardly, with several days old beard, dirty clothes, and scuffed boots.

"I've waited too long to mess this up. That little girl is going to learn she can't mess with me. That money should belong to me. Her mother cheated on our pa, so she will have to pay the price. Bob, you stay where you can see us and cover us if anyone tries to draw a gun. Charley, you come with me. We will go through the back of the barn and be ready to grab her. Bob, move that extra horse to the trees behind the stagecoach. That is where we will bring her. Keep a close watch on the cousin. He's the one we have to worry about."

Moving quickly to get in position, they waited for the right moment.

They watched as Belle came close to the barn. She peeked in the door and seeing it empty, moved towards the tack room at the end of the stable. Suddenly, a smelly horse blanket came down over her head. Then she felt ropes placed around her arms.

"Don't make a noise, little girl, and you won't get hurt."

They tied her hands behind her back and hobbled her feet. Tying a bandanna across her mouth to keep her quiet, they sat her in one of the stalls. Then in unison, they moved to the barn window to see what was happening. Mary was standing by the stagecoach. They saw Bob behind the stagecoach moving towards her.

"What is that fool doing? He's going to mess the plan up," Marcus said under his breath.

Suddenly Bob moved and grabbed Mary. She was fighting him, twisting to get away from him. Mary let out a stream of cuss words and moved away. At the same time, Brett came out of the way station, quickly assessed the situation, and drew his gun.

"Let her go!" he shouted as he moved down the steps.

As soon as he hit the bottom step, Marcus shot at him from the barn, causing Brett to duck and move behind the porch. The driver and the other passenger in the building saw the action and moved to the back door, heading to the back of the barn.

Bob yelled, "Hey cousin, throw your gun down, or I will

hurt Mary. We don't want any trouble. We will just be relieving you of the trouble of guarding Mary. She's our sister, and we will take care of her. Stand up and throw down your gun."

As the driver and passenger entered the back of the barn, they saw the two men at the window, with Belle tied up and thrown across a bale of hay.

"Misters, put your hands up and turn around. Don't reach for the gun, or you will find yourself full of holes."

Slowly the men turned around. Marcus, seeing the shotgun, lowered his gun to the barn floor. Charley looked at Marcus and turned to shoot. There was a loud bang as the shotgun went off, striking Charley in the chest.

Marcus became angry after seeing his brother on the ground.

"Why did you have to shoot him?"

He stooped to elevate Charley's head. Charley looked at Marcus.

"See, I told you it was a foolish idea. We should have settled with what Mary gave us in the beginning. It was plenty and more that we deserved."

With that, he collapsed. Marcus stood up with his hands curled in a fist. Grabbing the shovel next to the doorway, he moved towards the men. Just as he was swinging the shovel, the driver shot his arm, causing Marcus to lose grip on the shovel.

Bob, hearing the noises in the barn, threw Mary on the ground and mounted his horse.

Mary shouted, "Don't hurt him, let him go!"

As he ran to her, Brett helped Mary to her feet.

"Are you okay?"

"Yes, those are my stepbrothers. I know they are awful, but don't hurt them." Looking around, "Where is Belle?"

The driver tied Marcus's hands and led him out of the barn.

"Damn, now we have two bodies to bury."

Brett ran into the barn and found Belle gagged and tied. She had twisted herself up to a sitting position and was furious.

"I don't know if I want to untie you, girl. It looks like you are about to boil over."

Brett laughed at the sight of her. She kicked at the floor and fell backward over the hay bale.

"Here, let me help you out of this mess. You never brought the shovel. Don't you know how to do a simple thing like bring someone a shovel?" Brett continued to smirk.

As soon as Brett untied her, Belle stomped her feet. Whipping the bandanna out of her mouth, Belle let loose a string of unladylike words.

"I'll have you know I am not a servant. I don't like having my hands tied, and I sure don't like someone making fun of me." Then looking worried, "Is Mary alright?"

Grabbing her by her shoulders, he bent down and kissed her. The kiss was not a slight brush of his lips but a deep, lingering, soul-searching kiss. As he hugged her, he saw the confusion in her eyes.

"Belle, don't ever worry me like that again."

Not knowing what to say or do, she removed his arms from around her, turned, and ran from the barn to find her friend. She heard him chuckle in the background. Holding Mary, she cried when she saw how red her arms were. Belle gently touched Mary's cheek, where her stepbrother slapped her.

"Mary, why are you feeling sorry for these guys? They tried to kidnap you!"

"Belle, I know they are no good, and I shouldn't waste tears on them, but their dad was nice to my mother. I just hate that they are behaving like they are. I just want to get out of here and reach Sacramento."

Then a new gush of tears fell from Mary's eyes.

Brett and the other two men buried both the way station-master and Bob. Mary cleaned Marcus's wound. Brett tied him to a horse to follow the stagecoach to the Baton Rouge marshal.

Belle, holding her mouth, tried to settle down. She slowly climbed back into the stagecoach but was still dry heaving from the bandana. As soon as she was in, Brett and other passengers were fast behind her. Still in shock over being hog-tied and Mary's kidnapping attempt, Belle was shaking as she leaned against the seat. *Was she upset over being tied up, the kidnapping, or was it Brett's kiss?* Too numb to speak, she closed her eyes so none of the passengers would talk to her. Brett watched her intently.

"Belle, there was nothing you could do back there. Be tough. We are not out of the woods yet."

Several miles down the road, the driver stopped the stage-coach to take care of the horses. He watered them, fed them, and then gave them more water. He did not rest as much as he wanted to in order to put as many miles as possible between them and the last incident. Baton Rouge was only a few more miles. There he would turn over Marcus to the marshal, and they would be able to close the door on this chapter in Mary's life . . . hopefully.

# CHAPTER 11

*Baton Rouge was a pretty and quiet town,* thought Belle as the stagecoach followed the river. There seemed to be heavy river traffic, and many roadhouses were visible as they came around the river's bend. As they came nearer to the town proper, the girls could see buildings with vivid signs and carriages with well-dressed ladies and gentlemen. It was different from what Belle had seen before. In Natchez, most of the town was concentrated in a small area and had few shops. Stately homes sat in the middle of large parcels of land edging the town like the ones in Natchez, but these were much more significant and on larger pieces of land. Stately oak and magnolia trees with Spanish moss were gently moving as the breeze caught them. There were flowers everywhere, making a carpet of color to greet them. The magnolia trees stood like grand ladies, giving off a gentle scent that cleared the dust and dirt air. Belle saw Union soldiers walking up and down the sidewalks watching the pedestrians, but not seemingly bothering them as they went into the town.

Belle tried to concentrate, but her thoughts raced through her head. *The war is real. I hope we leave here before it becomes harmful. Mom and Pa fought so hard not to have this happen. I hope Aunt Hester will be okay. Where can Jeremy be? I hope he doesn't become a part of this.* Sadly, she turned to Mary.

"I see them too," looking towards the Union soldiers. "Let's just hope we can get out of here before trouble comes."

Belle and Mary quietly recognized it was essential to leave this area before the war broke out. The rest of the drive took a sad note as the impending war's reality settled on the two girls' minds.

They did not stay long in Baton Rouge, just long enough to eat, freshen up, change horses, and then get on their way towards New Orleans. Belle continued to watch the soldiers as they passed. *This cannot be good for our country. No one I know owns slaves. The Maryville area freed them years ago and now paid them wages and their living expenses. I hope Sally will be safe.* Belle reached over to Mary and patted her hand. Mary gave a weak smile, but it was easy to see a sad air in the stagecoach as they left Baton Rouge.

Belle stayed quiet, not talking to anyone. She had thought she was strong and that she could handle anything. Now reality was staring at her. The truth was this was not a fun and games situation any longer. She didn't want to pretend anymore. The reality was closing in around her, and she was not sure she was strong enough. *Between the mess back there at the way station and now seeing the soldiers. How can I deal with my inside feelings? I feel so alone.* Looking sadly at Mary, she put her head down to hide her tears. Mary held her hand as they traveled. No one said anything for a long time. The reality hit her hard. For the second time, she thought, *this was not a game any longer*. As for Belle, she made some decisions on that ride. She wanted to be who she was, not someone playing a false match. Life is too hard to playact or play games. If boys had to be brutal and fight wars, she would rather be a girl.

Brett watched the girls closely. Not understanding the

cause, he had a lot of questions in his mind about this girl. The more Brett watched them, the more aware he became of his feelings for Belle. Holding her in his arms brought feelings he had not had for a long time. No one had been able to break through his hard shell since his wife died. Why this girl? She was nothing like his sweet wife, Adele. Belle was tomboyish, outspoken, and focused on goals that she had not shared with anyone but Mary. What kind of girl would dress like a boy, be wicked with her rifle, or want to leave a comfortable home and trek out west to the unknown? Opening the curtain enough to see out, he watched the scenery for a while, then leaned back on the bench, still conscious of the support Mary was giving to Belle.

As they arrived in New Orleans, Belle pushed the horrors of the kidnapping and the rough treatment she had received to the back of her mind. Even still, when she least expected it, she found herself thinking about it. *I don't understand how I let them capture me like that. I am not as challenging as I thought.* Looking around as they entered the city, she was surprised at how pretty it seemed as they traveled towards the station. Even the air, though humid and fragrant, seemed cleaner. Mary started chattering as they drove by the homes. It had some of the same attributes as Baton Rouge but had a different charm. The streets were cobblestones. As the horses pulled the coach, a rhythmic clapping added a soothing sound to the birds singing. Leaning out the window, Mary was excited to take in the scene.

Belle, still subdued, sat quietly in the stagecoach. The homes were sheltered with tall brick walls providing privacy, only giving small hints as they passed by. Passing the beautiful intricate gates, they could see through the iron patterns to the beautiful, lush gardens beyond. Flowers dominated the scene. Even the smaller homes had front yard gardens full of trees and luscious flowers. The yards were neatly clipped, and everything looked clean. The heavy and sweet flower scents delighted them. The flowers had them forgetting the long hours of a dust-filled carriage. Belle and Mary looked around them, amazed at the scene. As they entered a more populated area, everyone they saw seemed to be in some rush. There were many carriages and horses in the streets. Women were coming in and out of the shops with parcels and often had their maids loaded down with packages.

There were sounds of laughter and singing. Several areas had men sitting at tables on the sidewalk, talking and playing instruments. The scene around the stagecoach was a clamor of sounds. The music was different. Accordions, trumpets, and saxophones blended to provide an uplifting spirit. In one corner, she saw a man dancing with loud metal on the bottom of his shoes. That was different from what they had seen before. Smiling and keeping a beat, Mary laughed at the merriment. Some dressed in bright colors, and others in tailored suits. Still, many had loose-fitting dresses with feathers, sparkling stones, and ruffles, lots of ruffles. The carnival atmosphere lifted their spirits immensely.

The sweet, salty air of the ocean made the humidity strong. Within minutes, Belle and Mary felt the heat. Not the heat they knew in St. Louis, but a sweltering, wet heat that caused them to drip with sweat. Their clothes became damp and limp within a few minutes. Mary's beautiful curls were falling from her hair arrangement. The humidity caused Belle difficulty breathing at first. Still, breathing here was more manageable than the dusty trail as she adapted to the air's heavy moisture.

The driver told them it would be two days before their ship left, so they hired a carriage to take them from the station to the hotel. Brett told them he would walk around, and he would see them later at the hotel.

"Clean beds, hot food, that's what I want!" Mary exclaimed.

Belle was in total agreement. The horse took them to a boarding house near the bay, where the scenery was so appealing.

"Wait, stop," Belle asked the carriage driver. "This is so beautiful. I just want to watch a minute."

Sitting on the rise, they could look down at the boarding house nestled in the beach along the cove.

"Missy, there is a beach for the residents at the boarding house right behind it. They have food and tables if you are hungry, and a nice sandy beach to walk on. You will like what we have here in New Orleans. Just enjoy it," chattered the driver. "Don't worry none, it is safe here. Whatever you do, don't go near the Quarter. It is not a good place for lovely ladies like you."

As Belle and Mary looked at the boarding house, they could see directly beside and behind the two-story white house was a long stretch of golden sand. The water gently washed up on the beach, with birds running in and out of the waves. There were beach tents set up for the hotel guests with large umbrellas and small tables. The water was different from the water seen along the trail. It was blue-green, turning darker blue as the water was further from shore. Small bubbling waves washed gently against the shore. Seemingly stretching to the skyline, the ocean looked never-ending. In the distance, they could see shrimp boats with their nets poised off the side.

The waves seemed to be playing with the swimmers. Belle watched a woman with two children running along the waves, picking them up as the waves hit their feet. The little ones were squealing with delight each time the mother lifted them. *This is what I need to help me forget. It is so lovely here. Good thing we have a few days before the ship sails.* Looking towards

Mary, she could tell she agreed. As they reached the entrance, they watched the bellhop take their trunks out of the wagon. They paid the driver and went for a short walk on the board-walk along the beach. Breathing in the salty air, being free from the stagecoach, Belle felt herself beginning to relax for the first time in days.

Riding in a stagecoach for hours at a time caused both girls to be stiff and sore. As they strolled down the boarded sidewalk, they soon felt the fatigue escaping as they bathed in the sunlight. As they reached the door to the boarding house, both were ready for a good sleep. The resident manager arranged for hot water to be carried up to their rooms and told them the dining room would be open later that evening. Still, he would have a light dinner to tide them over in case they couldn't wait for dinner.

In their rooms, they quickly stripped their dirty clothes off and put on robes. The manager sent a tray loaded with fresh fruit, egg sandwiches, and fresh hot tea. There were also small triangle pâté sandwiches, with a few pieces of fried chicken and a cabbage salad. Drawing straws, Belle won to be first for the tub. Mary checked the bed for vermin, then settled in a chair, watching Belle as she delighted in her bath. Sinking in the warm water, Belle sighed, settling down for a good soak. Thoroughly washing the grime and dirt from her hair, she not only felt different but looked like another person. For the first time in days, her hair was clean. The shorter hairstyle caused her regular curls to fall becomingly, surrounding her face and barely touching her shoulders.

Standing, drying herself from head to toe, she felt a peace come over her. Her feet felt good to be out of the boots. Setting them on the ledge of the window, she pulled out the linings and washed them, wrinkling up her nose at the smell of trail dust and foot sweat. She used the rest of her bath-water to wash her clothes, hanging them on the clothesline stretching out the back window of their room to the building next door.

As they waited for the chambermaids to empty Belle's bathwater, Belle laid on the soft bed, enjoying the comfort and the cleanliness of their room. Mary sat quietly watching her friend and reading her book. When fresh water arrived, Mary sighed as she slid down into the clean water. Mary, giggling with pleasure, let the water surround her, the hot water comforting her sore bottom from the bench's rough ride in the stagecoach. Belle was surprised when washing the dust out of her golden hair as she noticed that Mary's curls weren't natural. *I guess it is true. You always want what you don't have.*

As soon as the water surrounded her head, it was easy to see that her hair was straight and different from Belle's. Later, while Mary laid on the bed enjoying the quietness, comfort, and feel of being clean, she sat up and looked at Belle standing in front of the mirror.

"Belle, you look so different from before. I would never guess that you were the boy that I've known for the last few weeks."

Belle stood in front of the mirror with her red curly hair, noting the light dusting of freckles across her face.

"Well, at least our curls are in common," giggled Mary.

The hot sun had indeed made the patches of freckles stand out across Belle's nose and back. The copper curls twined down onto her shoulders, glinting in the light. Turning, she looked at Mary.

"Mary, I wanted to talk to you about that," she turned to look again at the mirror. "The scene back there at the way station was beyond belief. I can't get it out of my mind. How can anyone think that it was okay? Every time I close my eyes, I see it repeatedly. I was terrified when I had the blanket pulled over my head. Then to be tied up, and a bandanna stuffed in my mouth. Still not able to see who they were. It scared me until I heard their voices, then I just got mad. I discovered I am not as strong as I thought I was when we started this trip. Most of all," pausing, turning to look at Mary, "it made me realize that I am not the person I thought I was. When we first started, I wasn't aware of all the horrible things that could happen. I just want to be me. I am tired of the pretense. What do you think? Would you think it was terrible if I went back to being Belle?"

Putting her head in her hands, sitting on the seat, she began to tear.

Mary crossed the room and grabbed her hands, brushing the hair out of her eyes gently, then wiping her tears away, and sat down on the seat beside her. Sitting on the edge, both girls hugged each other.

"Belle, you can outshoot most men I know, and you are strong and dependable. We will still be friends, even best friends. It doesn't matter what you wear, we have always had each other. That is not going to change. We will get through this trip, and I know we will be happy." Grinning, she teased Belle, "I noticed your glances at Brett. Are you falling for my dear cousin?"

Turning around suddenly, Belle looked stricken.

"My gosh, is it that obvious? At first, I thought he was another older man. However, now I see a real man. Not like all those guys Aunt Hester kept throwing at me. Do you think he notices me?"

Laughing, "Belle, how could anyone not notice you?"

Hugging Mary, sighing over the clean sheets, they went to bed, feeling like they had just come out of a deep nightmare into civilization. That night Belle laid in bed dreamily thinking of Brett and how much she wanted this trip to be over. However, each time she thought of Brett's name, the face of Tomas appeared. Angrily, she punched her pillow. *Why would I think of that no-good womanizer? He couldn't walk in Brett's shoes. The whole goal of this adventure is to find a man I want, not some no-good man who is full of himself or someone telling me who to choose.* Frowning, Belle drifted off to a night of deep sleep. She saw Brett's face throughout her dreams, saying her name, putting his arms around her, and leading her back to the stagecoach. The following day, she remembered the feeling of Brett's arms around her, causing a sense of warmth and confusion.

After eating a light breakfast, they headed to the shops to prepare for the next phase of their trip. Belle being light-hearted, looked forward to buying girly things and stopped at each window looking at the wide variety of wares. She swore she would never wear the boy's clothes again. As they walked through the town, they noticed the change in New Orleans's atmosphere compared to the other cities where they had stopped. Many uniformed men walked on the boardwalks, occasionally asking for identification from the people walking to the shops. Frowning, Belle and Mary hurried through the crowds, occasionally stopping to look in store windows as they shopped. The soldiers mingled with the masses, watching the shoppers with interest.

However, they were not the only ones watching people. Brett stood at the edge of a building with a puzzled expression on his face as he saw the two girls giggling as they went inside the store. Confused, when he saw Mary with the red-headed girl, he scratched his head, staring straight at her, trying to place the new girl. Brett watched through the store window as the two girls looked at the dresses and other women's accessories. Suddenly, he recognized the girl with Mary. Quietly, Brett mused as a slow smile came across his face. *Our little boy is quite a looker when cleaned up.* He sat down on the bench outside the store and watched as they shopped.

Belle and Mary found several dresses while shopping that

only needed minor alterations and would last the months at sea. Pleased with their finds, they bought petticoats, shoes, and matching bonnets. However, Mary did not buy as many things as Belle. They were happy and giggling as they asked to have the packages delivered to the boarding house. As the store owners approached them, they agreed on one thing. No corsets. They crossed the street to look in the windows of a store that sold outerwear. The sales clerk brought them to the back of the store when they told her they would be at sea for a long time. Looking through all the different materials, Belle and Mary both bought a smooth beaver coat to withstand the seas' coldness. A Bonney hat and scarf with matching gloves completed the ensemble.

As Belle noted all her purchases, she purchased a new trunk to store all her new items. Tired from shopping and the excitement of buying new clothes, Belle and Mary left the shops. As they walked back to the hotel, still more Union soldiers walked on the streets and sidewalks. Trying not to make eye contact, Mary and Belle walked quickly back to the hotel, not noticing Brett a short distance behind them. While passing one building, they saw the recruitment posters and the soldiers standing at the door. There were a few men in line, looking very serious. Belle and Mary slowed to watch the process.

Leaning into Belle, Mary whispered, "It is good that we are leaving this area. War is never a good thing for either side. I am against slavery and am glad we freed Sally. I hope she will be safe."

Quietly after they were further down the street, Belle let out a slow breath.

"My heart breaks, wondering if Jeremy is safe. He's foolish enough to be caught up in the fighting. Somewhere he has to be safe."

Both girls hurried back to the boarding house.

She hated to part with her brother's clothes, but she did not need them any longer. She kept the jacket, gun, and holster with the rifle. However, Belle decided to leave the pants, hat, and shirt in the room as a donation even though she could not imagine anyone wanting to wear them. At the hotel, the girls settled down to eat and rest before leaving the following afternoon. While in the dining room, neither girl saw Brett two tables away, with a newspaper in front of him, watching them.

As they ate, the ladies heard the other diners discussing politics, often heated discussions concerning the states' secession. The other hotel guests shared their views concerning the premise of war looming.

"South Carolina already seceded, our legislators are talking, and I heard several other states are going to leave the Union as well."

Other murmurs around the room were just as disturbing.

"War, they want to free all our slaves.."

"My maid and houseboy are scared to death. They will have no one to take care of them. Worst of all, what will we do without them?"

Some were vocal concerning the slavery issues; some were against the owning of others. Silently, keeping to themselves, the girls waited for their dinner.

The food was a hearty fresh roast cooked with onions and vegetables. Served with popover rolls and fresh milk and butter, Mary and Belle fell quiet, enjoying their food. As a server passed their table, they noticed a different type of plant they had never seen before. Pointing it out to their server, she identified it as okra and gave them a small plate to try.

"Okra," repeated Mary after the server gave her the sample. Crunching down on the crisp, salty food, "This is exceptionally good. I have never eaten this before. Maybe the farmers in California will grow some of this in their gardens so that we can have it all the time."

Mary closed her eyes and enjoyed the fried okra. The waitress enjoyed discussing the okra and gave them a packet of seeds before they left the room. The noise in the dining room was becoming louder, with people arguing their views back and forth. Belle and Mary picked up their fruit, glasses, and the pies and cream to take to their room to eat later. Reaching their room, Belle and Mary suddenly felt the rush of fatigue which overcame them. Neither had much to say that night. As they ate the dessert, the evening routine was quick so that they could go to bed early.

The following day, after a hearty breakfast of fresh eggs, toast, and cured ham, the kitchen sent up a food basket for their trip as they packed their things. When they opened the basket, they found meat sandwiches, crackers, cheese, pickles, fruit, and a jar of fresh plum jam to take on their trip. The basket was large and heavy, so the porter added it to their baggage. As they waited for the carriage to take them to the ship, the porter took their trunks and packages in a different wagon. Also in the wagon were other passengers' belongings.

Brett walked towards them.

"Well, ladies, are you ready for the next stage of the trip? I think you will find it quite different from riding on the stagecoach."

He could see the excited flush on their cheeks as they walked with him.

"Brett, are you riding with us?" exclaimed Mary.

"No, I am stopping by the store to pick up a few things, but I will see you there."

Tipping his hat, he walked out the door.

Excited about the future, Mary and Belle had the driver take them by the ocean one last time.

"If you girls are going on the big ship, I think you will get your fill of water by the time the trip is over," he told them, smiling.

Stopping at the dock, they saw the *Flying Goose* for the first time. Holding her breath at the wonder of the ship, Belle compared it with the schooner docked next to it.

# CHAPTER 12

As Mary and Belle approached the harbor, the driver pointed out the ship they would be traveling by. The clipper ship was smaller and narrower than the schooner, with tall masts at both ends. Men were hurrying on the decks, shouting orders, and pulling on ropes. Other men were coiling ropes or carrying boxes into a large hole in the deck. Like a fire bucket brigade, a line of men started passing boxes of supplies up the gangplank. Belle and Mary moved to the side, trying not to get in their way, admiring how the crew was singing as they passed the boxes along. The rhythm of the song matched the passing of the packages. The gangplank was narrow and swung to and fro as they hung onto the railing and moved upward towards the ship. Clipper ships were designed to carry limited bulky cargo and this one was outfitted to carry six passengers. The slim, graceful shape of the hull, the projecting bow, and the ship's streamlined appearance showed it was made for speed. Belle and Mary both agreed the clipper ship was a thing of beauty even without the sails up. The captain met them on the gangplank and explained the vessel setup with its twenty-five crew members, mainly to handle the sails. Continuing to instruct, he told the passengers of the crew's different work shifts and how the men ate and exercised to stay healthy while the ship was at sea.

The captain revealed there were four other passengers.

"My, my, ladies, I have gone on enough. Please allow me to show you your cabins. I am sure that you are tired of listening to an old sailor," he laughed.

As they walked down the steps into the lower section, the ship's pitch seemed to mimic the waves against the beach, even though the harbor was deep, causing them to lose their balance. The passengers' main reason to go to their cabins was for the crew to have the space to handle the sails. Getting out of the harbor was sometimes tricky, and the crew did not need the distraction of the passengers. In the main cabin below the deck, four other passengers sat at a center table.

The *Flying Goose* was a beautiful ship with trim lines, shaped out of iron and mahogany, to make her "tight as a cork in a bottle," as the crew described her. The sails were made of double sewn canvas and welted with hemp roping. The *Flying Goose*, designed for speed, looked beautiful with her sails in full action. She flew two flags at the top of the mast, the American flag and the captain's personal flag just below it.

The ship's first mate continued to welcome the passengers.

"I'll try to make this brief, as we are leaving the port shortly. It will take us approximately thirty-eight days to reach San Diego, then another three days to reach San Francisco. Since the winter season is approaching, there may be times where we will hit rough seas. We will need you to stay below during those times so the men can do their jobs without worrying about your safety if you are on deck. We have been approached several times by renegade pirates, but we have a safety action plan we will go over later following the evening meal. When the bell rings, you will join us here in the recreation room for meals and evening games. Please take this time to settle into your cabin, and we wish you a safe trip."

The first mate saluted, turned, and went up the stairs towards the deck.

Belled looked around the main cabin. There was a long table with benches all secured to the floor. In the center of the table was a narrow trough to hold the serving dishes and bowls. There were indentations to place the plates along the table's sides, so the food stayed in place while the passengers or crew ate. Towards the ship's bow, there were four cabins opposite each other for the passengers.

As they entered their assigned room, Belle and Mary discovered it was a small space, with two narrow beds and limited storage for their trunks. Each bed had high sides to keep them from rolling out of bed during rough seas and a rope hanging from the side. They noticed each piece of furniture in the room was bolted to the floor. Their trunks were placed behind a short ledge against a wall, keeping them from sliding into the room during rough seas. The captain had left a weighted jug of water, some salt crackers, a bag of English muffins, sweet rolls, and cake to tide them over until the evening meal.

Along with being bolted to the floor, the tabletop had three-inch side rails around the edge to keep things from tipping while traveling through the sea. There were holes to set their teacups in to prevent them from rolling off the table. Tiered plates, anchored to the table to avoid sliding off, completed the set up. Under their desk was a small credenza with drawers where they put their treasures away to keep them safe. Taking off their coats, Belle and Mary left their clothes in their trunks and draped the outerwear over the chests. Mary noted there was not a lock on the door but rather a sliding bolt. Looking into the basket from the boarding house, they were astonished as they dug deeper. In addition to the sandwiches, pickles, and jam, they found fresh bread, small tea containers, sugar, dried milk, a set of small spoons, a teapot, and dainty teacups.

"Well, home sweet home for a while, not much to look at, but beats jousting in the stagecoach," stated Belle with a dubious look on her face.

Hugging Belle, Mary tried to reassure her.

"Do not worry, Belle. We will manage simply fine. After all, we are closer to the end of the trail than we were a week ago. At least I don't have to worry about my stepbrothers."

Walking around the cabin, they discovered drawers in the side walls with a single small knob on each one of them. The space inside was not exceptionally large, but it would hold things they used every day. As they pulled on a higher knob, they discovered it loosened and stretched across the cabin, hooking to another hook to form a clothesline to dry clothes. *How convenient for them to think of all the details for daily life,* Belle thought as she tried another set of knobs. There were hooks on the back of the door for their coats. Under the beds were large drawers for storage. Taking a book out of her trunk, Mary turned the lantern up and settled on the padded bench as she started to read. Even though it was noon, the room was dim due to only one porthole for the cabin.

Belle, looking out of the porthole, wondered what adventures lay ahead of them. *I wonder if Aunt Hester got upset that I left. She is probably glad that I am gone. It couldn't have been easy for her to take on a teenager to raise, not having children of her own. I need to write to her so that she does not worry, I guess.*

Doubt was creeping into her mind. Belle was overcome with a sensation she could not identify. She found her thoughts wandering back to Brett. Mentally shaking herself, she scolded herself to get a hold of her feelings. Belle had not seen him much since New Orleans, only a few minutes when they first boarded the ship. She had to stop letting Brett into her thoughts. She shook her head. *I am sure I was only interested in him as he was the only halfway decent man around. No telling what he thinks of me.* She squirmed in the chair. Belle reminded herself that Brett was only with them to guard Mary, to see that she made it safely to Phillip. *What could he possibly see in me?*

Out loud, she started talking to Mary.

"I decided to keep a daily journal while we are sailing. Maybe that will keep my mind busy. I have some needlework and projects I can work on in the evenings. The quiet life aboard the ship will be hard after all the excitement we have had so far," Belle smiled.

A cloud hovered overhead as her thoughts moved quickly through many subjects.

"Mary, I wonder what Aunt Hester did when she found me gone? I hope she wasn't too angry. I think I will write to her so that she knows I am okay."

She said this more to herself than to Mary. Mary looked closely at Belle and decided not to say anything. Belle had a distracted look on her face and probably wasn't looking for an answer.

The ship crept out of port and headed towards the open sea. The gulf waters were quiet, and only the gentle rolling gave them any indication that they were not still in port. Through the porthole, Belle watched the land recede in the background. Feeling a little queasy as they left the harbor, she lay down.

"What's wrong, Belle? You don't look good. Are you all right?"

Mary stood over her, full of concern.

"I will be fine." Belle hid her head under the covers. "I have to get used to the rolling, that's all. Don't fret. I will be okay. Leave that bucket close, however. My stomach may not agree with what I am saying."

Belle was not better the following day. Mary left the cabin to seek help for her. In the narrow passage, she met the captain.

"Good morning, Miss. Is everything okay?" he asked.

After hearing Mary's story, he assured her that this was common on a passenger's first voyage and that he would send some ginger tea and crackers around to the cabin. He reminded her that all passengers should stay in their places until they were on the third day. Then they were only allowed on deck for exercise between seven and nine o'clock in the morning and again in the evening from six until eight o'clock. The captain reminded Mary that the sailors needed to continue working the sails without passengers underfoot. The first time the captain said it, it sounded reasonable. *It was a sensible idea,* thought Mary, but now she felt imprisoned. Again, it could be worse, so she decided that she would work with the rules.

When the ginger tea arrived, Belle took one look and turned her head to the wall.

"Maybe later, Mary, not now," she whined.

That evening Belle, still feeling the motion of the ship upsetting her stomach, nibbled on the crackers and after a while, drank some of the cold ginger tea. She had to admit that she did feel better after drinking the tea.

In the evening, Mary walked around the deck with the other passengers. Looking over the railing, she became overwhelmed at how large the ocean seemed. There was nothing but water, no matter which direction she turned. Other passengers stopped to talk to her and told her stories of the other travels they had taken. They were a lovely couple heading home to California.

They lived near San Francisco and they had been on their

honeymoon to New York. As they chatted, Mary kept feeling like someone was watching her. When she looked around, there was nobody but the other passengers. The third passenger was a businessman who had been to New Orleans to buy supplies for his San Francisco store.

"Best emporium in San Francisco," he bragged.

The fourth passenger was not up on deck.

*Oh well,* Mary thought. I am sure I will have plenty of time to meet whomever it is when the time comes. Standing beside the rail, feeling the warm breeze on her face, she could hardly wait for the trip to be over. The weather was holding up well. It was sunny, warm, and with a gentle breeze.

The ship was still pitching and rolling, but nothing as she thought it would be on the open water. She became used to the feelings, walking back to the cabin, she had plenty to tell Belle. *I need to get Belle out of the dumps. She has allowed herself to wallow. I'll give her another day, but then it's back out into the world.* That evening Mary told Belle about the other passengers and their stories, trying to get Belle in a better mood. In turn, Belle curled up in a fetal position, slightly green, and held onto the bucket handle in case she needed it again. Sipping on the tea and munching on crackers all afternoon did not seem to help. *Nothing seems to work. This trip has not been good so far.*

After four days of nausea and just feeling terrible, Belle started to feel better. Mary encouraged her to go for a walk on the deck for the fresh air. Still a little queasy, Belle tried to clean up and be a bit more presentable to the other passengers. She decided to wear an everyday dress. It was pale pink with white rosettes around the bodice and hem. Looking at herself in the small mirror on the wall of the cabin, she shook her head. Not exactly the look she envisioned before getting on the ship. She was pale, and her hair seemed lifeless. She discovered how weak she was when trying to dress. *However, it beats wearing my brother's clothes.*

As Mary came through the door, she picked up a brush and walked towards Belle.

"Your hair is a mess, but we can fix it just like this," she whispered.

Mary comforted her and started to brush Belle's hair. She fixed it into a bun on the back of her head.

"There," she said, looking at her work. "You can hardly tell how short it is. Unless they see it down, they can't guess the length of your hair under these rolls."

Belle looked again in the mirror.

"Well, it is better. This is all I can do at this point. I am tired. Let's eat."

She wrinkled her nose and frowned.

"The cook said that he had prepared some robust broth to go along with the dinner, in case I can't eat," said Belle as she stood up to try to get used to walking with the floor moving.

Mary grabbed Belle's elbow to lead her out of the room.

The clipper ship rarely took but a few passengers because mainly it functioned in transporting cargo. There were boxes in the main hold but also stacked around the deck. The load remained light as the clipper ship moved fast. The other passengers talked about many things at dinner, but the most prevalent was the fear of civil war soon.

"I heard that the army is asking for volunteers, but I think it is too soon to be gathering troops. Several states are threatening to leave the Union and that is unheard of. We just got together as a country."

The women stayed quiet, worrying about their families and if this was a good time to leave them.

"If there is a war, at least in California, we will not have to be a part of it. They will settle their differences one way or another."

Belle tuned out the conversation as she noticed only five of the passengers were at the table. She still had nausea but ate every bit of the broth and crackers to regain her strength. Belle was not interested in discussing war. She just wanted to get this trip over with and to try to live a healthy life, whatever that meant. *My first requirement for my future is to be stable and not move around all the time.*

Stumbling from the table, Belle went back to the cabin. She was not interested in walking around the deck yet. *Maybe tomorrow.* Belle took off her clothes and put on her sleeping gown. Laying down on the narrow bed, making sure the bucket was near her, she held the rail as she drifted off to sleep. Trying to visualize Brett, the image of Tomas kept coming to mind. Punching her pillow to get rid of the image, she fell asleep.

The following day after breakfast, Belle and Mary strolled around the deck. Belle was much better. Still, she had nausea when discussing food, but Belle felt much better overall. The weather continued to be warm with a light breeze. Looking across the port side of the ship, all Belle saw were waves and more waves. Choosing not to watch the waves moving, she watched the sailors as they worked. Still leaning on the rails, a familiar voice spoke behind them.

"Good morning ladies, beautiful day isn't it?"

As they turned around, Belle's heart did a little jump. It was Brett.

Her heart gave a thundering noise; she thought sure he could hear it. Taking a couple of deep breaths, she tried to hold her excitement at bay. Noticing the profound change in Belle's looks, he tipped his hat.

"How are you doing this fair day?"

Looking at Belle, he saw the fine lines around her eyes,

the paleness of her skin. Belle shyly held out her hand as he reached over to kiss the back of her gloved hand. Holding it a few seconds longer than he should have, he looked into her eyes.

"You sure have changed since the last time I saw you. Mary told me you were sick. It will get better."

Blushing, Belle accepted the compliment but refrained from explaining. Mary chattering excitedly, started questioning Brett concerning his trip so far. At once, Belle felt the rush of nausea. Holding her handkerchief to her mouth, she turned and ran across the deck and down the steps to the precious bucket.

# CHAPTER 13

The next day, when the girls met Brett on deck during their morning walk, Belle held back and did not talk. Brett tipped his hat toward Belle, not saying anything to her. He strolled past them, walking towards the other passengers. Belle felt flustered and confused, looking at him as he walked away. Mary gave her a knowing look, and Belled flushed.

"It's not what you think," Belle said, turning away so Mary wouldn't tease her.

Later that evening as Mary and Belle took their walk, it was different because the other passengers were still at dinner. Looking around the ship, it was the first time Belle had a chance to look at it without wanting to hurry back to her new friend, the bucket. The bridge was oiled and polished to a high sheen but notably not slippery. She held onto the side rail, willing nausea not to return, even though she still felt queasy. She watched the crew as they went about their tasks, marveling at how precise their movements were as they worked. Each one of their movements seemed like a well-rehearsed dance routine.

*The breeze helps*, she thought as she closed her eyes and

took deep, slow breaths. The salty air, the soft movement of the waves all seemed to clear her head. When she opened her eyes, she found Brett standing beside her, leaning on the rail, looking out over the ocean.

"First time, huh?"

She heard his voice over the noise of the waves.

"It will get better." Winking, he smiled. "You look much better as Belle than when you did as Sam."

She noticed the twinkle in his eyes and his smile.

"When did you first figure it out?" Belle looked at him closely.

"Actually, from the beginning. Della gave it away when I came by the house to get the information concerning your trip. However, it was apparent in the barn back at the last station. You were so mad. Well, when you came out of the barn, your voice was a little high pitched, and you felt very soft to be the boy you pretended to be. I have to admit, the clothes, the shooting, and the shabby appearance could have fooled me for a while if I hadn't known already. But seeing you now, it makes sense. As I said, you look very nice."

"So, why did you keep quiet?" Belle quizzed him.

Turning her head, she was puzzled by his friendliness. Turning back to the rail, he said very quietly.

"Figured you had your reasons, and it would come out sooner or later. People always have reasons for what they do. I just figured it was your business. Besides, I wasn't sure if I wanted to let the other guys traveling with us know there were two pretty women."

Belle, flustered, looked at him for a few seconds, then smiled. Saying goodbye over her shoulder and gathering her skirts, she quickly turned from him and hurried off to find Mary.

When she entered the cabin, Mary was working on an intricate needlework piece.

105

"I saw you with Brett. Find out anything interesting?"

She kept her eyes on her work.

Belle felt her heart pounding and found herself short of breath. Taking some deep breaths, she turned to Mary.

"Brett is very relaxed about this ship. Somehow it seems much safer than the stagecoach. However, I notice he is always alert. It's as if he feels something is going to happen. It's probably my imagination. I still have queasiness. Will I ever get used to the ship?"

"Come, Belle, he's not the only one watching someone out of the corner of his eye. I had seen you many times watching him when you thought he was not looking. Can't fool me, Belle. You have feelings towards him."

Red-faced, Belle flopped down on the edge of the bed.

"I think he is worried about you, Mary. Have you known him for long? I mean more than just family gatherings. What is he like? He probably thinks I am just a child."

Mary looked at her worriedly, "I have not noticed it. When I have seen him, he was looking our way, but it was hard to tell whom he was looking at."

Leaning back on the bed, Mary quickly got up and went to the washbasin.

"I think I will read for a while in the main cabin. I heard they are playing a lot of games tonight. Let's see if we have enough to play cards or something. I don't want to stay in the cabin all the time. Come on, Belle, let's get moving."

"I will be along in a little bit. I want to catch up on some writing."

Belle sat down at the small desk. Taking out the pen and ink blotter, she wrote a letter to Aunt Hester to let her know that she was fine and to share her plans so that Hester wouldn't worry about her. Belle also wrote letters to her friends. Wondering how long it would be before she could mail them, she decided to add a short note to each of them every day and to send them when she had the chance.

The captain did not join them for dinner that night. He sent word by his first officer that there was a storm on the horizon, and he would prefer if the passengers would stay below. Belle and Mary joined the others playing cards at the dining table to pass the time. After a while, it became very noticeable that the ship was rocking from side to side more than usual. The crew tightened the hatch to prevent water from coming into the hull.

"Folks," the first officer reported, "there will be rough seas for a while, but it is a small storm, and we should be through it soon."

The deck started to creak, and Belle could feel the dampness coming through the boards above her. Deciding to return to their room, they secured the lamp in the hold with the straps on the table, turned it low, and climbed into bed.

"I forgot to tell you. When you were sick, the other passengers told me that the rope attached to the bed secures us in the bed during rough seas. See, here's how to do it."

Taking the rope and fastening it to the hook on the wall above the bed, the rope was in place. Letting the rest of the rope hang down, they could watch the movement of the ceiling as the storm tossed the clipper ship. Mary got out of bed and blew out the candle in the lamp, afraid it would tip over and start a fire.

Mary whispered, "Belle, I am scared. Surely we will be all right."

"Mary, the first mate said that they go through these little storms all the time, so my suggestion is that we try to get some sleep. We know where the lifeboats are, we have those silly vests, and we are not far from shore somewhere so that we will be all right."

Despite her bravado, Belle said her prayers more fervently

that they would be safe. The ship tossed and turned through the night. The loud creaks of the deck and the noise of the swaying of the mast kept them awake for a long time that night.

Towards early morning, the rocking of the waves slowed down, and the gradual quiet of the ship as it sailed through the waters awakened Belle. As she lay there, she could hear the sailors as they worked. *Thank God we made it through the storm.* She slowly drifted back to sleep.

The next few days were routine. Dressing, eating, and walking around the deck filled their days. Belle wrote in her journal and fashioned little bits of fabric into roses, daisies, and other trims in the afternoons, saving them for use later. Taking tiny beads, she embroidered them on the petals and leaves. It was a quiet time for them to think and settle in their minds about the past and let it go to be ready for the future. The passengers were cheerful, and the shared meals were laced with chatter about their plans.

The cook became creative with the food. After several meals with different servings of potatoes and soups, she joked about being on an Irish boat. Mary laughed but agreed. They did have fresh bread, at least one or two fruits a day, and various other lamb and chicken dishes. At least the food tasted good with all the spices and salt. Several times Belle saw Brett walking on deck, but she did not make conversation with him. She found out that he ate his meals with the crew, so he was not around for the other passengers' discussions. Mary was busy making different linens for her new home and kept mainly to herself, leaving Belle with much time on her hands. *Eighty-six days from the start, now sixty-four days until we reach San Francisco. This trip seems like forever. I need to keep doing things to occupy my time in order not to become crazy before this trip is over.*

As the days passed, the passengers fell into an easy

routine. After the meals were over in the evenings, the passengers often met at the dining table to play games, cards or just to talk about their excitement of facing a new life. Mary often shared stories about her home and how she grew up, leaving out the parts about her stepbrothers. However, remembering her home and her family caused her to become homesick. When Mary had those spells, Belle would encourage her to play games or cards. Belle loved to play cards. As time moved forward, she became much better than when she played with her aunt Hester. When playing the games, Belle noticed Brett often sat in the corner, reading a book. Belle didn't see Brett watching her as she played the games. Often, he would smile, seeing her competitiveness and her need to win.

Other evenings, Belle and Mary sat comfortably in some of the rocking chairs in the main cabin, working on their projects. Belle spent a lot of time drawing hats, decorations, and styles she saw when they were in Natchez and New Orleans. Mary sat quietly, embroidering items for her trousseau. Currently, she was working on a white-on-white camisole to wear with her wedding dress.

"Mary, those flowers are so pretty. I like the way the daisies are in satin stitch around the edges of the pleats."

Belle thought of using a similar design around the edges of a mantilla with matching gloves. She leaned over to watch Mary work. Holding up her drawing, Belle asked Mary's opinion.

"Belle, I have an idea. Let's go into our room so no one will hear us."

Rising and gathering their things, they went quietly to their room while the others continued playing cards. Brett watched them, then went back to his book.

Once inside the cabin, both girls began to talk at once. Shushing each other, Mary started first.

"Belle, just an idea, why don't we work together on some ideas. I can do the dressmaking and accessories. I think we should give it a shot."

Belle trying so hard to get a word in edgewise, was nodding vigorously in agreement.

"Let's work on our plans. Then we can work out the problems later."

Pulling out their pens and papers, they started on their ideas.

The couple from California shared stories about living in San Francisco and how they started their business. They owned a mercantile store near the pier and serviced the many boarding houses and apartments along the oceanfront.

"If you decide to open a store, we can sell you silks, spices, and grains no one else would have in your area."

Belle whispered to Mary. "What do you think? Should we tell them our plans?"

Smiling at the couple across the table, Mary bashfully shared their news.

"Well, actually, we are thinking of starting a business together."

Looking at some of the drawings, the couple showed their enthusiasm.

"These drawings are good. I think we can help. We have plenty of different silks, linens, cotton, and laces all the time. When we get them in, we will send you a sample, and you can decide what you need."

They smiled at each other.

"I think we can sell your stuff when you have it ready. I am sure it will be a success. We can talk more about this later. Give us a chance to think this through."

As the dinner bell sounded, the passengers and a few off-duty crew members met at the dining table. As a routine, they talked about the weather, the storm, and ideas of what they would do when they got to California. It was a quiet night for the most part, but Brett watched the girls closely. He saw them smiling, whispering, and more chatty than usual. *Wonder what they are up to now,* Brett wondered. As soon as the meal was over, the girls rushed back to their room, whispering and giggling. Belle and Mary went to bed happy that night, talking about their enterprise throughout the night.

# CHAPTER 14

Sometimes when on the deck, other ships passed them from a distance. The captain always had his spyglass out to check the identity. When he was sure the other vessel was not a threat, he would relax and go back to his cabin to work on the maps and cargo lists. The *Flying Goose* was carrying supplies and equipment destined for California. The captain usually didn't have passengers aboard and was focused on the transport of the cargo. However, he was friendly to the passengers but also aware of the dangers of carrying them. The captain was tall, lean, and had a short white curly beard covering his chin, with short mutton-type side whiskers. Wearing a short-billed cap, he looked as if any moment he would burst out laughing. His eyebrows were curly and bushy, covering his whole brow. He was cheerful and always had a smile on his face. The captain prided himself on still being clean and neat, no matter what was happening on the ship.

The ship's clinic was next to the captain's office, where the surgeon treated the various cuts, tears, sunburns, and at times did emergency surgery. He made each crew member go through an initial examination before coming on the ship and then weekly visits while sailing. His motto was to treat everything immediately before it became a problem. He often bickered with the cook about serving healthy food and decreasing the amount of tea they drank. However, the tea was a form of socialization and uplifted the passengers' morale during the long journey. Late in the evenings, the crew often sat on deck relaxing, even though they needed to prepare for what could happen next.

The crew dressed in thick long-sleeved shirts, even when warm out, as the sea had a sharp and cold sting to the skin when the salty spray washed up on deck. When working the sails, they faced threats to survival daily. There were dangers in climbing the nets, hauling them upwards, or letting the nets roll down. The first mate was skilled in first aid, as accidents often happened. At times, it took both the surgeon and the first mate to resolve a medical problem. The ship itself repeatedly tried to run through the waves, not caring if it was at an angle or not. The *Flying Goose* was a gentle but stern lady. At times, she was temperamental and fought the waves, letting the waves crash over the deck or swamp the poop deck, and sometimes flooding, sweeping sailors off the boom and throwing them into the sea. It was common to send a tiny lifeboat to rescue a sailor before continuing the trip. Other times, the *Flying Goose* danced through the waves, gently parting them, imparting only a gentle rolling feel. As she flew her course, her sails billowed like chiffon skirts.

The captain fought for control of the ship as he would fight a war. Often the passengers heard him yelling orders to keep the men working as a team. He tried to shave every minute off their time to maintain a fast clip. He had a cargo deadline, and he meant to keep it. When he hired his crew, he not only picked the best men possible but spent time training them to work together like a well-oiled machine. Spending the extra time with them resulted in men with loyalty and steadfastness. Rarely did one of the crew leave to work on other teams. They were paid well, received good rations, and knew their captain would do the best he could for them. There were other ships where the captain ruled with an iron hand and often a pistol or whip. Those captains often shorted the rations and tried to order the crew with a heavy hand, and many lives were lost while sailing.

The *Flying Goose* crew appreciated the captain and they felt the rules were tough but fair. Paying good wages meant many sailors signed on for more than one cruise. That advantage resulted in a crew that worked well together and knew their tasks. Often, they taught each other, so they could switch out places if needed. At the end of the cruise, the captain paid bonuses when they reached their delivery date on time. The captain did not allow his crew to drink spirits while working with the sails but allotted a pint of ale each evening at supper. Often Belle spotted them taking their mugs with them when they went to their quarters.

When on deck, the passengers had a safety line tied around their waists to keep them connected to the ship in case of rogue waves. As Belle stood beside the deck railing, she noticed the captain looking at something intently on the starboard side. Her eyes followed his gaze. She could barely see a small dot on the horizon growing more prominent as she watched it. Brett stood beside the captain, speaking quietly. Suddenly using his speaker, the captain cautioned all the passengers to move towards the stairs and stay below the deck.

Mary turned to Belle.

"What is going on? Why are we asked to leave?"

"I don't know, Mary, but something is going on. Let's get below."

Coming up behind them, Brett assisted them down the narrow stairs.

"Ladies, I think we need to secure our belongings and try to find a safe place to wait this out. The captain sees another ship headed fast this way. Currently, it is difficult to identify the vessel, but foolish not to take precautions. It could be another clipper ship with supplies, a privateer, or pirates. No matter what, it is better that he concentrates on the vessel's safety rather than to have to worry about the passengers."

They entering the dining area, and the crew gave instructions. They all left quickly to go to their cabins. Brett knew the situation was dangerous, but he went back up on deck to offer his assistance.

Belle and Mary put away all the personal items into their trunks and secured the belts that tied the trunks to the floors. Holding a sheaf of papers, Mary looked around the cabin for a hiding place. Looking confused, Belle watched her look under the bed and behind the door.

Standing, looking worried, she said, "Belle, these are patterns for my dresses. I can not afford to have them taken."

Leaning over the chest, Belle pulled a board away from the wall. She motioned towards the wall.

"I noticed this the other day. Quick, hide your stuff in here. They will not find it. I have all my patterns and Mother's jewels in there as well."

Taking off her necklace and her pin from her dress, Mary quickly stuffed them into a bag and hid the stuff in the opening. Belle took her shoe and hammered at the nails after she put them into place.

"They may take our clothes, but they will not have our life possessions."

Taking her quill pen, she placed a small mark on the edge of the board, so she would not forget which panel to pry open later. Gathering her guns, she made sure each one was loaded and ready for whatever they faced. She hid one under her pillow and her rifle beside her next to the railing. Mary did not have a gun, but she did have a knife for cutting fruit. It was not much, but at least something. Now all they could do was wait.

Up on deck, the captain gave orders, pushing the ship to move faster through the waters.

Leaning over to Brett, he mumbled, "They are not close enough to identify, but they are coming fast. At least we can try to outrun them."

The ship on the horizon was gaining on them. It was still too far away to see her honors to make an identification. Motioning to the first mate, the captain told him to dismantle the figurehead and let it fall into the ocean to increase the speed by reducing the drag and the ship's weight. The captain turned the clipper ship so the figurehead would miss the boat when falling and then fix a hard right to the starboard side. As the sails ballooned outward, the captain adjusted the ropes to catch the maximum wind to increase the speed.

"We will be a little off track, but we can make it up after we lose this ship," the captain motioned to the first officer. "The sun is almost down. Darken all the ports, and also on deck. We will disappear in the dark. The problem is, they will too. I suggest we all do a little praying."

As the skies darkened, the crew lowered the sails and hoisted black sails. As each sail caught the wind, the ship began to move quicker through the water. The final sizeable black sail caught the wind. With a jolt, the ship moved faster and further away from her initial course. The passengers felt the movement and secured themselves to the bunks to avoid falling to the floor. There were no fires lit that night. Belled covered the porthole to diminish the light. The cook came to each room with bread and ale but did not prepare hot food.

During the night, the crew quickly and quietly moved the booms to guide the sails to maximize the wind. Each crew member moved with renewed vigor and was poised to keep the *Flying Goose* in top form. As the wind rushed the sails, Belle and Mary felt each surge as they moved forward. The sailors' work shifts were changed from 12-hour shifts to 6-hour shifts to allow the sailors to rest between the change to recover from the additional hard work.

As the dawn rose, the captain scanned the horizon. Not seeing any ships, he ordered the cooks to prepare hot food for the crew and passengers. He placed the wheel in the hands of the first officer and went below for a much-needed rest. Brett offered his services to keep watch as the crew was busy with the sails, to which the captain agreed wholeheart-edly. Brett secured himself on the deck with the spyglass to scan the horizons. As far as he could see, there was nothing but rolling waves. The ship maintained the charted path. As daylight broke, the crew pulled the black sails and changed them back to the white sails. Again, as the sails hoisted, the vessel regained her speed. Brett wondered at the tactics of the captain but was glad he was prepared. Throughout the next several days, the ship gradually moved back onto course. The captain noted that they had higher speeds further away from land as they followed the currents. The captain's goal was to chart paths allowing his ship to stay within a day's reach of land in case of emergencies, for either the crew or passengers.

Later, he told Brett that he heard the French had attempted to build a series of locks across Panama that would cut weeks off the trip from New Orleans to San Francisco. They had failed and the hope was that another company would take up the challenge, but that had not happened yet. Tamping down his pipe, Brett lit it, causing small whiffs of smoke to trail forward with the boat's speed. Their next goal was to stop at the nearest port to pick up supplies.

As the ship steered closer to land, several unknown ships

appeared on the horizon. Most of them had friendly flags, but the captain became wary of one of them. He saw it closing in on one of the clipper ships that had lagged behind the others. The captain was not sure, but it seemed to be the same ship that was following them. As it came closer, he saw the cannon portholes open. Three of the other ships turned to help their sister ship. Pulling the covers off the gun ports, they readied the cannons for loading. Watching the drama ahead of them, the captain decided to stay on course for the safety of his ship but slowed down in case the other ship needed help. The *Flying Goose* crew watched closely as the privateer ship closed in on the crippled ship. The privateers did not expect the clipper ships to assist each other. Still watching the sails as the other ships joined their sister ship, the crew tried to outmaneuver the privateer ship. It was a fierce battle. The privateers boarded the disabled ship before the other ships arrived to help.

With his spyglass, the captain could see the passengers being hurried below by the crew. The others were fighting for their lives. The *Flying Goose* was close enough to hear the shouting and the pistol shots as the privateers attacked the crew. The other three ships closed in to assist. As they surrounded the two vessels, they opened cannon fire on the privateer ship. One ship was close enough to board the privateer ship, with bayonets and swords drawn. Scurrying up the boarding ropes fastened by grappling hooks onto the privateer ship's side, the sailors entered the battle. One of the other ships started shooting cannons into the privateer ship to sink it, wary of the crew fighting.

Within minutes the privateers were imprisoned on the captured ship, with the privateer ship sinking fast. Whatever treasure was on that ship sank to the bottom of the ocean. The privateers held the captives in front of them for protection, hoping to save themselves. As the *Flying Goose* crew watched on, the prisoners joined their crew, encouraged by the privateer ship's sinking, and fought hard to take back their craft. Other shipmates from the other vessels started boarding the attacked ship to quickly overtake the privateers.

Seeing the fight's results, the captain waved his flags at the other clipper ships as a salute and eased the *Flying Goose* back into its charted course. One of the destinations on the way to California was Jervis Bay, where they expected to pick rations for the rest of the trip.

After watching the scene, Brett discussed what they had witnessed with the captain.

"It worries me that the privateers attacked the ship so close to a port."

He shook his head.

"It's clear that they were not expecting the involvement of the other ships."

The captain shook Brett's shoulder.

"The privateers are encouraged by the talks of war and think that the cargo ships would rather lose their cargoes than their ships. The old 'better to lose now but gain more later' theory. But now, the ships are starting to fight back. The cargo vessels need to reach the West, or they won't survive. There is a lot of money at stake. I think we will see more ships traveling together for safety as these fools in Washington fight their wars. There are other ways to fight the privateers. You will see that we take care of our own if the government doesn't."

Moving away from the rails, Brett went below to rest after the excitement of the battle. The passengers were crowded around the table, waiting for news. Brett looked around.

"The ship is safe. It seems they had a plan."

Sitting down, the cook handed him a cup of coffee.

"They are traveling in groups now to protect each other. Organizing and working together, they destroyed the priva-

teer ship and captured the privateers. They will hold the prisoners until they reach San Francisco for trial. If they make it
there," he said quietly.

The passengers were quiet the rest of the evening,
thinking of what they would have done if it had been the
*Flying Goose* instead of one of the other clippers. Belle and
Mary went back to their cabins, each in their thoughts as
they went to bed.

As a safety measure, the captain called the first officer and
surgeon to meet in his cabin.

"I am concerned about the privateers' bravado in striking
so close to the land and ports. It would be better to anchor
outside of the harbor and send a small boat in the night
before we dock to check out the situation. These times are
unsure, and I do not want to walk into something that would
endanger our cargo and passengers."

Each man agreed and signed the roster to go ashore. That
evening, the captain explained the schedule change to the
crew and passengers. They would wait until the landing crew
returned to the ship.

The next morning both the crew and the passengers were
in good spirits. The sun was out, and they could see land on
the horizon. All were looking forward to having their feet on
the ground again.

"I hope they have shops where we can replenish our extra
food supply. We are almost out of crackers and biscuits,"
whispered Mary to Belle as they stood near the rail.

Belle had been quiet since the drama unfolded with the
pirates the day before. She nodded but continued to be in her
private world. She sensed him behind her before she saw him.
His scent was of ale, pipe tobacco, and old leather. Thinking
to herself, she inhaled the aroma, the same scent as she had
smelled on the stagecoach. *I would recognize it anywhere,* she
thought.

"Ladies, I would like to offer my services when we go ashore, the port can be very lively, and the thoughts of two beautiful damsels on their own are concerning. I will make sure you are safe and offer to carry your packages if you would like."

Mary turned and tilted her head courteously, whereas Belle kept facing the waves.

"Are you sure that will not be a problem? We haven't been shopping in a long time," Mary winked towards Belle.

Tilting his hat, he watched Belle walk off.

Turning back to Mary, "No, ma'am, it would be my pleasure. I will meet you at the gangplank when the captain says we can disembark."

With that, he turned and walked towards some of the other passengers, also standing by the rails watching land as it moved closer and closer.

As she leaned towards the railing, Mary looked sideways at Belle.

"What has come over you? You never even looked at him."

Belle lowered her head and pulled her mantle closer against the wind.

"Mary, I did much thinking last night. We could have been on that other ship, and maybe we would not have been so lucky. I need to get myself straight and quit mooning over a man that has not even given me a single reason to think that he might be interested in me. Brett Sanders is out of my league, no matter how much I am attracted to him."

With that said, she turned and went down the stairs to their cabin. Mary stared after her with thoughtful eyes and, with a shake of her head, followed her.

What they didn't see was Brett, who overheard their conversation, looking attentively after them. *Well, Mr. Sanders, what are you going to do with that information?* Unaware that

Belle was genuinely interested in him caught him by surprise. *That will change things for sure.* He rubbed his chin. Wistfully, he leaned on the deck railing and thought about his dreams of a slender, redheaded girl that caused him to have thoughts he had not had in a long time.

# CHAPTER 15

As they reached the port, the captain asked them to stay below, as the crew needed the room to work the sails. At sunset, as planned, the landing crew left in search of information. The night was calm, and the ocean was more ripples than waves. The *Flying Goose* rested quietly in the outer reef near the harbor entrance, rocking gently, giving a safe lulling peace the passengers had not had for a while. When the landing party returned, they met with the captain on deck to share their story. There were no signs of military nor signs of unrest. The town was open and as active as most coastal towns.

The next morning as the dawn appeared, the captain called a meeting for the passengers and crew.

"I feel that we will be safe to dock today. This is the natural course for our trip and normal for going around the horn. We stop here on each of our trips, and I have not had problems in the past. Nevertheless, I want to caution all of you. This country is in unrest, the same as our country. It seems that Paraguay is contemplating war with Brazil, Argentina, and Uruguay. So far, it has just been small battles, but I do not want us to be involved. We will be taking on supplies and water.

"For safety, first, I want you to be back on the ship by sunset. We will leave the harbor at that time and then sail through the night. We will only stop one other time before reaching San Francisco. If you do not make it back, rest assured you will be on your own, as we will be gone. These peoples are our friends and will not harm you. However, be aware of thieves.

"When we leave the port for our safety, we sail close to land until we reach San Francisco. The areas between here and San Francisco are prime for pirates and privateers. They usually stay in the larger towns along the coast as it is easier to hide. I do not want anyone to think of us as a target in the open ocean. I am sending a crew member with each of you as you leave. Be careful, shop, and get back to ship. The crew will go ashore by taking turns in small parties, the majority staying to protect the ship. If you hear the church bell, come back to the ship quickly."

The girls had washed their hair the night before, so getting dressed was a short adventure. Mary leaned over to tie her shoes.

"Belle, there will be a lot of walking, so wear comfortable shoes."

Belle stood up and grinned at Mary.

"Can you see my shoes?"

As Belle lifted her skirt, Mary laughed as she saw Belle had her brother's boots on under her dresses.

Twirling and smiling, Belle said, "These are the most comfortable shoes I have. Can you see them under my skirts?"

Mary giggled. "Not unless you raise your skirts. I would never have dreamed that you would have them on. You are the belle of the ball."

Belle laughed. "I am glad I saved them."

Belle reached into their secret hiding place in the wall and drew out some of the savings she had carried from home. She turned around, trying to see herself in the small mirror.

"Come on, Belle, let's meet our escort, and hopefully discover new adventures in this port."

Still giggling, they linked their arms and left the cabin. As they arrived at the meeting place for Brett, they laughed at their little joke when he first saw them.

"Well, you ladies sure sound cheerful. Are you ready to go? The others have already left."

Walking down the gangplank, they marveled at the site of the city. The city itself sat on the side of the hill, winding upwards to the top. They could see houses and shops lining the way.

A wooden plank sidewalk wound up the hill into the town. As far as they could see, street vendors lined the cobblestone roads sloping upwards into the city proper. The homes were made of adobe and painted in bright, passionate colors, giving the town a festive feel. Passing by the open-air stands, many vendors approached them to buy their wares. Colorful bowls, scarves, and toys lined the market stalls. Belle noticed Brett staying close to them, watching each vendor as they approached. Children played games between the vendor stalls, smiling or crying, depending on who was winning. The noise alone made this site different from what the girls were used to when shopping. Women approached the ladies offering brightly colored jewelry, often handmade beaded pins, necklaces, and bracelets. Street troubadours were singing and playing their instruments as they walked up and down the streets. Belle and Mary were fascinated by the colorful hats and scarves.

Mary bought a scarf with tiny crocheted pastel flowers around the borders. The scarf would match one of the new dresses she had bought in New Orleans. Belle bought a cream-colored lace parasol with ruffles gathered around the bottom edges. Mary purchased a man's hand-tooled billfold at another stall and a matching knife case to give Phillip as a wedding gift. At other booths, Mary found brightly colored fabric, silks, and lace. Brett took their packages to carry back to the ship so they could continue shopping. Still thinking about her future, Belle looked at the different bobbles, buttons, and lace at the various stalls.

As Belle wandered the stalls she thought about her future. *I spent many afternoons working with Aunt Hester in her millinery shop. I have those skills. I will open a millinery shop until I find the man of my dreams.* She pictured Brett's face. *Taking some time will give me a chance to make the right decision. I have my savings. We hardly spent anything on the trip so far.* Because they decided to go into business, shopping took a new perspective. Looking around at the different stalls, she found many other types of silk flowers and leaves, lace ribbons, and colorful ribbons she could use in her hat-making venture. At one booth, Belle saw many special different bobbles she would have loved to put on hats. Gathering a bunch of the bobbles, she gave the shy young vendor her money. Mary stood daydreaming in front of the stalls selling silks and satins, using her imagination to design women's clothing. At another stall, she found thin batiste, different pieces of cotton, and colored netting.

Loaded with packages, Brett steered the girls into a small outdoor café.

"Lunch is on me. I need to put all these down."

As he sat the packages under the table for safety, they sat at an outdoor table on the streets to watch the passersby. No menus or signs displayed what they were offering, but there were stands with many dishes, the smells drifted into the aisles and drew their attention. Smiling, Brett saw the confusion on Belle and Mary's faces. He described and translated the food choices for them. Most of the dishes were either chicken, fish, or pork. They all ordered chicken, as they were not sure they could handle any more fish or seafood.

"Where did you learn Portuguese, Brett?" inquired Mary.

As the server sat the dishes in front of them, the girls took deep breaths.

"Mmm, this food smells delicious."

As they ate, Brett smiled and shared stories of his youth.

"I lost my father early and left home to work on several ships so that I could send money back to my mother. This town was one of my favorite stopping places."

Pointing towards the houses behind them, he continued to share his story.

"If we go into the town proper, there are many houses, stores, and churches. When there are no ships in port, the town is quiet and home to many growing families. The families make their wares for the markets, selling them to tourists to support their families." Brett continued, "On the other side of town there are fine orchards, farms, and many fresh-water wells in the countryside. The people are a combination of Portuguese, Indian, and Hispanic, which melded together many years ago."

Finishing their meals, Belle looked at the space, committing it to memory for the future. They gathered their parcels and headed back towards the clipper ship. Passing a stall with many baked goods, the girls delighted in picking out different pastries for their afternoon teas. Brett, making a few purchases, suddenly became aware of two small boys who followed them, not noticed by the ladies but well under Brett's eye. He watched them note where the ladies put their monies and how they were careless with their attention to their surroundings. Paying attention to their hand signals, he kept a close eye on them. Brett shifted his packages from his dominant hand to the other hand in preparation for trouble.

Suddenly one of them moved in front of them and fell to the ground. As Mary and Belle bent over to assist him, the other grabbed their reticules and tried to break them loose from their grip. The girls slipped on the cobblestones, falling on top of the boy trying to pull their purses from them. Neither one let their money or parcels loose. The boy moved himself out from under them as they scrambled to regain their footing. Brett stepped between them, grabbing the boy by his shirt and lifting him off the ground.

In Portuguese, he asked the boy, "What do you think you are doing? Let go of the lady's belongings."

Seeing the scared look on the boys' faces, he let go of the boy, and he fell to the ground. Quick as a flash, the boy was up and running down the side street. His companions were running fast behind him.

As Brett assisted the girls off the ground, he couldn't help but notice Belle's boots. Brett asked them if they were okay as he helped them up, trying hard not to grin. Belle and Mary both dusted their skirts, gathered their packages, and turned to Brett.

"Thank you so much; we did not know what was happening. This is the first time we have been in a village like this. First, we were trying to help the little boy. Then, next we were joining him on the ground."

With a look of concern, Brett helped dust the street dirt from their dresses.

"Are you hurt? Did they get anything?" Watching as they dusted off their clothes and picked up their parcels, Brett was relieved they were okay. "I think we should head back to the ship."

As they were getting up, two sailors from the ship passed by with a wagon full of packages bought by the other passengers. Loading their parcels with the others, Brett turned to the girls to ensure they were okay. Waving the sailors on, they returned to their walk.

Taking each lady by the arm, they strolled back to the ship. Several times they stopped along the way to buy more pastries, biscuits, and fruit to replenish their cabin supplies. They noticed Brett stayed on alert and did not seem interested in purchasing anything else. He saw the worried looks on their faces.

"Don't worry. I will keep you safe, but we should get back. Dusk will be soon."

Once back on the ship, the girls relaxed and tried to rest. *I think I have had enough adventures for the day,* Belle thought as she carried her packages into the cabin. Looking around at all the parcels, Belle and Mary sighed as they began to put things away.

"Mary, I've been thinking. We have been friends for a long time. I have never lived outside of Maryville, even when my parents were alive. I feel very naïve about things. I still believe I made the right choice. I did not want to end up in the same place all my life. I think about my brother all the time. I know he is safe; I have never felt otherwise. Aunt Hester meant well, but this was my chance. Since I have you and your cousin Brett, it is much safer than if I just left on my own."

"Belle, I think you made the right decision. This gives you a chance to find someone on your terms. I saw how Hester kept pushing you towards different men. You would have been miserable." Mary smiled. "You will always have Phillip and me. You can come and stay with us!" Mary exclaimed jubilantly.

"That's kind, but Mary, I think I have to be independent for a while. I've never had the chance to be on my own. Aunt Hester spent most of her life single. For several years I worked with Aunt Hester in her millinery shop. I know how to make hats that women love. When we were shopping, I bought a lot of accessories to make the hats. I think I will have so much fun doing this. I have money saved that will support me for a few months."

Twirling in a bit of dance, Mary couldn't help but feel the excitement of Belle's idea. *I can hardly wait to share this with Phillip. It would be such a good partnership, my dressmaking and Belle's hats. We could be such a good team. Wonder how much of this will include Brett.*

Looking around the room at all the purchases, both Mary and Belle shook their heads. Belle put her hands on her hips.

"Well, we should have bought a couple more trunks. I think if we stack them carefully, we can move around a bit, but not much. We will have to spend a lot of time in the main cabin."

Laughing and hugging each other, it was plain to see the girls were happy.

The other passengers boarded carrying their packages, tired and ready to go to their cabins. As Brett leaned over the deck railing smoking his pipe, he smiled, remembering Belle's boots. *Guess she still has a little tomboy left in her. Where in the world did she get those ugly boots, and are they important to her? I can hardly wait to see what this woman does next.* He shook his head. *She is full of surprises.*

The evening meal was quiet as most passengers, including Belle and Mary, were tired after their excursion. Only half eating their meals, they excused themselves and went back to their cabin. Within minutes, they were both in bed, dreaming.

# CHAPTER 16

The next morning the ship left the harbor. Following the shoreline, the passengers saw beautiful jungles, forests, and brightly colored rare birds they had never seen before. As the clipper ship passed by small towns and villages, often small boats paddled out towards them to offer handicrafts, fresh fruits, and vegetables. However, the captain did not stop the ship. Captain turned the clipper ship out to sea. The bustle of the villages stayed in Belle's mind as she watched the ship gradually turn out to sea. She would miss all the excitement, but she wanted to get the trip over with and arrive in California. Only fifteen more days until they reached San Francisco.

Day by day, Belle felt the anticipation of arriving in San Francisco. The closeness of the passengers on the ship deepened their relationships. Belle, Mary, and Brett seemed to be together constantly. At every turn, Belle saw Brett, and her attraction grew for him. Looking at him standing by the rail, smoking that infernal pipe, she admired the way his cheek crinkled when he was in deep thought, the way his eyes narrowed when he was concentrating, and most of all, the sound of his voice. His voice was deep and thoughtful, with a tinge of huskiness. The draw towards him was one she could not seem to break.

Later in her room, she shared her attraction to Brett with Mary.

"Mary, please don't tease me. I need to share how I feel, but I am not sure of my feelings. I do not understand why I am feeling this way. Have you ever had thoughts about someone you couldn't explain?"

Putting her head in her hands, she bent over the table in despair.

Mary looked at her friend and wondered at the confusion Belle was having.

"Belle, when I was young, I never had any doubts about Phillip. He has been the one since I was seven, when he pulled my hair. But when I look around at other girls, I have found that not everyone has had that experience. I think you have feelings for Brett, but how will you ever know if he is the right one if you don't talk about your feelings with him? There is a big difference between infatuation and love for someone."

In her heart, Belle was already falling in love. *How can this be, she wondered? I barely know the man.* Yet, every time he was near, she felt flushed, short of breath, and had a desire in her. She did not realize she had that ability within her. It was all she could do not to touch him. *If this is just attraction, then I am attracted.* She cried inside.

After several days of solitude in their room, Mary convinced Belle to walk around the deck even though she was fighting her feelings.

"Goodness, Belle, being a hermit will not change your feelings. You need to face them head-on and do something. I see the way he looks at you when he thinks no one is watching. Just talk to him, get it out in the open, for both your sakes."

Predictably as they were walking, Brett tipped his hat and joined them.

"Good morning, ladies. The weather seems good again today."

Belle looked at him, thinking how crazy it was to be talking about the weather. Mary, sensing they needed to be alone, moved to another group, leaving them standing by themselves. Guiding Belle over to some trunks placed on the deck for the passengers to sit on, he tipped his hat and sat beside her. Moving close so she could inhale his scent, she tilted her head to try to hear what he was saying. Later, when Belle tried to remember what they talked about, all she could remember was the sound of his low voice, his smile, and his eyes when Brett looked at her. She was fighting a longing she could not explain when he was near.

The next day following dinner, Belle joined Brett for a walk around the deck. They stopped in one of the small areas arranged for the passengers to relax. As they walked towards the railing, she found her breath was hard to control. Leaning forward, watching the never-ending waves, he placed his hand on her elbow. The tingling feeling traveled up her spine, causing her to shiver. She immediately felt the glow moving towards her face. Turning, she looked at him and saw the responsive feeling in his eyes.

Forcing her to a more private place, he started to speak.

"Belle, I think you know that I am interested in you. Could you possibly have any room in that pretty little head for an old cowboy who has come to care for you a lot?"

Taken by surprise, she looked tenderly at him.

"You are not so old. Plenty of good years left in you."

Then feeling embarrassed, she put her head down. Brett placed his finger under her chin, raising her head so that she was at eye level.

"Belle, I know you are young. You will want to do many

things before you get married, but I hope you will start thinking of me as a possible suitor. My wife died several years ago, and I have had time to place those feelings in the past. Can we give it a shot? I promise I will move slowly and give you a chance to fulfill your dreams. Belle, let's give our love a chance. Admit that you have feelings for me too." Leaning towards her, he lightly brushed her cheeks with his fingertips. "This deck or even the ship is not the place to discuss our feelings or our future. There is no privacy on this ship. However, I can promise you that you are not making a mistake to give us a chance."

Looking around, the other passengers and crew members seemed occupied and not looking their way. He gathered her close. So close to him, she was afraid of her feelings for him. The smell of leather, pipe tobacco, and shaving soap lingered as she felt the security of his arms around her. Pushing him back gently, she reminded him of the other passengers.

"Never mind the others, Belle, I need to have you in my life. Regardless of your problems, my love for you is more real and more important than any issues you may have. Give us a chance. We have this time together to explore our feelings. Let's not waste it."

In her heart, she knew that he was right, but she was afraid. Afraid of what the future would be like with him, but worse, she was fearful of what life would be like without him. She placed her two fingers in front of her lips, kissed them, and laid them against his cheek. Then she laid her head on his arm. He pulled her closer and listened to her heartbeat. All he could think of at that moment was to have her near.

After enjoying his nearness, she became aware of how the situation would look to the other passengers if they saw them. *What a mess,* she thought. Slowly disengaging herself from his arms, she looked at him. Giving him a timid smile, she turned and went back to the others.

Brett watched her as she walked away. Turning back to the never-ending waves, Brett wanted Belle in his life. He had stayed away from temptation all these years. When his wife died, he had told himself he would never allow himself to be involved with someone else. The pain of losing someone was more than Brett thought he could handle. Now he wanted to take another chance. To his relief, this one little slip of a girl had awakened his heart again. Watching the waves dance on top of the water, he contemplated how he would win her over, not knowing that she was already in love with him.

The days seemed to pass too fast for him with the need to spend every moment with Belle. However, time was slow for the other passengers who waited and waited for it to be over so they could move forward with their plans and lives. Every chance he had, Belle noticed him appearing at her side. He traded places with the other passengers so that he could sit across from her at meals. While others played board games in the evenings, Brett sat on the side, pretending to read, but watching her play. He noted every smile and laugh when she made a mistake, and the gentleness she showed when she let her friend win the game. This girl was not the young boy that he had first met. *How could I ever have thought she was a boy?* He watched her deal the cards, carefully passing the correct number to each player.

Brett was short of breath anytime she was near. When she wasn't near, he couldn't stop thinking about her. Some would only see her from the outside, her actions and her gentleness. However, he knew differently. He remembered and was still amazed that she climbed on top of a runaway stagecoach and shot at her attackers. He marveled when she slept on the floor so that her friend could have the bed. Most of all, he admired the fact that she was willing to pass off as a boy to avoid whatever or whoever was trailing her best friend. *Belle had the nerve and was not afraid to go after what she wanted.* What

Brett couldn't identify was what her goal was and who was trying to stop her.

Leaving the boisterous group below deck, Brett went up the stairs to watch the stars and to try to come to grip with his feelings. *Since when have I ever let someone dominate my mind, my thinking, and my heart? Was I like this before with my wife? I just can't remember. But I do know I need Belle, whatever it takes.* When he arrived on top of the deck, he noticed there was unrest among the sailors. He looked to where they were looking and saw a speck of white on the horizon. It bobbled between the waves, hardly noticeable unless you were looking in the right place. Walking over to the captain, who had his spyglass out, he leaned on the railing.

"What's out there?"

# CHAPTER 17

The captain lowered the spyglass and looked towards Brett.

"Someone has been following us for the last few days. Occasionally, we see them on the horizon when the sun is either rising or setting and hits their sails just so, but they never get closer or disappear. The ship could be innocent; however, preparations for battle are in place. Please do not get the passengers alarmed. Let them enjoy their trip. We can handle this problem."

Giving orders to the crew, the clipper ship slowly changed course and moved closer to where land was in sight, still moving on their chosen track north to San Francisco.

Brett spent a long time that evening watching the horizon and wondering how he could make the girls safer if it turned out to be something dangerous. That night, he cleaned his guns and placed them in reach if he needed them. His knife was sharp. Making sure his ammunition was in order, he laid his saddlebags on the floor near the bed. Laying on the bunk, he tried to sleep. Still, he only had visions of Belle—fighting off the gunmen, the look on her face as she came out of the stables at the way station, and how she looked with her fancy dress and her boots in town. He mumbled to himself. *Man, what have I done? I am in love with a wild woman. At least she is never dull.*

The following morning, he was lucky enough to see Belle alone, sitting on a bench on the deck, reading. As he approached, she looked up with a shy smile.

"Good morning, Brett. Isn't it a great day? The air seems different somehow."

He tried to make small talk beside her but found he could not. All he could do was try to figure out a way to win her heart.

"Belle, I know we haven't known each other exceptionally long, but in these times, sometimes, time doesn't make a difference."

"Brett, you do not understand my situation," Belle said very quietly. "I care deeply about you. Give me a little time. I need to make sure of our feelings. My parents died when I was young, leaving just my brother and me. Oh, Aunt Hester tried her best to raise us, and we were a handful. But when Jeremy left home, it broke my heart. He taught me almost everything I know. He has to be somewhere near San Francisco, and I need to find him."

"I'm not talking about a short whirlwind relationship. I want us to be together forever. Belle, take your time but take a good look at what we could have. We can work things out."

He stood looking down at her for a long time. Afraid to look at him, she stared out across the ocean.

"This will not be the end of this conversation. You will see that my feelings are real. I will not give up, and I am not going away."

With that statement, he walked away. Not quite as confident as before, but with a new resolve.

Sitting on the steps, Belle thought to herself. *How do I*

*explain? I know I have strong feelings for him, but it feels similar to the situation with Aunt Hester. Everyone seems to know what's best for me. That is the problem. I want to be the one making the decision. I want time to work it all out.* Stopping, then sitting on the steps, she slowly put her head in her hands and let the tears slowly run down her cheeks. After a while, she rose and went back to the cabin.

As she sat down at the small table, Belle heard Mary behind the dressing screen.

"Are you ready, Belle? I thought you had already gone up. I am excited. Only three more days until we reach San Francisco. I hope that Phillip hasn't changed too much. It has been two years since we have seen each other."

Mary chattered away, not noticing Belle was not answering her. Coming from behind the screen, she stopped suddenly. Looking at Belle's face, seeing the raw emotion, she walked swiftly to her.

"Belle, what happened? Are you okay?"

That just started Belle to flood with tears again. Wringing her hands, she cried until she couldn't cry anymore as Mary stood beside her with her hand on her shoulder.

"Mary, I am such a fool. I flirted with Brett, just wanting him to notice me. Then something terrible happened. I became trapped by my own game."

As she sat down, a change came over her voice as she said quietly, "I saw how the wind blows through his hair. I noticed how he places his fingers in his vest pocket when he is thinking. I noticed the dimple in his left cheek but not in his right cheek. How he stands with his pipe unlit, leaning on the rail as he watches the waves. Whatever is he thinking? I love the smell of him when he is close. I still see him watching you and everything you do. Oh, Mary, what am I going to do? Is this how you are supposed to feel?"

Following this outburst, Belle started to cry again, heavy sobs shaking her body.

Mary saw the devastation of her friend but felt helpless to change the situation. Holding Belle by the shoulders, Mary helped her to stand up.

"Belle, I have only known you for a short time, but during that time, I have seen a strong, honorable woman. You can work out these problems. As I see it, you need to be honest with Brett. Maybe if you tell him how you feel, you can work out the problems together. Now wash your face and get pretty, and let's go up on deck before it gets too cool."

Sighing deeply, Belle followed her advice.

Walking around the deck with her friend, Belle tried to figure out how she would articulate her problem.

"Mary, I had no idea that I would fall in love. What does that mean? How do I work this out? I am between the life I thought I wanted and the life offered to me. How do I find Jeremy? How do I find out if I can be independent? What is wrong with me?"

Mary watched her walk away, again feeling helpless in comforting her friend. *My dear Belle, your problem is that you are in love.*

The following day was beautiful. The sun was out, no clouds were in the sky, and the waves were calm and peaceful. As Brett looked out over the ocean, he suddenly focused on a white sail on the distant horizon. Turning to the captain, who stood on the deck above him, he noticed the captain had focused his spyglass in the same direction.

Meanwhile, Belle looked around the cabin as if seeing it for the first time. *So much has happened,* she thought, and she sat at the desk. *When I first started this trip, I thought it was an adventure. I was going to find my brother. I was going to make a place in the world. The world is so large. How will I find him? Maybe he doesn't want to be found. Since then, I have watched men and animals get killed for no reason. In the towns that we passed, I saw the appearance of the women who lived in the small towns who quit before they made it West—depressed and looking like they had lost hope. How will it be when I reach the frontier?*

Looking at her lap, Belle scolded herself for thinking that all of this would be easy. *Life was so much more predictable when I was living with Aunt Hester. She made my life more manageable than I realized. I never knew how lucky I was to have her as a guardian.* Tears began to fall down her cheeks. *I can never go back to be that person again. How do I handle this mess?*

She sat there and thought and again felt the tears rush down her cheek. Suddenly straightening her shoulders, she washed her face in the basin on the desk, dried her tears, and looking in the mirror, she scolded herself.

"You are not a child anymore but a woman who has traveled across a country to marry a man who trusted you enough to ask you to be his wife. You need to be a strong woman and stop this nonsense."

Staring at herself, she felt she had needed that said out loud. She gathered her skirts, opened the door to the cabin, and walked up to the deck. Once on the deck, she saw Brett talking to the captain. Walking up to them, she tapped Brett on the shoulders. As he turned, Belle saw the love in his eyes, which almost broke her resolve. Taking a deep breath, she told him they needed to talk. He led her to a quiet place, where they sat down on a box leaning up on the stairwell to the hatch below.

Brett took both of her hands in his.

"What do you need to talk about?"

Resolving not to cry, Belle held her head high and began.

"Brett, this is so hard, but I have to be honest. When I first saw you, I felt strongly for you. I liked how you handled a gun, the way you walked, and the half-smile you gave when you were pleased about something. When your arms are around me, I can think of nothing else."

Moving closer to her, he put his hand through her elbow and looked into her eyes.

Pushing him back a little away from her, she continued.

"Please listen. I'm trying to be honest with both of us. I began this trip to find my freedom and independence and not have to depend on anyone."

In her head, the words were fighting with her, proving she was making a big mistake. *The problem is that I love you. I can't stop thinking about you.* Preventing him from speaking, she placing her fingers across his lips. Putting her head down, she was afraid of meeting his eyes again. She felt a profound loss after telling him the truth. Slowly, Brett put his arms around her shoulders, drawing her near. He let her cry until she couldn't anymore.

"Belle, well, you want honesty, then I need to share some information with you as well. I met you under pretense. It was not only Della that wanted me to travel with you girls, but Phillip hired me to keep an eye on Mary and to protect her until she reaches San Francisco. Being close to Mary also meant I was close to you. Remember, I thought you were a boy at first. I was suspicious that Mary had brought a boyfriend with her. You do not know how relieved I was when I discovered you were a girl. At first, that is all that it was. Then watching you go into the barn, and then terrified when I saw what happened to you. I felt I needed to protect you too. When I discovered you were a girl, I was relieved and pleased. Seeing your bravado endeared you to me. When I comforted you, I knew something was wrong, but I couldn't figure out my feelings. Why would I care about a stubborn young woman who dressed and fought like a guy with no sense? Instead of watching Mary, I couldn't get you out of my mind. I am in love with you." Putting his fingers under her chin, he tilted her head upwards. "We will work this out somehow. I need you to be in my life as my wife."

Leaning on him, smelling the manliness of him, trying to imprint her need for him in her mind, took all her reserve not to tell him she wanted him. Belle knew that she did not want to lose him in her heart, but she also knew that she had to be serious concerning her needs or could never commit freely. How would this work out? She stayed in his arms for a long time, letting the comfort of his arms make her forget. That is how Mary found them. She saw them and silently backed up, leaving them alone in the darkness of the deck.

The days passed quickly, and her love for Brett increased with each day. They sat together in the evenings, holding hands, talking about how their future could be. They walked the decks in the evening. He told her of his parents' orange groves and how he wanted to work there. They spoke about the home they would build and the children they would have.

The ship on the horizon stayed the same distance from them, never gaining but never gone. The captain was always watching, always alert.

As the clipper ship moved closer to San Francisco, the tension of possibly seeing Tomas overwhelmed Belle. Several times she reread his letters. They were full of promise and talk about the future. A future she did not want to be a part of. She did not want him in her life. Belle wanted Brett. Each day, Belle was feeling worse and worse. Again, she approached the subject of the turmoil she was having with her decision. Brett tried to be understanding and compassionate, but he did not want to lose Belle. He decided it was time to stand his ground and made her listen to his reasoning on making the right decision of choosing him, of course.

Later that evening, as they walked on deck, he looked out across the ocean as he held her in his arms. She loved the feel of his arms, the security, and the love that surrounded her. She nuzzled into his shoulder, lost in the sense of him.

As he gently raised her hair off her neck, he whispered, "I want this moment to live forever. I do not want to ever forget the love that you have shown to me over the last few days."

Belle turned around and looked deeply into his eyes. His love for her was evident in how he held her and how he cherished her enough to be willing to wait until they were married to go further.

With his arms around her, he pulled her close to him, his lips hungrily devouring hers. Belle leaned into him, matching his need with a need of her own. Praying these moments would last forever, she settled into his arms.

"Belle," Brett whispered, "you have to make a clear choice, and then we will live with that choice, no matter what your decision."

Letting her go, he turned to the railing.

All the love that she had been feeling over the last few minutes seemed to evaporate at his words. Looking sidewise at him, not being able to meet his eyes, she lowered her head and whispered.

"Brett, that is not fair. You know how I feel, but I also have a feeling of commitment to myself. I want to know that I can take care of myself independently before I commit to someone. I don't know how to come to terms with all of this. Please, let us enjoy this trip together."

Taking a long look at her, sighing, Brett was aware of the conflict in her.

"I am sorry, Belle, it is all or nothing. Life is full of commitments. What about the one between us? Where is our future while you worry about someone you don't even know is alive or his whereabouts? Make a decision, Belle. You are not a little girl anymore, but a woman. A woman that I love and want to be with for the rest of my life. It is real, not a fantasy. I am here, right here in front of you. What I am offering you is a commitment for life and a love that is enduring. Clear your doubts, little girl. I want you to make the right choice. I hope that it is me."

With that, he turned and left her standing by the railing. In shock, Belle stood there, watching him walk away. *He thinks this is about Jeremy? How will I straighten this all out?*

Slowly, she descended the stairs into the cabin. Mary took one look at her and rushed to her.

"What happened? You look terrible. Did you argue with Brett? Come sit down. I will get you some water."

Belle waved her away.

"No thanks, Mary. I just need some time to think. I don't want to eat this evening. I want to stay here and try to figure out the mess that I have created."

With that, Mary left her and went to eat.

All during the dinner, Mary could not help but watch Brett. He was quiet and hardly made eye contact with the other passengers. Following dinner, instead of staying behind and playing card games, he went back to his cabin. None of the passengers seemed to acknowledge that something had happened. *Maybe they didn't notice*, Mary thought as she walked her way back to the cabin. When she reached inside, Belle had curled up in her bed and was facing the wall. Not wanting to disturb her, Mary undressed in the dark and went to bed.

The next day was not any better. Mary wandered around the deck both in the morning and afternoon by herself. She saw the captain looking at something in his spyglass, but when she looked in the same direction, all she saw was endless waves. They seemed to roll continuously, some large, some small. Growing tired of the scenery, she sat down on one of the boxes and started working on some of the needlework she had brought. That is where Brett found her.

145

"Mary, are you okay? I am not used to seeing you without Belle."

Looking at his face, she saw the sadness and the dejected manner of his shoulders. Patting the box, she motioned for him to sit.

"Brett, what is going on? You and Belle were happy. Now both of you act like you are at a funeral."

Bending over, putting his head in his hands, Brett told her what happened. This situation was something that he couldn't fix. It was up to Belle to make the decision. Hugging him, she told him how upset Belle was and the difficulty she was having.

"Mary, it is simple. Either she wants me, or she doesn't. How do I make Belle understand this? I just have to wait for her to grow up."

With that, he stood and walked away. Mary watched him. He was a man with the weight of the world on his shoulders.

Belle told Mary that Phillip had hired Brett to protect her on the trip. *What he didn't do was defend himself,* she thought. With a sigh, she walked to the railing. There on the horizon, she caught a glimpse of a tiny white sail. Then it disappeared. *That's upsetting, but I probably imagined it.* She moved back from the railing and walked to the main cabin with hopes of joining a card game. She didn't notice the captain's worried look as he held his spyglass towards the same area she had watched.

Following their evening walk on deck, Mary quickly completed her evening routine and dressed for bed. Belle looked around the room as she tidied, getting ready for the following day. As she wiped down their table, she looked at Mary with a smile on her face.

"Remember when we decided to make this trip? As I looked at you, I thought you were the loveliest thing I had ever seen."

"Well, Belle, what a nice thing to say. I'm sorry, I can't say the same," she laughed with glee. "At first, I couldn't figure out why you decided to dress as you did for this trip. I know you ran around in the woods like that when you were hunting. I always blamed Jeremy for putting those ideas in your head. By the way, that hat amazed me."

Belle joined her in laughter.

"I have, you know. I thought I looked like the best pretend boy I could be. What gave me away? Was it the hat? The jacket, or the pants with the rope around the middle?"

Both girls laughed and giggled.

"You were trying so hard. Yet, it was obvious that you were not who you thought you thought you were. It was so easy to see through that getup. Then I knew right away. But why did you want to be a boy?" questioned Mary.

Not knowing, their giggling and laughter passed through the thin door of their cabin. Brett moved his chair up against their cabin wall, lit his pipe, and opened his book. Hopefully, the other passengers would think of him reading. As the smell of the pipe floated through the open room, Brett listened to the girls enjoying their stories.

"Oh Mary, like you, I guess if you think about it, we all have stories to tell. My brother, Jeremy, left home to find himself in California. I missed him so much when he left. Like you, I lost my parents as well. However, I was lucky. Aunt Hester took us in to raise. She wasn't the wrong sort. She fussed about the house, so I spent a lot of time on chores. But now I understand why it is crucial to learn to look after yourself after all this mess. One thing I did learn from Aunt Hester was how to design and make hats. She owned the most pleasant little shop. I loved going there to work with her. Taking small bits of lace, tulle, and making flowers was so much fun. If you could see what she could do with a basic form, you would cry out at the beauty of her hats.

147

"However, we didn't have much money, so I learned how to make the most of everything. I thought it was horrible that we had to scrimp and save. But we would have never had anything if we hadn't learned to make the most of what we had. Anyway, I had this grand idea to go to California to find Jeremy. Since I didn't have any way to pay my fare, I got the bright idea of getting there when I saw the mail-order bride ads. But then your problem came along, and it seemed like the right path."

"But Belle, wasn't that a problem? I understand your situation, but taking a chance on missing the love of your life over your brother who chose his path is a mistake. I am so glad you did not take that path your aunt was trying to choose for you. I have known Phillip my entire life. You have been around Brett for several months now and have gotten to see him in many situations. I see him as a man of honor and it is obvious he has fallen for you hard."

Mary watched Belle.

"That was my plan before your mother died, Mary. Anyway, it has all worked out for the best, I think?" Belle looked over at the closet at the pair of boots in the bottom.

"Oh, those boots belonged to Jeremy. The pants, shirt, and jacket as well. I didn't have time to fit them. I just put them on and hurried out the door while Aunt Hester was asleep and left the next morning. Oh, I left Aunt Hester a note. But I bet she was glad to get rid of the responsibility of having me."

As she was resting her chin on her hand, Mary smiled.

"I'll never forget when I first saw you with that ugly plaid shirt and those hitched-up pants before we left. I was so upset that I had to leave my home, but at the same time anxious to go to Phillip. I was not sure I wanted you to come along with me." Mary wrinkling her nose and sat down beside Belle. "When I first found out that Brett would meet us later,

I was not sure I could go by myself. When you agreed, my heart lifted, and I knew this plan was the right plan."

Interjecting, Belle responded, "Mary, your tears overcame me. When I saw you sitting on that bench, dabbing tears with your handkerchief, looking like a lady, all I could see was this beautiful porcelain doll sitting on a bench crying. Why wouldn't that bring anyone to the point of helping you? You smelled like marigolds and heather at the same time. I figured if I traveled with you, no one would give me a second glance. Then when you fell into cahoots with me, and we watched all those men walking . . . . Going into the alley to practice their walks was hilarious. I never had so much fun. I remember one guy, the one with the shotgun. He walked with his toes out and his knees bent. I tried so hard to do that, but all that happened was that I fell."

Rolling with laughter, the girls made faces as Belle tried to do the walk.

Outside, Brett had to smile. *So they were both in it with each other. Well, they sure had me fooled. At least until the barn incident. Belle was just a little too scared, a little too soft, and the scream was a dead giveaway. That was the first time I realized that Belle was playing a game and a true lady. Then to hold on to me as she did. Yes, little Belle played a good game.* As he heard them continue to talk, he pretended to be engrossed in his book. The other passengers were playing card games, not noticing Brett sitting against the wall with his book.

"Brett is the one I love. I used to think I didn't need romantic love, but I need someone to be nice and take care of me. Now I realize I want to be more. I want to be an equal partner and share in the work and whatever it takes to make the situation work."

Brett looked deep in thought as he replaced the chair near the dining table, closed his book, and went back to his cabin. *This information makes things a little complicated but exciting.*

As for Belle. It took a long time for her to go to sleep. Whenever she closed her eyes, she could see Brett. *How am I going to handle this situation? Oh Mary, if you could only know what is on my mind or in my heart, you would know what a hard time I am having.*

# CHAPTER 18

Belle and Mary awakened early the next morning to the scuffling and running noise on the deck above them. They heard shouts and a bell ringing. Sitting up in bed, they looked at each other in alarm. A sudden knock on the door and then a cry for them to prepare for rough sailing caused them to spring from their beds and run to the porthole. What they saw caused instant panic. There was another ship coming towards them. As it came within view, they saw the privateer flag flying.

"Oh no!" they both shouted at the same time.

Scurrying to get dressed, they quickly hid their valuables in their secret hiding place. Then they strapped themselves into their beds and waited. The captain was trying to evade the other ship by turning towards land to a nearby village. They felt the ship tip and speed up. A giant swell made them think they would tip over. The clipper ship changed directions quickly, causing the ship to lean far to the right. The privateer ship came closer and closer.

There were the sounds of the gun bays uncovering and the cannons loading. The crew was shouting, and the captain was hollering orders. When the batteries went off, the noise shook their cabins and caused them to tremble. At the same time, they heard a cannon firing from a long distance. Looking at each other, Belle and Mary were unable to determine the direction of the noise. Loosening the ropes, they ran to the porthole to see what was happening, ignoring the orders to prepare for a battle. The clipper ship turned suddenly again, causing Belle and Mary to slide to the edge of the room. Scrambling to hold tight, they righted again. At the same time, they heard the other ship returning fire. The cannonball passed over their ship, heading towards land but fell short. The *Flying Goose* turned sharp again, throwing Belle and Mary to the floor. Confused, Belle scrambled to look out the window. The ship had turned so that they were looking at the shore rather than the other ship. The firing was coming from a cliff on the shore, not the ship chasing them. Then another loud cannon sounded, exploding near them but closer to the privateer ship. They felt the *Flying Goose* speed up, then make a turn again. In the distance, they could hear the sounds of cannons and firearms, and smell the smoke. There was shouting and cursing.

Hiding further under the bedcovers, Belle became frustrated that she could not see what was going on but was too scared to look out the window. They felt the ship move faster and faster. Many explosions were hitting around them but most whizzed past them. Then suddenly everything became quiet.

"Either we are sinking, or they left," whispered Belle.

Mary looked at Belle.

"There is no noise. Surely they haven't boarded us."

Slowly they rose out of the beds and tiptoed to the porthole. There was no ship in view.

"Well, I don't know about you, but I am going up to find

out what has been going on," whispered Belle as she opened the door to the cabin.

As she came into the main cabin, the other passengers were coming out of their rooms.

The first mate met them and told them to take a seat.

"The captain is busy, so he sent me to explain. He did not have time to report what was happening as it happened so fast. There has been a privateer ship following us since we left the last port. It stayed just beyond the horizon, but last night, it started moving toward us fast. In this business, the safety of the ship, passengers, and cargo is of the utmost importance. Therefore, we have arranged for protection from the forts along the coast. The captain ran the signal flag up so the fort on the cliff could see we were in trouble. All he had to do was get us near the coast, lead the other ship in close, then make a sharp turn so that the cannons on land could get a clear view of the other ship. They scared the privateers off, so we are back on track. We think we crippled their ship, but they are out of sight. We do know they pushed some of the passengers overboard, so we are on the lookout for them but cannot stop. Hopefully, if they are alive, they can make it to shore. We should reach San Diego by tomorrow evening and disembark the following morning. We will continue near the coastline so the forts can offer protection."

As the captain joined them, the passengers cheered loudly, each taking turns to tell the captain thanks and shake his hand to avoid what could have been a disaster. The captain explained that his company had taken great care to build in safeguards for their ships.

"Our ships only have to make it within the range of the protection forts scattered along the coast. That is the reason for staying closer to the shore, rather than sailing in the open seas. We carry much-needed cargo, and it is our job to make it to our destination, not necessarily beat time records. I want to thank all the men who helped during our crisis."

He looked directly at Brett.

With that, the first mate turned and went back on deck to organize their sail's final leg.

That evening, Belle decided to speak with Brett and tell him her decision. It was the honorable thing to do. *Nothing in my life seems easy*, she thought.

Suddenly the passengers heard a loud cry, "Man overboard!"

Pointing to a piece of wood riding the waves, they could make out a man draped over the side of the log. The captain lowered a lifeboat, and several of the crew went to his rescue.

"Ladies, it will be safer to go below. The crew is going to have their hands full getting back up and on course," requested the captain.

Taking one last look over the ocean, Belle and Mary returned to their cabins to relax over a cup of tea. That evening at dinner, the passengers were energized and talked about the man rescued that afternoon.

In the sick bay of the ship, a blonde-haired man lay unconscious on the bunk. The ship's medic was dressing several wounds on the survivor's back. He looked at the captain.

"I don't know who he is yet, sir. He has not awakened since we pulled him aboard. Whoever he is, he has had a hard time with it. I have dressed his back and the gash on his leg. It looks like he went through a lashing."

Walking over to the bunk, the captain pulled back the blanket. Turning his head away, he covered him.

"I will send a couple of men to take turns watching him.

Let me know when he wakes up. We need information, not only about him but about the ship."

"Aye, Captain."

The man on the bunk lay quietly, barely making out the surrounding words. He felt gentle hands apply some cooling salve on his back wounds. The relief from the burning wounds subdued him, and he fell back into a blissful subconsciousness that allowed him some comfort from the previous three days of torture.

At times, the man would call out names or grunt in pain. When this occurred, the medic carefully measured small amounts of a mixture of laudanum. He was careful to only give a small amount over a long period to dull the pain. Gradually he woke up and began gaining his strength. When he was able to talk, the captain came to his cabin.

"Sir, good to see you are recovering. Do you have a name?" asked the captain.

"Thank you for rescuing me. I didn't think I could hold on much longer. My name is Tomas Cavelier. I live on a small farm just east of Sacramento. I had been back east visiting my relatives. While sailing back to California, privateers attacked our ship—pirates, whatever you want to call them." Taking a drink of water, he continued with his story. "They raped and killed the women right away but made the men help with the ship. When I refused, they put me under the lash, then threw my body overboard. I watched them sail away, leaving me for the sharks. Luckily, I found the log and could get my back out of the water, so the blood would not attract the sharks. Then you found me. I lost count of the days, maybe three, four until you found me."

Looking at Tomas carefully, the captain was unsure of the story, but the pieces seemed to fit. In his mind, something wasn't right.

"I don't have any more rooms onboard for passengers, but

we will be in San Francisco in three days. You can sleep here in the medic's room until we get there."

"Captain, if it is passage money you are worried about, I will assure you payment."

"Mr. Cavelier, it is not the money I am concerned about. We are not safe yet. I still have concerns about the privateers for this ship."

As he left the room, he told the medic to keep a close eye on the patient. He wanted to make sure this was not a trick of some kind from the privateers.

As she packed and went over each of her purchases she obtained on the trip, Belle often looked at Mary, amazed at the glow and happiness her friend exhibited.

"Mary, I swear, you are almost bursting at the seams with all your humming and smiling. I know, I know, you will see Phillip in three days."

Laughingly, Belle stopped her tasks and enjoyed observing Mary labeling each of her items to Sacramento.

"I know that it's not true, but I feel the ship is suddenly going at the slowest speed it can go. Maybe I could swim faster." Turning, she laughed at Belle. "I know it is my imagination."

"Mary, the man we picked up a few days ago, they said he would join us this evening. Wonder why he was floating on that log? Somewhat strange. Oh well, it is nothing to us. Brett is going to walk with us this afternoon, so we need to get ready."

Hurrying up to the deck, the girls took a deep breath of the fresh salty air. Brett joined them, smiling.

"Good to see you girls. Mary, you look fresh as a daisy."

He leaned next to Belle, "And you, my lady, cause my heart to jump, you are so pretty."

As a slow blush covered Belle's cheeks, she smiled back at him.

"I think we should find time to talk."

"What's wrong with right now?"

He led her over to some boxes to sit.

"Brett, I am sorry, I have been such pain on this trip. I am in love with you and think of a future with you every day. I just want you to give me a chance to prove to myself that if I need to, I can take care of myself independently."

As he took her in his arms, he held her close.

"Belle, I will wait as long as you need, as long as I know that when you have worked all this out, that you will be my wife. I will still court you and help you with whatever you need. I have the patience to get what I want and what I want is this pretty little hardheaded redhead who is holding my heart in her hands. Do your thing, make your fortune, be mine."

"Brett, you have my heart, my love, and my dreams," whispered Belle as she stood in his arms.

Across the deck, a blonde-headed man watched them intently. *Well, little girl, we meet again. It looks like you are not the stiff person I thought you were. So you like older men. You won't miss him after we get together. Once you are with a real man, you won't want anyone else.* Smiling, he went back down the steps to the medic room.

# CHAPTER 19

The following day, Belle and Mary stepped up onto the deck. It was a clear day, the breeze was gentle and the sun teased its warmth on the afternoon. Standing by the rail, they did not see the blonde man standing on the other side of the ship behind one of the masts, watching them.

"Mary, I can hardly wait until tomorrow. It's like it will be the first day of our new life."

Leaning over the top of the rail, she could see the fish swimming alongside the ship.

"Belle, I am getting so anxious. I haven't seen Phillip in two years. Do you think he will notice any changes in me? It has been so long. I don't remember how I looked two years ago. Do you think he has changed?"

Turning to face Mary, Belle couldn't hide her amusement.

"Mary, calm down. You have known Phillip all your life. Everything will be fine."

Suddenly, she noticed a shadow falling over them. They turned to look; both Belle and Mary were surprised.

"You! Where did you come from? What are you doing on this ship?" exclaimed Belle as she saw who it was.

Mary noted his appearance. He was wearing a shirt too large for him from one of the crew members, and his pants were too long. He had a bandage around the top of his head and another as a sling for his right shoulder.

"Are you the one they found in the ocean the other day?" Mary asked quietly, aware of the tension between Tomas and Belle.

"Yes, my ship was attacked. I was taken prisoner but managed to escape. I couldn't believe it when I saw you two on board. It is nice to see old friends."

"Don't call me a friend, Tomas," Belle uttered. "I told you before that I did not care for your charms."

Taken back at the severity of her tone, Tomas took a step backward.

"I think we got off to a bad start back there in Missouri. Belle, give us a little time to get to know each other. I am sure we will become friends."

"Never!" Belle exclaimed as she turned and left the deck. Mary followed her quickly to their room.

"What was that all about?" whispered Mary.

"We got off to a bad start, all right. Tomas was rude and very pushy at the dance where we met him. He was arrogant enough to think I would swoon and fall into his arms. Mr. Tomas's intentions were not honorable. Do you know he tried to get me to walk around the garden with him? There is something about him that gives me goosebumps. Never let me be alone with him. He is bad news."

With that speech, Belle almost stomped her foot. She was so angry, she could feel a flush rising in her neck.

Brett was reading a book in the main cabin as Belle rushed to her room, with Mary close behind her. A few seconds later, Tomas came through the main cabin with a scowl on his face as he headed to the medic room. Watching the three, he could only wonder what it was all about. He didn't remember ever seeing Belle that angry, except when Mary's brothers tried to kidnap her.

That evening as they pulled into port, all the passengers were on deck for their first glimpse of San Francisco. It was late evening, and the docks were bustling, even at these late hours. They could see stacks of cargo boxes lifted from the other ships lined along the docks. Each lift had several men pulling on the cables to guide the cargo to their assigned spots on the pier. Others were moving the freight into wagons. A steady stream of wagons was loaded heavily with cargo boxes, moving slowly up a slight slope towards the town's lights. Brett stood at the other side of the ship, looking off into the sea, not a part of the group of passengers crowded around the deck.

Belle looked longingly after Brett. *I know that he wants our relationship to move faster, but I have to prove things to myself before moving forward with him. But what if I am wrong?* The question nagged at the back of her mind. Inside of her, she felt the loneliness of the confusion in her heart. However, she was stubborn enough to think it had to be her way.

Later, while packing her clothes and things to leave the ship, Mary chattered excitedly.

"Belle, you have to join us as soon as we get everything set up. I want you to be a witness to our wedding."

Without giving Belle a chance to answer, she went directly into her wedding plans.

Belle sat and looked at her friend. She was happy for Mary but couldn't help feeling a lingering sadness for herself. Looking at Belle, Mary shook her finger at Belle. Sitting on the edge of the bed, she watched the torment in Belle's eyes. Wiping her eyes, Belle agreed. After she laid out her prettiest dress, Belle cleaned her face and prepared to meet her future the next day. *Hopefully, Brett will understand.* Mary continued to chatter long after Belle fell asleep.

The morning air smelled of fish, salt, and ocean. Belle stood near the rail, watching the scene before her. There were so many activities, she hardly knew where to look next. There were ladies with umbrellas walking along the pier, looking in the different fish stalls choosing their dinner. There were stalls full of vegetables, fruit, and other wares for sale. Cooks in their white caps and aprons were shopping at the various fish stands, weighing and buying their fish. She watched them point at the different varieties, and then the fish was wrapped in paper and stuck in their shopping baskets. The rattling carts, yelling vendors, and hurrying of sailors was almost too overwhelming. Everything seemed to be happening all at once. She watched a young boy feeding one of the wharf cats leftover fish from the markets. Each time he held the piece of fish out to the cat, she hooked it daintily with her paw then gently laid it on the ground to eat. The seagulls swooped down, trying to get their share, but they were wary of the cat. *Must have had dealings with her before*, Belle mused.

Mary slipped up behind Belle, watching the scene.

"What a beautiful cat. We must get a cat when we get to Sacramento. I love them so much!" she exclaimed as she clapped her hands. "Phillip had cats when we were growing up, so I am sure that he wouldn't mind."

It was easy to see how excited Mary was for the trip to be over. As Mary spoke, Belle couldn't help but notice her elation. Mary almost did a little dance as she watched the activities on the dock. Suddenly, Mary grew quiet, grabbed Belle by the arm, and told her to look towards the pier's far end.

"Oh my," taking a small gasp, pointing to a man walking down the dock. Mary exclaimed excitedly, "There is Phillip! He looks handsome dressed up in his suit. Oh, Belle, he takes my breath away."

Clutching Belle's arm, Mary started walking towards the

beginning of the gangplank towards Phillip. Mary had little dance steps as she crowded the gate. Taking Belle's hand, she almost cried.

"I can hardly wait until we are off this ship, and I can go to him. Belle, it will all work out. I know it will."

Belle smiled at her joyfulness.

"Remember, I did not move to Maryville until my mother died, so I did not know Phillip before, just heard plenty about him."

Belle looked where Mary was pointing. Phillip was tall and blonde with a tan suit and bowler hat. His skin was tan from the sun, and he looked strong and healthy. Phillip was searching through the people until he saw Mary. His eyes settled on her, and a slow smile crossed his face.

"Wow, Mary, he is all that you said he was." Winking at Mary, Belle smirked and said, "What a good-looking man, I would set my cap on that one. If he didn't have his eyes on you, of course."

Mary looked at her strangely until she noticed the smile and then started laughing.

"Keep your hands to yourself, lady. That one is mine."

Moments later, Belle watched Brett leave the ship and walk up the steps to the pier. He did not look back. She saw him shake hands with Phillip, then disappear into the crowds. With a heavy heart, she looked away and knew that would be the last time she would see him for a while as he had told her he was going to visit his family. *Strange, it seems like this was no more than a job for Brett. They must be good friends as she watched them smile and talk. Buck up, little girl, you committed to self-sufficiency, and you need to make the best of it. Brett's not the only man in the world if he decides not to wait.* But in her heart, she knew better.

As soon as the hotel porter came and took their things, Belle and Mary walked down the gangplank. The minute

Mary saw Phillip, she gave a little gasp and ran to him. He picked her up in the air and held her in his arms for the longest time. Kissing her gently, Phillip slowly let her down. With his arms around her waist, he still welcomed her as if he never wanted to let her go. Abruptly, Mary realized Belle was standing beside them.

Turning and pulling Phillip around to Belle, she excitedly introduced him.

"I have so many stories to tell, but Belle has been not only my companion but my best friend. Without her company, the trip would have been boring," Mary gushed.

Phillip shook Belle's hand.

"I appreciate you being with Mary. She said you met in Maryville? If you mean that much to Mary, then I am sure we will be friends. I was worried that she would have problems being a woman alone, but she insisted she couldn't wait for me to have time to come and get her. For once, I am glad she won the argument. Is someone here to pick you up?" he said, looking around the crowd.

Before she could answer, Mary gushed to Phillip.

"I hope you don't mind. She traveled with me the whole trip, and I promised her she could stay with us until she could get settled."

Belle noticed a tall, thin man dressed in jeans, a plaid shirt, and boots came towards her looking around the pier. His blonde hair shone in the sunlight, his beard was short, and his whiskers long. Deeply tanned with deep lines around his eyes made him much older looking than she expected.

"Belle, before you get upset again, just listen to me for a few minutes." Tomas pleaded.

Taking his hat off, he looked at Belle.

"We got off on the wrong foot. I was wrong to treat you the way I did at the dance in Maryville. Since we will live in the same area, I would like you to give me another chance. If not as a couple, but as friends. I promise no more wrong moves."

He saw Belle stiffen.

"Sacramento is a small town. We will probably see each other around town. At least we can be pleasant to each other."

Tomas felt very awkward with the others watching them. Belle looked at him for a long time.

"Tomas, you are right. Sacramento will probably be a small town, as we will see each other, but not as friends. I forgive you for your prior actions. Just never try them again."

Tomas left her standing at the dock as he joined Mary and Phillip, leaving Belle to follow them. Tomas and Phillip started talking animatedly about their work. As she stared at their backs, she felt the tension between the two men. *I wonder how they know each other. I don't want to cause any trouble for Phillip, but I will be watching Tomas cautiously.* When she turned, she saw Brett walking behind them. Motioning to him, she asked him to join their group. Brett, seeing Tomas with Phillip, became leery.

"Why is that guy with Phillip? It looks like they know each other."

"I don't know. That guy is the one from the dance in Maryville. I don't like him, but Phillip asked him to join us since we are going to the same place. It looks like they know each other. I am surprised to see him here, is all."

Smiling at Brett, she suddenly felt the stress building inside of her. Brett joined the other men, leaving Belle and Mary to walk together.

As Belle walked down the sidewalk beside Mary to the hotel, she felt faint. Mary, so happy to be reunited with Phillip, did not notice her distress. Suddenly Belle's world was spinning; she felt short of breath as she fell to the ground.

When she awakened, she found she was on a bed in a

strange room. Lace curtains were blowing gently at the window. Mary, Phillip, Brett, and Tomas were all sitting around the bed. Tomas was holding her hand. Mary had placed a cool cloth to her head.

"Belle, are you okay? You fainted. It must be from all the excitement." Mary patted her shoulder. "Just rest. You don't have to do anything right now."

Tomas, looking concerned, continued to hold her hand. As Belle tried to rise, she felt the darkness overcoming her vision and quickly laid back down. She felt embarrassed about the situation.

"Please, I will be okay. I guess the excitement was more than I expected. I will be okay."

Mary looked at Belle's pale face. The moisture had beaded on Belle's forehead like tiny pearls. She looked so small and helpless on the bed. Mary replaced the cool cloth on Belle's forehead as she waved her arms towards the men.

"Why don't you go downstairs and eat? I am sure you have plenty to discuss. I'll stay here with Belle, and you can bring us something to eat later."

She stood to hug Phillip, and Brett reluctantly left with Tomas.

Sitting down beside the bed, Mary pulled her book from her bag.

"Belle, the last few months have been hard for both of us. Rest a little while. I have a few pages left to read in my book. I am sure that the men will be back soon."

Belle gave Mary a weak smile and closed her eyes. *The turmoil I feel on the outside is nothing like the turmoil in my heart. No matter how long I rest, I know I have to be at least cordial to Tomas. However, in my heart, I know that Brett is the one for me. Why is it so important for me to be independent? What a fool I am.* Belle lay quietly with her eyes closed. She was unable to rest because all she could think of was Brett and how it could be for them.

As Phillip and Tomas entered the dining room, Phillip saw Brett sitting at one of the tables.

"Glad to see you, Brett. I wanted to make sure to thank you. I know that it was not an easy trip. I was so worried about Mary making that trip by herself. Sit with us. I will buy us lunch. By the way, this is Tomas. He arrived on the same ship you came in on."

Tomas frowned as Brett joined them, both men passing judgment on each other.

Taking his hat off, Brett held out his hand to Tomas.

"Ah yes, you were the privateer captive. That must have been a rough time. I heard they were tough."

Taking his hand, Tomas gave a firm handshake.

"I have scars to remind me not to allow myself to get into that situation again. How about you? I noticed you were on the *Flying Goose* as well."

"Yes, I was there. My job was to escort the two lovely ladies upstairs to this gentleman."

He motioned towards Phillip.

"From what I saw, you were friendly with the redhead. I don't blame you. I met her in Maryville and was stunned by her looks."

Tomas winked at Brett.

Frowning, Brett looked closely at Tomas.

"There is much more to Belle than just her looks. She is intelligent, loyal, and we are looking towards a great future."

"Whoa, man. I didn't mean anything by what I said. All I can say is good luck. She is a little headstrong."

Then turning to Phillip, he started to give an order for supplies which he would pick up after they arrived in Sacramento..

Brett watched the two men talk as he sat across from

Tomas. He noticed the lines around the eyes, the calloused hands, and the skin's dull coloring. *Yes, I am jealous. I can't let this man around Belle. I can tell he is interested in her. He can never treat her the way I will. Belle has to accept the reality of our love.*

After ordering, the waitress set their dinners in front of them. Tomas grabbed his fork like a weapon and started shoveling the food, not waiting for the others. Staring at Tomas, then turning to Phillip, Brett began talking about the trip.

"We had several adventures, but Mary was very calm throughout each one, quite a girl you have there, Phillip."

He smiled as he picked up his fork.

Tomas watched Brett as he ate, casually watching Phillip out of the corner of his eye.

"What kind of adventures?"

As Brett told Phillip about the trip, Brett talked mainly about Mary. Brett left out the stories of Belle because they were personal. He just didn't want to share them.

Near the end of the story, he said, "Phillip, I did not tell Mary that we knew each other until we were on the ship. It didn't seem to matter to her, knowing she had a support system. I told Belle first as she was suspicious, even though Della told her she had asked me to be with them."

"Don't worry about it. I agree. I think Mary was just glad that they weren't just two women alone on the trip!" exclaimed Phillip.

Tomas raised his eyebrows at the mention of Belle's name.

Looking up from his food, Tomas joined the conversation.

"Now that they are near Sacramento, I guess you won't have to stick around, huh?"

He looked at Brett as he spoke.

Ignoring Tomas's rudeness, Brett continued with the story of their adventures.

"I watched Mary and her friendship with Belle. When I

first met them on the stagecoach, I thought Belle was a guy. She wore these old dirty boy pants, hat, boots. Like she was a boy around fifteen. It amazed me when we had to fight off some gunslingers. She climbed up on top of the stage, just like she knew what she was doing. She can shoot."

With that, Tomas looked alarmed. He leaned towards Brett.

"I thought you were supposed to be protecting Mary. How did Belle become involved?"

"I'm not sure myself," Brett answered. "The pair seemed like really good friends, which proved right later. But when I discovered she was a girl, I was amazed at her gun abilities. I don't think she will let any man be around her if she doesn't want them. She can shoot better than most men and doesn't take too much guff."

Remembering his run-in with Belle at the dance, Tomas changed positions and looked nervous.

Standing, Tomas tipped his hat to Phillip.

"Since I will be leaving, I will go say goodbye to the girls. Belle did not look very good when she fell."

Phillip, turning to Tomas said, "I will try to have your order completed when we get back to Sacramento. I will finish here and then bring the girls some dinner. When did you say you were leaving for Placerville?"

As he rushed from the table, Tomas looked over his shoulder at the two men, not answering the question but instead running up the stairs. Upon entering the room, he found Belle still on the bed but awake.

"Mary, could you leave us a few minutes? I need to talk to Belle."

"No, Tomas, I will not leave you alone in the room with Belle. It is not proper. How could you even ask?"

Opening the door, she motioned him out.

"If you need to stay, then be quiet. Belle, you know I have

been crazy about you. I am offering you marriage and a home. You will be an honest woman and will be happy."

As Belle pulled the covers tighter around her body, her face became red, and she appeared angry.

"How dare you to come into my room and offer such an incredible proposition? You have never appeared to have any properness about you. As I told you before, leave me alone. I do not want to be near you, let alone marry someone like you. Please leave immediately!"

As Tomas took a deep breath, he grabbed Belle's arm to shake her. The girls could see his eyes squint, a flush rising from his neck.

"You spoiled little girl. You will be sorry you turned this guy down. You will marry me in the end because no one else will want you when I am through. Not even that old man downstairs you have your eye on. If Mary weren't here, I would show you what a real man is all about."

With that, Tomas turned and walked out the door.

Tomas hurriedly passed Brett and Phillip on the stairs without saying a word.

"Wonder what that was all about?" Brett said as he continued to climb, carrying a plate for Belle.

"He's a strange guy. Tomas comes into the store and buys stuff with cash, then leaves. No one knows anything about him, except that he runs some kind of farm up in the hills," murmured Phillip. "But enough of that. You are staying for our wedding, right? I want you to stand up for us. I know that Mary has already asked Belle."

Nodding his head, Brett had difficulty answering. He thought being close to Belle for several more days without holding her would be difficult. Seeing Brett's hesitation, he looked closely at his friend.

"What's going on, Brett? I have known you for a long

time and," suddenly, he stopped—the dawning realization as he looked at his friend. "Oh no, you have fallen for Belle."

"Don't say anything. This situation is hard for both of us. Belle feels she has to follow through on her commitment to be independent, no matter how hard it will be. I don't want to be the guy that stops her from doing what is right. Neither one of us could live over that. It would hurt us in the long run."

Looking downtrodden, Brett beseeched Phillip not to say anything.

"I want to gather her in my arms and get the hell out of town, but that would turn her against me, and I would have a hard time making things right for her."

Nodding in agreement with his friend, Phillip agreed with him and said he would keep a close eye out for her. Entering into the room, they saw Mary sitting on the bed's edge, looking out the window. She had been crying. Belle was also tearing at her handkerchief, and tears were rolling down her cheek.

As he took Mary in his arms, Phillip brushed away her tears.

"What is going on here between you two?"

At that point, there was a knock at the door. Opening the door, they saw Tomas standing there.

"I just thought I would check on Belle one more time before I left."

He entered the room acting as if he had never been there. He saw the confusion and that girls had been crying. Belle looked angry. Suddenly she turned to face Tomas.

"Why would you come back here? I told you I wanted you to stay away from me. I do not want anything to do with you."

Not saying a word, Tomas backed out of the room and

left. Both men looked at each other. Quietly closing the door, Phillip turned to face them.

"Okay, what is the problem? What is going on here? There is nothing that we can't work out."

Mary was the first to speak.

"First, Tomas thought he could ask Belle to marry him and she would fall all over him to be his bride. He upset her and now Belle is acting ridiculous. She is afraid that I am forcing you to take her in, and she wants to stay at some boarding house when we get to Sacramento. She is talking about leaving today before the wedding."

With that, Mary's tears started to flow again.

Belle looked at Phillip with tears running down her cheeks. Brett sat down. He knew this was going to take a while. Belle went to the window, watching the people walking on the sidewalk below.

"Mary, it is not quite like that. You have been my best friend for years. I just don't want anyone to feel sorry for me or feel they have to take care of me. You saw Tomas's act. I need to be away from him."

Mary put her arms around Belle's shoulders.

"Belle, no one is trying to stop you from your goal. We are your friends. We are here to support you in obtaining your goals. Relax. Everything will work out. You can stay with us for a while until we get the business running, then you can live wherever you want to live. You need to have people around to protect you from people like Tomas or at least let them know you are not alone. I have already spoken to Phillip. He will fix the upstairs room over the store for you. You can pay rent. It will be just like living in a boarding house only better. We will live in the back rooms of the store. It will all work out."

Taking a deep breath, Belle answered her.

"Mary, I've made a fool of myself again. I will accept your

generosity. When I saw Tomas leering at me and acting like we were more than acquaintances . . . he acted like I would be grateful for his offer. Then knowing how I have hurt Brett by not wanting to jump into marriage, it was just overwhelming to me. I lost control." Turning to face Brett, "I do love you, Brett. All I do is mess things up. I am so sorry."

Phillip and Brett stood against the wall, still amazed at the spitfire fury displayed by Belle and how fast she turned it off. Mary took Phillip's arm and guided him to the door, with Brett right behind them. Kissing Phillip lightly on the cheek, she opened the door. Taking the hint, they said good night and left.

As Mary closed the door, Phillip glanced at Brett and could see the thunder in his eyes.

"Come on, friend, let's have a drink and talk about the situation before you do something you will regret."

When they came down the stairs, they saw Tomas in the bar area. As they entered the hotel saloon, they saw him talking to one of the barmaids in the back corner. Tomas had a drink in one hand and his other hand across the barmaid's hip.

Phillip put his hand on the back of Brett's elbow, leading him to a corner booth, out of sight, but where they could keep an eye on Tomas. Tomas was smiling and had moved his arm around the girl's shoulders, laughing at something she had said to him. After a few minutes, they walked up the stairs together.

"Well, that didn't take him long, did it?"

Phillip was watching Tomas and the girl. It was all Phillip could do to keep Brett in his chair.

"Settle down, drink your beer. I think Belle has made it clear that she does not want anything to do with him."

～

"Did you see how Tomas looked at Belle? It was like she was an ice cream cone. I don't want that scum to touch her. I swear if Tomas touches her, it will force me to take action. Then I don't know if Belle will forgive me. I should march up those stairs and beat the pulp out of him."

"Settle down. None of this will help the situation. I have a plan."

As Phillip started to share his plan, Brett took several deep breaths and started to settle down. A little while later, they watched Tomas stagger down the stairs, disheveled and looking pleased with himself.

Suddenly noticing them sitting at the table, he doffed his hat at them and walked out the door with a smirk on his face. Again, it was all Phillip could do to hold Brett down in his chair.

"I have an idea," Phillip smiled at Brett.

Silently whispering the plan, Brett became more mellow.

"I like the sound of it if we can only convince Belle," said Brett quietly as he thought through the ideas.

# CHAPTER 20

The next morning Belle awakened and stretched. She looked out the window smiling at the warmth of the sun. It was all she could do to not sing. The sun was shining, and everything seemed so different from the day before. Thinking about the night before, she hung her head. *How could she have let her thoughts interfere as they did?* The idea of Tomas following them to the hotel, then coming to her room, like he had the right to be there, troubled her. *Brett probably thinks we were interested in each other. I knew when I first met Tomas, he was not the kind of man I wanted around me. Now he is going to Sacramento. Will I ever get rid of him?*

She bowed her head.

"God give me the strength to stay on my path and not be involved with a man like Tomas. I was hoping you could help me stay on track and, at the same time, show Brett how much he means to me. I love him so much and need him in my life. I am not the same little girl I was when I left St. Louis. As for Tomas, I will not go anywhere near him. I will not marry him, and I will not give him another chance to treat me like a Jezebel or to touch me."

His words had poured over her like vinegar on honeyed toast. Rising and dressing quickly, she awakened Mary.

"Mary, no matter what happens, do not let me be alone with Tomas. He is the kind of guy who thinks he is God's gift to women and that he can have his way. He has to know I will not tolerate his behavior, and I will never marry him under any circumstances. To be honest, he scares me."

Sitting up, Mary looked closely at her friend.

Seeing the bruises on Belle's arms where Tomas grabbed her, Mary whispered, "Belle, I think it is vital that the guys are around if Tomas comes near you again. I think he did not take you seriously last night. He may be crazy. Why would he come back to the room right after you threw him out? I'm not sure how he will take it if he sees you are determined to reject him, and I do not want him to hurt you anymore."

Looking at Belle's arms in the daylight, she saw the imprint of Tomas's fingers turning into dark purple patches and how Belle tried not to show she was in pain. Belle looked even angrier than the night before, but after a few minutes she agreed with Mary. Belle and Mary finished dressing and left to go downstairs to meet Phillip.

As Belle entered the room, she was surprised to see Brett at the table. At the same time, relief came over her, knowing she would be safe if he were near.

He pulled her chair out for her, stating, "We have something to talk with you about after breakfast."

Brett saw her discomfort.

"It's not about Tomas."

Looking at them, she smiled, and an instant sigh of relief escaped from her lips.

There were not many people in the dining room of the hotel that morning. Looking around, she was much calmer than when they were upstairs. The waitresses had laid the table with fresh linen and a small glass with violets. Still breathing restlessly, Belle settled down to eat. The waitress brought eggs and toast to Belle with a bit of flourish.

"Was that other man with you last night, your man?" The waitress winked at Belle as she sat the coffee down in front of her.

Even though she was speaking to Belle, the girl smiled flirtatiously towards Phillip and Brett.

"He sure knows how to treat a woman, yes indeed."

Standing up, Belle put both her hands on her hips.

"What do you mean?"

The waitress laughed as she strolled off.

Mary tugged on her skirt to get Belle to sit down. She looked at the men.

"Do you know what she was talking about?"

Both men looked the other way. Finally, looking embarrassed, Brett told her she should not pay any attention to the waitress. That seemed to set her off more. Rising from her chair, she looked for the waitress, leaving her food to get cold. Mary caught her hand and pulled Belle towards the door.

"I think we should take a walk and let you cool off."

"No, I am okay. I just let Tomas get to me. I know what she meant. I'm not dumb. I am fine now. It bothers me that someone should associate me with him."

Taking a deep breath, they walked back to the table. As Belle cooled off, she sat still in the chair. Belle could not help but watch her friend and the happiness she had found. *I will not ruin this wedding for Mary, no matter what happens.* Straightening her shoulders, she took Mary's hand.

"Let's forget all about my situation. I want this day to be all about you." Laughing, Belle exclaimed, "Mary, you're getting married tomorrow! Let's be happy."

Phillip sat next to Mary, gently holding her hand and looking at her adoringly as a different waitress approached their table. Mary blushed at the waitress, seeing them holding hands. Phillip took their hands under the table when he noticed the waitress. Turning and smiling, Phillip beamed.

"You caught us during a happy moment. We are getting married tomorrow."

The waitress smiled, "Yes, sir, we will have everything ready for the big day. What would you like to have for breakfast?" She noticed the untouched breakfast on the table. "I see the first breakfast didn't suit you."

After she took their orders and walked away, Belle caught their attention.

"Phillip, Mary, I have a favor to ask of you. I know that this is probably not the right time, but I need to get some things settled today."

Belle looked at them worriedly. Brett and Phillip looked at each other, hoping it would be easier than they thought.

"I have changed my mind again."

Each man rolled their eyes, then started to grin.

Timidly, Belle placed her hands on the table. She folded them together and seemed to grip them tightly.

"I am not going to leave. I am staying for the wedding. I was unrealistic and not showing Mary how much she means to me. I will take you up on your offer to stay with you until I have everything worked out. I do have a favor to ask, though. I do not want to be around Tomas again. If you don't mind, I would like to travel with you to Sacramento. I have some personal monies hid away. I have been saving for a long time. I want to see how that works out. I know that it will be difficult at first, but I want to be independent and take care of myself. I know that I need some support, and I hope to depend on both of you for a little while. Not for living support, but to be there if I need help. Even though someone," looking at Brett, "told me it was a mistake to not let friends help me, now I know it was not realistic to think I could do everything on my own."

Brett turned to Belle, disappointed that she had not included him in her request.

"What about me?" By the time he had asked, both Mary and Phillip stood up and reached for Belle to hug her. Looking at Belle, he realized she didn't hear him. *At least she will be near.*

"Of course, we will be there for you. That was our plan that we were going to talk to you about after breakfast." They both said it at the same time.

Then they turned and laughed together.

Phillip letting her go, let out a sigh and said, "I have space for you to work with me in the store for a short time until you get set up. There is even a room above the store I can fix up for you so you don't have to stay at the hotel if you would like. It won't take much. I have already fixed a nice set of rooms behind the store for Mary and me so that you won't be alone. We will be near enough to hear if you need us, but you will have privacy. This idea will work out great. The hotel is across the street to eat, or just a little way down the street is George's Kitchen. He serves delicious dinners. There, it is all settled. You don't have to worry about a thing."

Belle let out a loud cry of joy. Even though Mary had said the same thing before, it was different hearing it from Phillip.

Turning to Brett, she said, "I don't want any problems with Tomas. That is why I left you out. It would be better if we were not an item until all this settles. I care deeply for you, and I know that all of this drama will work out somehow."

He took her hand to his lips.

"I will always be there for you, Belle. It will work out if I have anything to do with the situation."

Embarrassed at the display, she turned back to Phillip and Mary.

"Mary, Phillip, I formally take you up on your offer. Let's

draw up a contract, so I know that it is a business deal. It's so nice of you to help me. I don't know what I would do if I hadn't known Mary. I have had few friends that would help me like that."

With tears swelling up in her eyes, she turned to Brett. "You understand?"

Looking into her eyes, he paused and then agreed to her suggestion, even though he did not agree with her reasoning. He knew that Tomas was a scoundrel, but he would be close to protect her. As he sat down, he watched her eat and interact with her friends. There was lots of laughing and happiness as they planned for the future. Brett wondered how he could have found a better match.

# CHAPTER 21

The rest of the day, Mary and Belle prepared for the wedding. There were preparations to decorate the venue, final fittings on dresses, and most importantly, to decide what to wear when they left the next day for Sacramento. Phillip had found a nice place by the river overlooking a valley. The trees were large oaks with lots of shade and soft grass under footing. Several of the women from the hotel built an arbor and decorated it with paper flowers.

As Belle worked on the dress fittings, she watched Mary. Her happiness showed in her perpetual smile, the glow on her face, and the dreamy look in her eyes. She lit up every time Phillip was in the room. Mary flitted from thing to thing. She seemed not to be able to concentrate on anything except that she was finally marrying Phillip. Mary had brought her dress with her, but it needed a minor adjustment, as she had lost some weight on the trip to California.

The dress itself was cream-colored linen with pale blue organza overdress, trimmed in cream lace and blue ribbons. The overdress had dainty tucks down the bodice with tiny buttons around the edging of lace. Mary's hat was satin with miniature silk roses along one edge, and a translucent veil tacked on the inside and on the crown. The veil draped down Mary's back and covered her shoulders. She had cream-colored shoes with matching buttons down the front. At the toes were tiny miniature silk roses. Mary did not have flowers, so Belle loaned her mother's white Bible. They tied a streamer from the bible, and it all blended perfectly. The Bible was the only thing she had of her mother's, other than a few pieces of jewelry, and she took it everywhere with her. Looking at the white leather of the Bible brought back happy memories of her mother and of them going to church and reading late in the evenings.

Later, when they went to their room, Belle dug through her trunk and pulled out a fabric bag, and handed it to Mary.

"I know that you are so happy that there is no room for anything but Phillip, but I wanted to give this back before something happened to it."

Cautiously Mary opened the bag. There she found the deed and her mother and stepfather's wills and all her dress patterns. A cloud fell over Mary when looking at the papers. She remembered her mother's smile and how happy she was when she married Mary's stepfather. Almost in the same instance, Mary remembered how mean her stepbrothers had been to her. Folding the papers back up, Mary looked at Belle. Belle walked over to her, taking her hand and smiling.

"That part of your life is over. It's something you need to share with Phillip, and then you can decide what you want to do. After all, he is the man in your life now, and he can help you make the right decision. After what I have seen of Phillip, he seems like the kind of person that makes the right decisions."

"Do you think I should be worried about my stepbrothers? They wouldn't try to do anything out here, do you think?" Mary asked worriedly.

"What difference would it make? They wouldn't get far with Phillip. Bullies are usually cowards. It was terrible what they did. They thought you would be weak and hand everything over to them. That didn't work."

Mary laughed. "I will never forget how brave you were, Belle, hanging off the side of that stagecoach with the horses running wild and men shooting your way. I thought you were crazy."

"Mary, now that I think about it, I was crazy to do that. Whatever possessed me to do something like that when, if I had died, no one would have known about me or known any of my kin. I would have been put in a hole somewhere without a proper name. Well, thank goodness that is behind us. We need to meet Phillip for dinner."

She picked up her shawl to leave the room. Still folding her clothes for the following day, Mary put them away and followed behind Belle, still smiling with happiness.

Phillip and Brett rose when the girls came down the stairs.

Taking Mary's hand, Phillip turned to Belle, "Thank you for helping her. I wouldn't have known what to do."

He couldn't take his eyes off Mary. It was almost embarrassing to Belle to see a couple so in love that no one else in the room mattered. Brett held her chair for her as she sat down. Belle thought, *if only that could happen to her*, not noticing the slight grin from Brett as he sat down.

He whispered to Belle as she looked at the other couple.

"It is good to see things working out for them. They have been in love nearly all their lives." Smiling, he took her hand. "Belle, we are different people from them, but I know our life will be as treasured as theirs. I have never loved anyone as I do you."

Turning, seeing his smile, she smiled back.

The next day was perfect for a wedding. The sun smiled

through the trees, casting light shadows over the field at the edge of town where they had built a small altar. As they approached, a slight breeze caused the leaves to dance circles on the ground. The minister, dressed in his best black suit, with a white shirt and a small flower in his buttonhole, stood at the altar. Several women from town had heard about the ceremony and showed up, never wanting to miss a wedding. The guests stood in a circle in front of the altar, dressed in their Sunday best. Belle couldn't take her eyes off of Brett as he stood beside the minister at the altar. He had a dark brown suit that showed his tan to perfection. His hair, freshly cut, waved back from his eyes. Brett held his hat in his hand and looked very handsome to Belle.

The couple approached the makeshift altar. The arbor behind the altar was decorated with paper flowers of all colors. There were a few witnesses. However, Mary and Phillip were unaware of anyone but each other. Belle looked on, hardly aware of the words but envious of the apparent love Phillip and Mary had for each other. As she looked at the couple, she prayed that someday she would have the same happiness with Brett. She needed a happy ever after in her life.

Belle left the happy couple to celebrate their vows that evening and walked around the shops. She found several ideas for hats by watching the passing women, drawing sketches for her shop. The town had placed benches along the sidewalks for tired shoppers to rest. It was the perfect place for Belle to observe the hats and bonnets as they passed. *The women dressed differently here,* she mused. *I will have to change my thinking about what is practical.* Some bonnets were simple and tied at the neck to protect the skin from the sun's hot rays during the summer. Since it was the beginning of fall, both seasons of hats were on display from the different women. The winter hats covered the ears with either turned-down

183

brims or individual coverings to protect them from the cold winter winds. She spied several Eastern-type hats with wide brims, netting, and flowers. To her, it was apparent that that style was more for show than was practical. She spent the whole afternoon watching, sketching, and thinking about the hats she observed as she sat on a bench with her drawing paper.

It was late in the afternoon when Belle returned to the hotel. She cleaned up after the day's work and went to the dining room. When arriving, she saw Brett stand up and motion her to the table.

"You look happy," stated Brett. "How was your day?"

"It was an exciting and productive day. I saw so many more hats than what Phillip said he has in his store. It makes me want to get started right away."

Putting her napkin across her lap, she looked around.

"I suppose Mary and Phillip are not coming?"

Brett grinned. "They are taking their dinner in their room."

Catching his smirk, she laughed. The waitress took their order, and they ate in silence. *It's nice to have a quiet dinner,* Belle thought.

Brett watched her throughout the dinner but did not intrude on her thoughts. *This is how it should be, just two people enjoying a nice dinner, no drama, no noise, and no one pointing guns at you.* He mused. *I hope there will be many others like this.*

"Would you like a nice stroll before retiring?" he asked.

Rising from her chair, she linked her arm in his, and they walked on the sidewalks of the nearby shops. Sitting on a bench in the nearby park, they watched the children sailing little boats in the pond and mothers pushing their prams through the park.

"Belle, I have been thinking about your situation. I think you are right." Holding her hand, he continued as he looked into her eyes. "Let's start from the beginning. We know that we care for each other, but let's get to know each other. My family ranch is near Sacramento. Even though I have responsibilities there, I checked with my friends and found an opening as a lawman when we return to Sacramento. So, I have accepted the job as the marshal in Sacramento to be close to you. When we get to Sacramento, I would like to court you the right way, not just little hidden moments like on the clipper ship. I overheard Phillip's offer to you concerning working with them in his store, with him and Mary. I think it is a good idea, but you decide what you want to do. Just understand that I am near to support you in what you choose to do."

Leaning on his shoulder, she agreed to his idea of a new start, and for a long time, they just sat on the bench, each in their thoughts of the future.

The following day, Mary knocked on the door and entered without waiting for Belle to answer. She sat on the edge of the bed, beaming with happiness.

"Belle, tell me that you are still coming with us tomorrow. Phillip and I both want you to come. I have never been as happy as this."

Belle, wiping the sleep from her eyes, watched her friend bubbling with joy.

Sitting up, she reached out and hugged Mary.

She said, "Of course, I thought you understood that I had decided to take Phillip's offer. I won't be in your way and I'll set up my shop as soon as I can get materials and grow my inventory. I have some money left over from the trip and some from my savings. If Phillip's offer is to work with him in the store and live in the space above, I will take the offer with pleasure."

Holding Belle's hand, Mary danced around the floor.

"It will be such a great life, Belle. Don't be upset about me wanting to make sure about you coming with us. My life is so perfect right now. It would not be if you weren't in it. We are leaving on the stagecoach tomorrow morning."

Handing her a ticket for the stagecoach, Mary cautioned Belle.

"This is for tomorrow. You can pay Phillip back when you get your first pay."

With that, Mary danced out the door with her feet hardly touching the floor as she giggled.

After washing and eating, Belle left the hotel for another day of observation and sketching. Belle felt a peacefulness she hadn't known since the death of her parents. She found bits and pieces of materials and supplies that she could use for hats at a few different stores. As she wandered up and down the main street, she often stopped at the windows to look at the fashions or items that caught her eye.

Later, Belle joined the newlyweds for dinner. Phillip told Belle that Brett had left early that afternoon after not finding her to say goodbye. At first, she felt disappointed that Brett did not join her and the newlyweds, but the couple's joy was infectious, and she soon forgot that he was not with them.

The next morning Belle rose early to pack her trunk. She did not have room for her sketches, so she put them in her handbag, intending to work on them on the way to Sacramento. She put her monies in her cloth bag under the waist of her petticoat, with only a few dollars in her handbag if she needed to pay for food. Her rifle, saddlebags, and pistols went into the new trunk along with her purchases. Belle looked at her luggage.

"I can't believe I only started with one. Now I have three. With the new stagecoach trail from San Francisco to Sacramento, the trip will only be another week."

Laying her sketches on the bed to organize them, she made a stack for each one she drew from the clipper ship,

New Orleans, and San Francisco. Belle contented herself with her sketches of the women's hats. Belle had an impressive number of drawings to start her inventory. On each sketch, she had carefully listed the materials needed for each hat along the margins, plus reminders of the techniques needed for the hat. Belle had also added any ideas for improvements or style changes when drawing them. Looking inside the trunk that held her treasures for the new hats, she saw she had ample amounts to get started on her inventory when she arrived in Sacramento.

For the other hats, if Phillip didn't have the supplies in his store, then Belle would have to order things from San Francisco or rely on the next clipper ship, which would take several months to obtain. Ever since she had this idea, she was grateful for her aunt's training in making the hats and handling the finances that go along with the business.

Belle hardly thought of Tomas and the horrible scene in San Francisco. As she headed for Sacramento, visions of hats, gloves, and accessories flooded her imagination until she fell asleep to the steady rocking of the stagecoach. Belle couldn't help but watch the joy between Mary and Phillip as the time passed on the trip. She sat wondering if things would work out between her and Brett. They never stopped holding hands. Seeing Mary dozing with her head laying gently on Phillip's shoulder, she was happy for them. She frowned when she thought about Tomas. That was a problem she still had to settle.

As they arrived in Sacramento, Belle had the first glimpse of her new home. The streets were wide, dusty, and in some places, muddy. There were only a few streets that had cobblestones. She watched as the stagecoach pulled up in front of the hotel. She noticed there were primarily men walking the streets, with few women. Phillip retrieved their luggage and handed them to a young lad to take to the store's wagon.

Then Phillip led them into the hotel for dinner. She remembered how the cities along the eastern stagecoach way stations looked. Sacramento was different. There were oak trees and various flower boxes in front of the buildings, but the air was dry. There was little humidity. Another difference was the missing patriot booths along the sidewalks asking for volunteers for the army. No men in uniforms were walking the sidewalks. She hadn't seen a single uniform since she arrived.

The hotel was not like the hotels in the East. Eastern hotels showed their wealth with crystal chandeliers and velvet sofas. They were clean with shiny tiled floors, and there were plants everywhere.

As she looked around, all she saw were canvas printed upholstered sofas and curtains on the windows. A fine layer of dust was evident across the surfaces. There were no crystal chandeliers but multiple oil lamps. The floors were bare and wooden.

Similarities between the two types of hotels were few. There was a large cherry wooden check-in desk, and the clerk was friendly. Belle kept thinking, *What is wrong? Why do I feel uncomfortable here?* She shrugged her shoulders. *I guess I am just tired. It will look better tomorrow.*

On the stagecoach traveling to Sacramento, Phillip said he would hire some workers to fix the store's upstairs room for her, so Belle decided to stay a few days at the hotel while waiting for her room. In her hotel room, she quickly wrote a letter to her aunt Hester, and then washed her face and hands to eat. She walked downstairs to meet Phillip and Mary in the dining room. The room was different from the rest of the hotel. It was cheerful, with lace curtains on the windows and quilted cushions on the chairs. She looked around. *Something is missing. I can't put my finger on it.* The waitress wore a nice clean striped pinafore. *Maybe that is it. It all looked clean.* The pale green tablecloths looked friendly with their small vases of yellow roses. Belle sat down. *At least I won't run into Tomas here.*

When she sat down, she felt relief from the travel. *Well, Sacramento is home now. I am not doing anything tonight but sleep. I am not going to think about my problems.* The dinner was refreshing; a nice chicken pie with fresh green beans and apple pie for dessert. Filled to the brim, she slept hard and long that night.

The following morning after breakfast, Phillip took the girls back to the General Store. The store was set off the main street on a short side street. It had a covered sidewalk with flower boxes under the windows. The building was three stories tall, white with green trim, and had a covered porch. At the top of the building was a sign that read *General Store* in large letters. Under it in smaller letters:

*We have everything you need. If we don't have something, you must not need it.*

After taking in the sign, Belle and Mary held their faces to keep from crying with laughter.

Looking embarrassed, Phillip quipped, "The owner before me hung the sign, and I liked it, so I kept it. Should I change it?"

He looked at each of them for their comments. Both girls straightened up.

"It brings class to the store. Leave it."

# CHAPTER 22

As she entered the store, Belle's mouth dropped open.

"I never saw so much stuff. Goodness, Phillip, how did you find all of these things?"

Walking up and down the aisles, Mary and Belle saw all the merchandise skillfully placed on open tables for display. The tables were clean and neat. The walls were painted a light sea green, and the floors' rough wooden rail ties were sanded and varnished giving them a substantial sturdiness to the building. There were lanterns, picks, shovels, and various other tools in one area. They saw tents and gold pans along with them. In a different place were dry goods—flour, sugar, buckwheat, and other grains in large barrels—with bags hanging on the sides ready to be filled. As she wandered along the side of the wall, Belle saw clothes like jeans, leather jackets, socks, shoes, ladies dresses, and accessories. There was even a small section for children that included hats, gloves, overalls, baby bibs, and blankets. There were hand-carved toys displayed on the shelves behind the counter.

Seeing Belle and Mary looking at them, Phillip explained,

"I had to put them back here. Whenever a child visited the store, I found the toys everywhere after they left."

Everywhere Belle looked, she saw more. Large jars of hard candy lined the counter. Penny candy was displayed in the same type of candy jars as the hard candies. There was a scale on the counter, and a yardstick nailed to the counter to measure.

"Phillip, this store is amazing! I never dreamed I would be able to find so many things in one store. You have done a wonderful job." Turning towards Mary, Belle said, "I am going to love working here. I owe both of you so much. A job, a place to live, how could I have become so lucky?"

Phillip seeing the wonder in Belle's eyes, walked over to her.

"I own this block. Later, when you are ready, I thought I would build another area attached to Mary's dress shop for your hat shop. What do you think about starting here in the front corner of the store? Then when I get the building addition finished, we can put the door here and move your ladies apparel in there. With large open doors the women can see you immediately, or they can come through another door in the front."

Mary was grinning ear to ear.

"Phillip, how could you figure this out so quickly? I only told you last night."

He hugged Mary tightly.

"I just seem to know what works from growing up in the store business. I want you to take a couple of days off with Mary before you start, so both of you can walk around and get used to the town. It is a little wild on Fridays and Saturdays when the cowboys and miners come to town, but it is nice the rest of the time. We have several churches, womens organizations, and town activities. One of the more surprising enterprises in Sacramento is one of the railroad hubs. Soon the railroad will be finished between here and San Francisco in December." Phillip walked over to one of the large front windows. "I know my store is not on the main street, but it is quieter on this side street, and my customers always find my store. Driving cattle to the rail yards causes a lot of dust and noise on the main street. I wanted the store to be out of their way."

Still walking around the store, Belle decided she could hardly wait to start.

"Phillip, what do you plan for our work schedule?"

"Well, if you don't mind, I would like you to work in the mornings and Mary to work in the afternoons. That way, you both have time to work on your projects."

Mary reached up to kiss Phillip on the cheek. "That sounds great." She turned towards Belle. "I think using our downtime from the store gives us plenty of time to work on our projects. If there are questions about the projects, we are still in the same area and not separated like if we were in a different building. I am so excited! This is going to be great."

Things had settled down over the next few weeks, with both Belle and Mary getting used to the routine. Their inventory increased, with both of them working each day consistently.

When Mary would finish a sample dress, Belle made sure she had several hats that would go with the dress. Mary would make gloves and use some of Belles's materials to decorate them. Mary and Belle both knitted mittens, scarves, and hats in the evenings for the upcoming winter.

One evening, after a long day of sewing, Mary and Belle looked at each other over the white work table they had put in their area. Mary winked at Belle.

"Who would have thought that our friendship could have gotten any stronger than it had before we started all of this?"

She spread her arms wide to encompass their area.

"We could have never done all this without Phillip," Belle said as she put down her needle. "We are able to live our dream. Now, if I could get the rest of my life together."

Mary looked intensely at her friend.

"Belle, it will happen. Brett's been working so hard to get his job organized. I am sure he will have more time soon."

"Mary, it's not that. My first goal of coming out here was to find my brother. I received a letter from Aunt Hester, of course admonishing me for leaving without letting her in on my plans, but she had received a letter from Jeremy saying he is going back there. She said she wrote to him somewhere in a town called Paradise and told him I was here. I hope he will come here before he goes home. Maybe, I can talk him into staying here?"

Phillip often joined them in their sewing room, doing the business's books. As the store prospered, Phillip bought more land and started investing in the town. Often, the light in the store would be on in the evenings while they worked which attracted people who were taking their evening walks. They would come to look at the various hats and dresses in the windows.

When women came into the store, Belle noticed they shopped differently than the men. Men usually came in with a list, left it with Phillip while they did other things in town, and came back later to pick up their orders. Women, on the other hand, spent time walking between the aisles looking at the goods. The table displayed as *New Items* caught the eye of the women more than the men. As they gradually noticed the women's corner of the store, their business started booming. They had a large assortment of day dresses, cotton work clothes, and fancy party dresses. With the purchase of a dress came free alterations. The customers could buy a new dress and matching hat. Some came in to buy just the hats.

In the evenings, Belle, Brett, Mary, and Phillip would walk through town after dinner. As time passed, they saw their creations on women as they walked. Often Brett made time to walk with them, knowing how much it meant to Belle. It was a good time of life for all of them.

# CHAPTER 23

Sacramento was a growing town with a population of over 13,000 people. The boom brought new problems. For years, the cattle were driven to yards at Sacramento's edge to go to San Francisco and Fresno for processing. As the population increased, the town grew around it. The young city's growing problems often clashed with the townspeople's needs compared to the businesses' needs.

Brett's new position as the marshal began with new rules to enforce and a vow to clean up the rising city and make the streets safe for the citizens. In the development of his plans, he discussed them with the mayor and his deputy.

"The first thing I want to do is reroute the cattle drives out of the main street in town to a new trail outside of the town proper. My deputy and I have placed signs and markers with fencing to designate the path. The fencing is set much broader than the city streets they followed before making it safer for the cattle. I plan to ride out of town and meet the drivers before they reach Sacramento to talk about the new process. I don't think the foremen will see any difference in the way they drive the cattle, but the drivers so far are not happy about the change."

"So, Marshal, how do we handle it if they cause trouble? It is important to have a plan," said the mayor as he looked at the drawings on the marshal's desk. "You know how they like to 'shoot um up,' especially after being on a long-distance ride. How are you going to handle their agitation?"

"Well, so far, we have arrested several of the drivers when they tried shooting up and down the street like in the past, but after a couple of nights in jail, they cooled off. They realize we have outgrown the 'Wild West' and are becoming a proper town. Word will get around. I have asked to increase our budget. With the new sections of town and all the buildings, we need to hire more deputies to maintain the order. Are you in agreement?"

The mayor was deep in thought.

"I see the 'no gun' rule in the saloons also upset many drivers. Each of the saloons has a check-in room at the entrance for guns, or they can leave them in their saddlebags."

"Well, at first, it was a problem, like any new idea. However, it is working in Dodge and St. Louis, so we can make it work here." Brett looked squarely at the mayor. "This town will be the center of the state at some time, so it is time to put in practice safety for the citizens that live here."

Clapping Brett on the back, "You are right, Brett. I see the town council chose the right man for the job. Every town has growing pains."

As the disturbances in the town decreased, the towns-people felt safer. There were always newcomers not knowing the new laws, but the marshal or his deputies quickly corrected their mistakes. The jail expanded to ten cells from two when he took over as marshal. The new regulations were posted outside of town on each road at one-mile intervals for five miles.

~

In the spring of 1862, the rains began. Mary and Belle sat on the benches outside the store.

"Where are all these people going? Oh Belle, look! That is the furniture from the new furniture store over in the old part of town," cried Mary as she watched the loaded wagon pass by.

They scanned the streets full of wagons. They watched many people traveling up their roads.

Turning to the store, Mary called out, "Phillip, something has happened in the older part of town. There is wagon after wagon carrying goods. Come look!"

Phillip looked outside the window, then wandered out on the sidewalk. When seeing the mayor, he asked what was happening.

"It's a mess, Phillip. The daily rains over the last several weeks have caused the river to rise over the banks. The river rose fifteen feet along the riverbanks, causing the older part of town and the boardwalks to flood." Watching more wagons pass, the mayor continued. "When the water receded, the mud was thick and the horses and wagons could not travel on the streets. Often the wagons were stuck in the mud with no way to release them until the sun dried out the roads. The horses had to be pulled out with oxen, leaving behind the wagons until dry weather. We've had floods before causing the city to build levees, but this flooding broke the levees and flooded the town." Stepping back to keep the mud from splashing on him, "We had an emergency meeting last night. The residents and founders voted to raise the streets fifteen feet. We will also build levees to hold back the Sacramento River during floods."

The plan to raise the town fifteen feet caused problems. Store owners built additional floors onto structures, creating basements from the original stores. Dirt was piled eight feet in front of the buildings, giving extra support for the pilings needed. The water lines and gas lines caused problems initially, but gradually progress was made. During this time of growth, new stores and shops were set up further along the edge of town, creating new shopping areas and bringing more shoppers to Phillip's store.

Brett stopped in a couple of times to pick up items to take back to the family ranch whenever he had time off from his job. Even though he enjoyed his job, his ranch and his family were essential to him. During this time, Brett was determined to help his family manage the citrus farm and harvest the crops. He spent as much time as he could there during his off hours from law enforcement.

One Sunday afternoon, Brett invited Belle to the ranch to meet his family. As they arrived at the ranch, Brett explained, "We are at the end of the harvest season for most of the citrus fruits. You will be able to see how they worked the fruit."

She was amazed at the process of harvesting and sorting. The long tables were spread across the courtyard, with workers on each side to sort the different types of fruits from large bins brought in from the orchards. Some of the fruit was sorted for jams and jellies, with others packed for shipment to the East Coast by clipper ship. The rest of the jam was sold to the hotel, Phillip's store, and the other small shops in town.

Holding Belle's hand, Brett introduced her to his mother, who reached out and pulled her in for a hug.

"So you are the one that has finally caught my son's fancy.

We have waited for this day. Come, let me show you around our home. Please call me Isabella."

Belle admired her mid-length full flowing skirt showing her ankles, brightly colored in oranges and yellows with a matching top. She was not wearing petticoats and seemed so relaxed compared to the full-length skirt, petticoat, and bodice Belle was wearing.

Brett's mother was slender and seemed to have a perpetual smile. Belle could see in her eyes the same blue as the summer sky. Leading Belle by the hand, his mother took her into the sizeable old adobe home. Belle saw paintings of the orchards, embroidered wall hangings, family pictures on the mantle of a massive fireplace in the communal room, comfortable furniture, and tiled floors. Windows along the back wall gave a view of the orchards and brought the light into the large rooms. A large patio on the back of the house was complete with an outdoor cooking area, comfortable furniture, and a long table with chairs.

"During the warm days, we cook and eat outside. It gets hot here in the valley. The vines covering the patio are original grapevines to make the wine we drink with our dinners."

Leaning towards Brett, Belle whispered, "What a lovely home."

Hugging her, Brett said, "This is our family home. My grandparents built it, my parents added to it, and we will raise our children here someday. Our family has always been close. We take care of each other."

At that time, much loud laughing and talking occurred as several young people entered the patio.

"Uncle, we heard you were back. It's about time! You left us working while you took a vacation?" Patting Brett on the back, the young crowd smiled and looked at Belle. "You brought back a souvenir?"

Belle looked surprised and turned to Brett as he laughed and told them to behave.

Belle met Brett's sisters and their children on the patio, each working on some part of the meal. Brett's mother and sisters prepared lamb kebobs, mint dressing, orange cream pie, along with roasted potatoes, creamed corn, beef stew, and a platter of fresh fruit. Wine from the patio grapes completed the dinner. Belle knew she had much to learn living in California, as she noticed the lemon slices in her drinking water. A peace fell around her as she watched the happy family interact with each other. *This family would not understand the loneliness of an only child living with a maiden aunt. Life should always be like this.*

Watching the playful laughter among the family as they joked with each other, all while working, Belle realized this was the kind of life she wanted in her future. The children joined them after playing lawn tennis or a new game of marbles. This family understood the value of friendship. She felt accepted by them and warm inside.

Later as they sat on the patio, they discussed their futures. Belle told Brett about her plans for the shop, and Brett told her about the farm. As she watched him talk, she noticed how strong he felt about the orchards and the harvesting, and the importance of teaching his family the skills needed to run the orchard.

"Look at Juan over there," as he pointed to a tall young man leaning against a lemon tree. "He has just started learning how to manage the trees and how important it is to be in the orchards every day. Someday he will have his own orchards to run and be able to take care of himself and his family."

Watching Brett talk made her smile inside. *He was so much more than she had thought when she first met him.* Brett discussed his plans to manage the farm and still be a lawman. On the way back to town, as she leaned comfortably on his shoulder, the horses' quiet clopping gave her peace she had not had for a long time.

# CHAPTER 24

Weeks passed, with Belle being busy in the store and Brett upholding the law as marshal. Settling into a daily routine, both Belle and Mary were surprised at the amount of business they had. Busily trying to keep up with their orders, they didn't have much time for other pleasures. They spent the working hours talking with each other as they worked and building plans for the future. Brett came to town two or three times a week to see Belle. They often walked in the park, sometimes eating lunch. It was a quiet time in their lives for both of them.

One morning, she put away some new merchandise that came in on the stagecoach when she looked up and saw Tomas staring at her through the window. Approaching Tomas, she noticed Phillip behind the counter, watching her.

"Can I help you?" she asked as Tomas stood at the door.

"What are you doing in there?" Tomas demanded.

Marching to her, he grabbed her arm and twisted her around to face him.

"I came to get you when I heard you were working here. You don't belong here. You were meant to be a wife, a mother. Stop wasting your time working in a store. I offered you marriage. You should be at my place taking care of my children instead of wasting your time here. You working here is not what I planned," he said wildly. "I will not let my future wife demean herself like this!"

Belled looked at him, shocked. Trying to move away from him, Belle kept talking, trying to distract him as he held tight to her arm.

"Tomas, whatever do you mean? I told you before I have no intention of even considering marriage with you. Are you crazy? What children? I don't remember you saying anything about children. I do not even know how to answer you. Why do you think you can march in here and demand that I take care of your children when this is the first time I have heard about them? Let go of my arm. As I told you before, we have no commitments. I will not come with you."

She jerked her arm away from him.

"I decided you were not a man I would be interested in at the dance back home. I am appalled at your behavior. You need to leave at once. Leave me alone. Don't bother me!"

Angry, with tears overflowing, she jerked her arm out of his reach as he tried to grab at her again and go through the door. He grabbed her from behind and tried to pick her up, but she kicked him in the shins and ran towards the living quarters' stairs. As he rushed to grab her again, he suddenly stopped as he saw Phillip had a rifle aimed towards him.

"Don't interfere in this, Phillip. Stay clear. This matter is none of your business. This is between us, a lovers' quarrel. Don't get involved."

Phillip stepped from behind the counter with the gun still on him.

"The lady made her point. She does not want to go with you. I have heard her twice in different conversations say she does not want anything to do with you. The term 'lovers' quarrel' does not fit here. My advice is to move on and forget about her."

Lowering his hands away from his hips, Tomas kept moving slowly towards Belle. She turned and ran towards the stairs. Tomas was too quick and was able to grab her leg and pull her off balance. What he didn't see was Mary coming up behind him with a pan. She stood her ground and walloped him on the left cheek with the pan. He turned and grabbed the pan away from her without letting Belle loose. Backing up, Mary heard Belle cry out.

"Don't get hurt over me!"

By that time, Phillip placed his rifle between Tomas's shoulders. Tomas stopped, letting go of Belle, and turned slowly with his fists still curled.

"Ok, you win this time," Tomas said. "I will be back to get you, Belle. I don't ask just anyone to marry me and then let them run away."

With that, he turned and left the store. Belle ran to the window and watched him get in his buggy and drive off.

Belle turned to Phillip and Mary.

"What can I do? How do I convince him that I will never marry someone like him?" She burst into tears. "I am so sorry I involved you in this mess."

Mary rushed and enveloped her into her arms, tenderly wiping the hair from her eyes.

"Belle, believe me, we will stand by you no matter what happens. It is a good thing Brett wasn't here. Tomas would be crawling back to his kids. Speaking of kids, what did he mean, kids? Did he tell you that he had kids? What is your relationship with that man? I was with you most of the time at that dance. How could he think you have committed to him? Next time I will hit him harder. Maybe that will knock some sense into him."

Wiping her tears, Belle sat on the seat by the window. She put her head in her hands.

"He never once mentioned kids. We've never been alone long enough to discuss anything personal. He's dreaming up a lot of stuff that never happened. I apologize for all this happening here in the store. Thank goodness there were no customers."

Mary helped her stand.

"Belle, why don't you go upstairs and wash your face, maybe take a little rest. We will put our heads together and think of what to do."

Phillip spoke with Mary quietly, alone. Since he had arrived and opened the store, he had heard several stories about Tomas and had a couple of run-ins with him in the saloon. To him, it seemed like Tomas was known to have a reputation for hurting women. He would keep a lookout for Tomas and talk to him when he saw him again. Meanwhile, it would be a good idea if Belle always had someone with her.

"I think it could be dangerous for her if he caught her alone."

The days following the incident went slowly for Belle. She was always watching out of the corner of her eye, waiting for Tomas to pull something else. Gradually she relaxed, and she started working hard on her hat inventory, and things started returning to normal. Belle continued to watch the women in town, especially the ones that went shopping in San Francisco. The townswomen were buying her hats and often came back for advice whenever they wanted to match something they had purchased or something in their closets. Phillip ordered supplies for her, and she spent her evenings happily making hats, bonnets, and gloves. However, she was cautious. She never went shopping alone as she had before. At times, the cloud of Tomas's threats bothered her, but she shook off the thought. *I will not let him know how it shakes me.* Nevertheless, she thought it best not to tell Brett about the problems with Tomas.

Phillip did not feel the same way about the incident. Walking to the marshal's office, he sat down to discuss the problem with Brett. After telling him about the incident and how rough he was with Belle, Phillip watched the slow flush rise in Brett's neck, his eyes narrowed, and he took a deep breath.

"Listen, Brett, before you do something rash, let's talk about it. Belle likes to feel like she is in control, but I don't think that's the case here. This Tomas feller is not acting rationally. I am not sure what happened when he and Belle first met, but for some reason, he thinks he has the right to coerce her into marriage. He's somewhat loco. You can see it in his eyes when he looks at Belle."

"I saw it too in the restaurant when we first arrived in San Francisco. But how can I protect her? She won't even tell me when he comes around. She thinks she can handle it." Sitting down at his desk, he looked towards the ceiling. "I don't want her ever to be left alone where he can get to her. How do we do that without her figuring out what we are doing?"

"Brett, we won't discuss it. We'll just do it. Tomas is bad news, and he is getting worse. I'll include Mary into the plan. The way he looked at her when she hit him with that pan was like he would hurt her too. I can't let that happen. It is going too far. We will have to do this ourselves."

With those words, Phillip rose from his chair, shook Brett's hand, and left. For a long time, Brett sat thinking, trying to work out a protection plan other than just being with her. For her own sake.

# CHAPTER 25

In the evenings, Mary enjoyed sitting at the worktable after dinner sewing and making dresses as samples for her customers. Belle would join her when she did not spend time with Brett. Phillip often sat at a smaller table working on store books. One evening, smiling, he watched the two girls chatting and working. Closing his ledgers, he walked over to them.

"Well, ladies, I have some good news. Your little business has taken off money-wise, and I have decided to expand your corner."

Watching the excitement, both girls jumped up to hug him.

"When?" both girls asked in unison.

Laughing, he sat down at their table with a blank sheet of paper.

"Let's do some planning. I think we should start having the new building started in the next few days. I already talked to a contractor. He's ready to begin."

"First," Belle exclaimed, "we need to sit down and discuss the business side. How much will it cost, how much can we put into the design, and how can we pay you back for the store and setup?"

"Ah, my Belle, always the businesswoman. Phillip, Belle, is right. We need to make this business our business," remarked Mary.

Sitting down, they wrote up a business contract between the three of them, making Mary and Belle the new store owners. Phillip agreed to delay the payments for the new store for six months to get them started, and to pay him a set amount monthly for their part.

The days flew by as the new store took shape. The actual construction of the building went quickly over a couple of months. The walls, painted a light green to match the rest of the interior of the main store, impressed Belle. Mary collected dresses, dry goods, fancy trims, and threads. There was shelving along two walls to showcase Belle's hats and glass cases to house the more expensive trims and jewelry needed to accessorize the merchandise. Two tables were set up in the back of the store to talk with customers about special orders plus a curtained area for the customers to try on the goods in private. There were mirrors throughout the shop. On one side of the store were display racks for the dresses and coats. At one point, Mary looked around, deciding that it looked bare.

"Belle, we need to work harder. Our supplies look meager in the larger space."

"Mary, it's not a contest. Relax. I swear you are worse than I am."

"I know, Belle," she laughed. "I am just so excited."

Phillip arranged large windows in the front with areas in the window to show the latest designs. He had mannequins brought from San Francisco to showcase Mary's dresses. To make the store more accessible, he put two large glass doors between the two stores so that the customers could enter either through his store or from the street into their store.

One evening, looking around the store, Mary and Belle were amazed at the appearance of their new space.

"What do you think? Are we ready?"

Mary turned and looked around. There were dresses on display with matching hats and gloves, even shoe decorations on some of them. As they admired what they had done, Belle smiled with delight.

"I think we are ready. However, we have been selling all along. Won't it seem funny to have a grand opening?"

Laughing, Phillip looked at the happy woman. *Who would have guessed the joy these two girls managed to have with materials, ribbons, and lace? Definitely not a man's world.* Smiling, he showed the posters that he secretly had made. A local artist had drawn a lady with one of their creations pointing towards their store, directing the public to the new business located next to the General Store. Both women were thrilled and could hardly wait to place them around town.

After several tries, they designed their advertisement for the local newspaper. They paid the fee to have it printed in the paper's next issue.

### GRAND OPENING:
#### The Two Sisters
A shop for women is now open for business.

Next door to the General Store on Elk Street.

Custom dresses, bonnets, and women's accessories.

The big day was the placing of the shop sign outside the new building. The sign was painted a dark green with white lettering to match the molding around the store's windows. Phillip had the sign maker paint pale pink roses along the border with two fancy ladies on the left-hand side. One of the ladies had blonde hair and the other red curly hair. Mary ran to him and clasped her arms around his neck in thanks, with Belle close behind her to hug him.

"Whoa, ladies," he said happily. "What if the customers saw me hugging the two prettiest girls in town?"

At that moment, two ladies walked into the store. Turning as they looked around at the merchandise, they saw the doors leading into the new store.

"What a nice idea. What do you have there?" They turned to walk to the area, turning slightly back to Phillip. "I see that your new lovely wife has ideas of her own in running the store. Good job."

Over the next few weeks, the ladies' corner had developed an excellent clientele as the women in town discovered their enterprise. The store business increased as ladies' husbands followed their wives into the store. As ladies went directly to the women's section, the men looked around and found things they needed.

Often as they worked quietly together, Belle continued to see the strong connection between Mary and Phillip. They were always kind to each other and they could not help from touching one another or holding hands when close. They shared little smiles often. She couldn't help but to think about Brett. *When we walk, he is always holding my arm or hand. At first, I thought he was a little forward, but now I feel the warmth of his protection. I am so lucky to have a man in my life that respects me and my wants. Someday, I will have what Mary and Phillip have, or maybe I already have it.*

Often, in the early evenings after visiting the ranch, Brett would come to town. They would sit on the porch outside the store, share their daily activities, and talk about the future. Sometimes he joined them in their work corner as Phillip and he spoke about their businesses. To top off the fun evening, tea and desserts were served. Belle had a warm feeling as she watched her friends share their lives. She had not told Brett about the incident with Tomas, hoping it would fade away, and that Tomas had accepted that she would not be his wife.

One evening, Brett was telling them about something that had happened in town. He did not notice the cloud over Belle's eyes as she suddenly thought about Tomas. Clasping her hands in her lap, she caught Brett's attention.

"What's wrong, Belle? Is there something I should know?"

Phillip came and stood, listening and watching as Belle told her story. He could see Brett becoming angry.

"I knew I should have taken care of him a long time ago. He cannot expect to be able to treat you like he owned you. Why didn't you tell me? I should have been here to protect you. You have to trust me, Belle, and tell me these things."

"Listening to you talk about your work, it just came to me. I worry about another confrontation with Tomas, and I cannot handle it the next time. Thank goodness Phillip and Mary were there when it happened. I am so happy now with the store, the business, our relationship, but there is always the dark cloud of Tomas hanging over me."

Looking down at the floor, Brett could see the worry on her face.

"Trust me, Belle, all of this will work out."

# CHAPTER 26

As the business grew and the customers started regularly coming, Mary designed a new wedding dress to meet her customers' demands. It consisted of a "Sunday Best Dress" created with a detached lace and net overlay pinafore. Since most women could not afford to buy a "special onetime wear" dress, this became popular. For each dress Mary made, Belle designed a matching hat with a detachable veil. These outfits were not only practical but popular. Before Mary and Belle set up shop, the ladies traveled to San Francisco for unique dresses. But now, after seeing their designs and the quality, they preferred to shop with Belle and Mary. They saved enough money on the trips to buy accessories to match.

Phillip was proud of Mary and Belle.

One day he said teasingly, "I am so lucky. When marrying Mary, I got two for one. Now that's a bargain!"

When he said it, they all laughed. The girls then asked for raises, so he stopped saying that phrase and just smiled a lot. However, when calculating his books, he was amazed at the store's profits since the women started assisting him. They were off to a good start.

Mary received letters from Aunt Della and Sally regularly. One particular letter told her that her stepbrothers were in jail for robbing a bank. Mary was not surprised. She wrote the solicitor of her estate in Maryville to stop the stipend to her stepbrothers and increase the monies to Aunt Della and Sally. *I want to set up a trust to be paid monthly for her lifetime.* The rest of Della and Sally's properties that were not lived in were to be sold and put into a trust. At this time in her life, Mary was happier than she had ever dreamed. Every time she looked at Phillip, a warm caress surrounded her, causing her to smile at her good fortune.

Brett hired several deputies to assist him in town. They divided the city into sections and rode their horses to patrol. As the town grew, Brett hired new deputies. The crime in Sacramento had decreased significantly. The Civil War became the most potent issue of the day. Many young men left their families to go back east to fight. Families and friends were separated and divided when taking sides. California's war efforts consisted of sending gold east to support the war effort, causing a new problem. Outlaws often tried to rob the special envoys of the gold, causing many deaths. In 1861, secessionists tried to separate California and Oregon from the United States but were defeated. Thus, California remained a state. Even the Pony Express had to worry about being either shot or robbed as they raced across the prairie. Most of them started traveling by night rather than chance traveling during the day.

The clipper ships often had to run through gauntlets of both Union and Confederate ships to get supplies to the western states. Letters from the East, full of news of the war, often carried sad news of lost family members. The Union viewed California as a vital asset because of its gold. However, few battles occurred because of the isolation of California from the rest of the country. Many of the struggling miners who had families back east, were leaving to go back to the South or North to fight as volunteers.

Entering the store, Brett saw Phillip helping a customer. As the customer left, Phillip poured Brett a cup of coffee.

"You look awfully down partner, what's going on?"

Sitting on the bench near the counter, Brett sipped his coffee.

"Just lost three more men to this war thing. It's getting worse. Sometimes I think we are losing more men than came out here initially. I just spoke to Henry over at the saloon. He's having problems keeping help. He lost the piano player last night. The Army has recruited about forty men to leave tomorrow for the trip back east. I heard part of the secessionist group down by San Francisco left by clipper ship to go back to fight for the Confederate group. Hope the businesses around here don't suffer."

Leaning across the counter, Phillip agreed.

"I think my part of the business is down twenty percent since the war started."

He pointed towards Mary and Belle busy sewing in their section of the store.

"However, the women are doing good. They more than made up for my losses. If I don't go over there once in a while, they wouldn't even know I was around."

Laughing, Brett agreed with Phillip.

"That's why I came in this morning to see Belle. We are two lucky guys."

Brett and Phillip walked towards the women working on a pale-yellow wedding dress with a cream-colored lace overlay. Belle smiled as she saw them, holding up a pale-yellow hat with pink and red roses around the band.

"I see you are just in time. Mary and I decided to take a break and go to the hotel for lunch. Would you like to join us?"

She winked shyly at Brett. Phillip searched under the counter and walked to the front of the store, then holding up a sign:

*Gone to lunch, be back by* ____

He penciled in the time.

"Let's go."

~

Tomas felt the same problems as the store owners in town. Looking over his fields, he saw his brother picking tomatoes to take to the hotel later.

"Bill, our sales are down with the miners since those fools seem to think they should go fight this war. We need to focus on stores and hotels. How can we package this stuff that would appeal to them better?"

Tomas scratched his head.

Bill, aware of the wasting produce, sat down across from Tomas and offered his suggestions.

"Maybe we should open a market in town for the towns-people. Sara could run it while we work the farm. Her mother could take care of the kids."

Tomas thought carefully, "Bill, you know how I feel about this kind of stuff. Your wife has kids and needs to stay at home to take care of them and us. She has her hands full, besides we need her to help us in the gardens. I'm not going to pay for people to work out there. It is our job, not for strangers. I made an allowance for those two hired hands, but I'm not sure we could make enough to cover the pay we would have to put out to replace Sara. Her mom's not well enough to watch the kids."

He thought about Belle. *That fool woman should be here earning her keep and taking care of the chores. She's all high-and-mighty now that she is with Phillip and Mary. I will make sure she learns her place.* Tomas sat on the porch and reviewed his books and tried to work out a plan. He often brought produce to sell in town but never approached Phillip's store. Belle saw him several times but avoided him and returned to the store as quickly as possible. He had changed. Tomas was sullen and angry most of the time. He could not control his need for alcohol and would frequent the saloons often.

There were times when Tomas would watch Belle through the windows of the store as she worked. Carefully ensuring that she did not see him, he contemplated what he would do about his perceived relationship. As he sat on the bench outside the store, Belle suddenly looked straight at him. She reached under the counter to ensure that her pistol was on the shelf and turned to Phillip.

"Tomas is outside."

As Phillip opened the door to the store, Tomas stood up.

"Is there something I can do for you?" Phillip asked, directly looking both ways up and down the sidewalk. As chance would have it, Brett was walking towards them with one of his deputies.

Pushing Phillip aside, he walked towards Belle.

"I see you have your little protection group around you. I want us to talk. Let's go outside."

"Tomas, I have tried to get you to understand. I do not want anything to do with you. Please accept it and leave me alone."

Belle stood close to the counter, with her hands on her hips. Coming closer, he saw she meant business. He tried to grab her hand, but she pulled back. Tomas backed up and looked at her trying to think of something that would convince Belle to see his point of view.

"I know things are not right with us. I don't know what I did. Could we at least try to figure it out so I can correct the problems? I had great plans for us."

Brett entered the store but stood back, watching.

Looking into Tomas's eyes, Belle saw the truth in what he was saying. He didn't know what he had done to turn her away from him.

"Tomas, no woman wants a man to mistreat her or to think of her like property. There is nothing you can do to change your behavior towards me. I am not in love with you, nor could I love you. When I first met you, I made it clear that there would be no 'me and you.' I want a different life. It would be much easier if you would accept that and find someone else to fit into your life. It just can't be me."

"You've found someone else. That's the whole problem. Who is this coward? I will teach him a lesson."

"You have to listen to me, Tomas. It doesn't matter whether I have found someone else or not. It just won't be you. We both have to live here. I can't be afraid of you. I plan to be here a long time without you in my life."

"I had plans for us," said Tomas as he looked around the store. "Now you are saying you are not interested. I don't care what you think. The minute I saw you, I knew I would marry you and have many children. You cannot stand there and tell me you are not interested. I see you looking at me whenever I am around. You are just trying to raise the stakes. This business stuff is not for women. You need to be in a home, taking care of me."

Belle, holding her ground, slowly moved the pistol closer to her body.

"You need to accept what I told you. I am sure you can find someone else. Just be honest with whomever you choose and treat that person well. It doesn't take much to make a woman happy. Right now, you need to leave and to leave me alone. Can you understand that? I'm trying to be honest with you."

Turning, Tomas saw the audience behind him. Noting the marshal standing beside Phillip, he put his hat on his head and stomped out of the building. As she laid the pistol back under the shelf, Brett walked towards Belle and held her in his arms, trying to soothe her trembling.

"I hope he understands. However, you can't blame yourself for his problems. It's time you live your life for yourself. When you are ready, I am here."

Mary and Phillip went outside to leave them alone.

"The reason I was on my way here was to tell you there is a couple here to see you, Mr. and Mrs. Campbell. I was coming out of the office when they stopped me. I think they are from the East. Do you know them? They are at the hotel and want you to meet them there for dinner. I told them I would carry the message."

Turning her head away from Brett, she slowly dried her tears.

"I don't think I know anyone by that name. Are you sure they were asking for me? Would you go with me? I am tired and emotionally drained. Figure out a way for us to leave early. If they have traveled from back east, it would be rude for me to turn them down."

Tipping his hat, "I will be glad to be the escort for a lovely lady. I will call for you tonight at six thirty."

Across the street, Tomas sat on a bench and watched them through the window. At first, angry feelings overwhelmed him. *What a fool I've been. It's been that lawman the whole time. He won't get away with it. All that talk about my actions and my behavior. When all along, she's been playing a game behind my back.* Standing, Tomas checked his gun and put it back into the holster. Then he checked the pistol he had hid in his belt under his shirt. Satisfied that everything was okay, he quietly strolled towards the saloon. *Belle played me for a fool. We will see who wins this game. She will be sorry.*

As Belle dressed for dinner at the hotel, Mary came up to her room to say good night. Seeing Belle dressed in one of her latest designs, she placed her finger near her chin and grinned.

"Going out with Brett tonight? You look nice."

"Brett said a couple from back east was at the hotel, some relative or friend. I'm not sure but he wants me to meet them for dinner. I wasn't sure I wanted to go, but now that I have on this dress of yours, it is heavenly. I love it."

She twirled with the fullness of the skirt billowing with its lace stripes on the bodice, then settling down into soft ruffles.

"Whoever it is will not know you, Belle. You have changed so much since I have known you. Remember when we first met? You were so sad about losing your mother. So often I saw you dressed in pants, trailing after your brother. Before we came here, you were so sure that you could pass for a boy. Learning to walk like a guy was a picture I will have in my head forever. Look at you now. A princess straight from a storybook."

Mary, lightly fluffing out the skirt, stood back and looked at her approvingly.

"What I would like is to go to bed. When will that Tomas get the message and leave me alone? But it doesn't matter, and I will not change my mind. This dress is beautiful."

Belle twirled a little to show off the fit of the dress.

"Good job, Mary."

The dress was a light shade of apricot, with tiny yellow daisies embroidered around the edge of the bodice. It fit tight at the waist but gave room to breathe in the bodice. It had a matching lighter shade jacket. With Belle's red hair, it was a good color for her.

As Belle and Mary descended the stairs, Brett was at a loss for words. Belle was beautiful. Breathtakingly beautiful. He hadn't noticed her hair had grown out, shining like a copper penny. As her hair fell loose around her shoulders, the light hitting it so perfectly, she didn't look real. Saying good night to Mary, Brett led Belle out of the store for the short walk to the hotel. They did not see Tomas watching them. He frowned when he saw how Belle looked, and then followed them as they headed to the hotel.

# CHAPTER 27

There was a soft glow of lights coming from the windows of the hotel. Guests conversed with each other in a gentle murmur at the tables filling the room. The tables were lit with candles and were decorated with small vases of pink roses. The glow of the candles on the ivory-colored table-cloths gave a festive feel to the room. As Belle and Brett waited to be seated, she was suddenly surprised and shocked to see her aunt enter the room. Running to hug Aunt Hester, Belle felt the tears of joy running down her face.

"Aunt Hester, I never thought I would see you again! You look different."

The gentleman with Hester had his arm around her waist, beaming with happiness. He let go as Belle threw herself into Hester's arms. Holding her for several minutes, she looked up to see her aunt smiling.

"Belle, I was afraid we would never find you. Shame on you for worrying me like that." Turning to the man beside her, Belle saw a look on Hester's face she had never seen before. "This is my husband. We were married several months ago, and it was the wisest decision I ever made. Meet Harry Campbell."

It was Belle's turn to be shocked again.

"Your husband, Aunt Hester?" Turning, Belle exclaimed, "You must be something extraordinary to talk Aunt Hester into marrying."

They laughed over the good tidings, and Belle hugged them again.

As she turned to Brett, she smiled and introduced him.

"Aunt Harriet, now I guess you are Uncle Harry? This is Brett Sanders. He is Mary's cousin and a good friend."

After shaking hands, the waiter came to tell them their table was ready.

As they sat down and ordered dinner, Belle wanted to know the whole story.

"Not so fast, young lady, your story first. Why would you leave without seeing me first, without a goodbye? My goodness I had to threaten Della with bodily harm before she finally gave in and told me the story. What were you thinking? You worried me to death."

Belle looked ashamed.

"I didn't even think you would worry. I always seemed to be in the way. I just wanted to find a way to California to find Jeremy, and most of all, I wanted to have an independent life. I did not want to marry anyone back home. They were so, well, young. Every time I looked up, there was someone else to consider as a prospective husband. Aunt Hester, so far, I haven't found a trace of Jeremy. In your letter, you said he was living in Paradise. Brett has been putting out messages trying to find Jeremy, but he seems to have disappeared after getting out here. Oh, sorry, I forgot my manners. Brett is the marshal of Sacramento. He also was the escort and protector for Mary and me on the trip."

Shaking his hand over the table, Aunt Hester looked at him with a critical eye.

"You are the man who fell into this young lady's crazy scheme? We need to have a long, serious talk."

Hester gave him her best look of intimidation.

"No, ma'am, you have the wrong story. I met Belle and Mary on the way to California. I just try to stay out of her way and support her through her messes."

Brett winked and settled back in the chair with a look of mischievousness. Belle looked at him with daggers. Hester winked at him, agreeing.

"Maybe it would be better if I tell my story first," said Hester quietly. "Your new uncle, Harry, is the attorney for your trust. Did I tell you about the trust? It was being saved for when you get married. When you left, I panicked. I contacted him so he could help me find you—what a crazy idea. Of course, I wanted you. No matter how many problems you caused, I will always love you. You were just like your mother. Still thinking up schemes, always doing things you shouldn't have. Not that you were a spoiled child, just a busy one. We checked all the stagecoaches, the wagon trains, every way we could think of you leaving. I almost caught you in Baton Rouge, but your stage-coach left just before I got there, and the next stagecoach didn't leave until the following day. I thought you might be trying to catch a ride in the wagon train, but I never thought of a clipper ship. We thought of that after your clipper ship had sailed. Spending all that time together, chasing you, Harry and I discovered we liked each other, and after a time, it grew into love. When I received your letters from San Francisco and Sacramento, Harry thought we should come as soon as possible. So here we are. We have a lot to tell you, but that can wait until tomorrow. So tell me again about this handsome man."

She winked at Belle.

Brett shifted his weight in his chair, waiting to hear how Belle told this story.

"Aunt Hester, you are so right about me. Being so naïve, I thought nothing about what I was doing. I was wrong to use someone to find Jeremy. I still haven't found him, but I found the man I can never leave. I discovered that life is not about parties, fine clothes, and games. I am so lucky to have work that I love and a way to take care of myself."

Hester looked at her worriedly. She saw a new level of adultness and concern that had never been on her niece's face before.

"My dear," spoke Harry, "tell me about the work you are doing that allows you to save money and support yourself all this time."

"Aunt Hester, I have you to thank for giving me a way to make money," started Belle.

Hester raised an eyebrow and looked back at Harry.

"Yes, I opened a millinery section of Mary and Phillip's store. Mary, who you know well, got married and I was her maid of honor at her wedding to Phillip. I work in the mornings with Phillip in his store, then in the afternoons, I make and sell my bonnets. They rent me a small apartment above the store where I live. Of course, the hats are nothing like yours, but I have been able to sell a lot."

"So little Mary married the love of her life after all. I always thought she was too young to say she was in love with Phillip, especially since she was a toddler." Hester sat remembering how interested Belle was in her hats and the time Belle spent working with her, she coughed and then smiled back at Belle. "I would like to see what you are doing. Can I come by tomorrow morning? But first, I need to tell you about Jeremy. You missed him. A few weeks after you left, Jeremy came home. He also brought his new wife, who is expecting, or should have had a child by now. Jeremy was so upset that you had left looking for him. He knows if anything happened to you, he would be the one to blame. Belle, Jeremy has changed. He is no longer the brother you remember. Getting married gave him stability. With the rest of his inheritance, he bought a small farm and made a home for his wife. Her name is Anabelle. He sent you this letter."

As Belle read the letter, she realized her plan had not been the wisest. But would she have changed her life if she could do it over? Not a chance. She liked her life now, her friends, and most of all the love of her life, Brett. Relief showed on her face as she realized her brother was safe and secure.

*Dear Belle,*

*I am sorry I missed you. I must have been halfway home when you left to find me. I have had the most wonderful adventures since I left home, and you were always in my mind. I wish you could have been with me to share them. When I left, you were just a baby. I understand you are all grown up and decided to have your own adventures. I hope you are safe and that you come home soon. I would like my wife to meet you. The next time you see me, I will be a father. I bought Mary's old farm and plan to raise horses and cattle, along with farming. Sally, Mary's nanny, agreed to help us with the baby for the first year, then she said we should have it under control. I miss you, little girl, and I hope you are having a wonderful new life.*

*Your brother, Jeremy*

As they ate, they each told their stories of the last year. It was evident to both Belle and Hester that the circumstances of both women had changed. Watching Hester look at her husband while he spoke, the little jesters between them, holding hands under the table, made Belle feel she had misjudged her aunt all those years. Hester, watching Belle, saw how the little girl she had watched grow over the years was now a grown-up woman. Belle spoke with confidence and assurance about her life.

Tomas leaned against a pole outside the hotel window, watching Belle talking animatedly with the strange couple at the table. He didn't like the marshal sitting with them, but he noticed the marshal was not participating in the conversation. Feeling inside his shirt to assure himself that his gun was in place, Tomas became more hostile as he watched them. He lit a cigarette and continued to try to figure out who these people were and why Belle was so friendly with them. Finally, the alcohol started to wear off. He just felt tired and angry. He kicked the pole and, after several tries, mounted his horse to go home. All the way, he thought of how he could force Belle to marry him.

On the way back to her apartment above the store, Belle felt content and happy. Brett held her hand like it was the most natural thing they should do when walking. As they returned to the store, the lights were out in the back. When stepping inside the store to say good night, he enveloped her in his arms and kissed her gently. As he held her, his caress awakened the senses in her body as she moved passionately towards him. Running her fingers through his hair, she responded to his kisses with a need of her own. Pulling her closer than she ever had been held, Brett started nibbling on her neck, her cheek. As Belle felt the heat rising in her, Brett began to kiss her passionately, as she let out a small moan. As Brett felt her breast tighten through his shirt and heard her little whimpers, suddenly, he stopped.

"What's wrong, Brett? Have I done something wrong?"

"No, I want this badly, but I wanted you to think about what we are doing. Is this what you want? There is no turning back if I continue."

"Brett, I have been in love with you for ages. I want you. I want all of you. Please don't stop. I can't explain how I feel when you touch me, it's like an all-consuming fire within me whenever you are near. I was honest with Aunt Hester. I found a man I could never leave." Kissing little kisses on his cheek, "that someone is you."

Kissing her gently on her forehead, he picked her up with her skirts dragging the floor, carrying her quietly up the stairs. He kissed her cheeks, nose, and lips, gently causing a rising fire within her. Opening the door to her bedroom, he laid her gently on the bed. She sat up as he undid the buttons of her dress. She slid the skirt to the floor, laying it on the chair. As she removed her chemise, he saw the creaminess of her skin, the slight pout of her lips—the consuming fire in her eyes. Struggling to get out of his trousers, he almost slipped on the floor, uttering an oath. Belle started giggling.

"Here. Let me help you."

Seeing her green eyes bright with amusement, he stepped out of his pants.

Laying her gently back on the bed, he slowly slid his hands up her body and started kissing her passionately. The feel of Belle against his skin tortured him until he felt he would explode. She had never been kissed like this before, which stirred her emotions. The little secret kisses behind the school did not even turn on her imagination like this one did. This kiss begged her body for more, and her mind wanted to belong to the person that excited this emotion in her. Removing her bodice, Brett felt like time was in slow motion. Looking at the soft neck he loved, he bent to kiss the nape of her hair, removing the pins, letting the golden-red curls loose onto the pillow. *This is how it should be, with the woman you love.* As the heat rose between him, he felt he was on fire. Taking her face between his hands, he kissed her.

"Belle, I love you beyond belief. I never want us to be apart."

She cupped his head between her hands, vowing to herself

never to leave. It was a game of no return, yet the game of commitment and love.

She woke to the sun rising and shining its sunbeams across her face. She felt Brett's arms around her with his head laying across her chest. Caressing his head, she gently kissed the top of his forehead. *This is the man I love. Just looking at him, watching him sleep, fills my heart with such overwhelming feelings. How could I have ever thought I could leave him and marry another? I was crazy and foolish.*

With a gentle rap on the door, the door opened and Mary rushed in. Mary's eyes widened and she stopped suddenly, taking in the scene. A smile ran across her face.

"Oh my, I am so sorry," she said as she put her hands across her face and backed out the door.

Rising from a deep sleep, Brett rubbed his face and looked at Belle. Belle's face was red and her eyes wide with surprise. She pushed him aside to get out of bed. Opening the door, she rushed out in her gown as Mary reached the bottom of the staircase.

"Mary, please come back. I am sorry."

Mary turned around, looking at Belle's stricken face.

"Belle, it's me who should be sorry. When I told you it was time to get your life straight, at least you took my word. I was just surprised, that's all. I just wanted to tell you, someone named Hester is on her way to see you. Phillip ran into her when he went to the post office."

Mary turned and skipped lightheartedly down the stairs, smiling.

Belle turned abruptly around, passing Brett on the landing and pushing him out of the way for the second time in five minutes. He stood there in his bare feet, rubbing his head. He turned and looked at Mary.

"Better get moving. Your future in-laws are on their way!"

A horrified look passed over Brett's face making Mary

laugh even harder. Phillip came over to see what was happening. One look at Brett still standing on the landing with his shirttail hanging, no pants on, and his boots in his hands with a horrified look on his face, caused Phillip to join Mary in laughing. Brett turned and ran back to Belle's room.

Belle was in a state of panic. Tossing dresses from the closet, pulling petticoats from the drawer, she was busy trying to get dressed. Brett stood at the door, not knowing what to do.

"Put your clothes on and try to straighten up. Aunt Hester will be here any minute," Belle shouted as she danced around the room.

Brett decided the best idea was to run, escape, and get out of there as fast as possible. As Brett ran through the store, Phillip saw his stricken face and opened the door for him, tipped his hat as he ran by, then busted out laughing.

A few minutes later, Belle descended the stairs like nothing was wrong. Greeting Mary and Phillip, they would have thought it was like any other morning if they hadn't known different. Belle wore a light blue dress. It enhanced her red curly hair, making the highlights stand out as the light from the window caught it. Wearing her hair in a twist at the back with her best hairpins gave Belle's hair a prim and proper look. Grinning, both Mary and Phillip turned their heads and went back to work.

Taking the covers off the counters and the different hat showcases, she dusted the area and cleaned while she waited for Aunt Hester. As she laid out her workbench to start on the day's orders, she noticed her hands were shaking. *Oh my, I need to get a hold of myself. I do not want her to think I am still that little girl back in Missouri.* Taking deep breaths, she willed herself to take tiny bits of satin to make rosettes for the bridal order she was preparing. Moments later, she heard the chiming of the bells on the door, announcing her aunt.

Walking into the store, Hester and Harry took the time to survey the store. At times they picked up items, then laid them down. Belle, trying not to hover, greeted them and then stood back as they went around the store. As they reached Belle and Mary's doors leading into their store, Hester reached out to hug her.

"My dear child, this place is amazing. Introduce me to your friends. I hardly recognize them. California seems to have changed everyone."

Following introductions, Hester motioned Mary to sit with her in Belle's section of the store. Belle had a small round white table with matching chairs, which Belle and Mary often used to talk with their clients. Hester continued to look at the hats, and then she noticed a dress in the corner which was one of Mary's new designs.

"This is amazing. How did you ever think this up? This idea would have sold a fortune in Missouri," patting Mary's hand.

The dress was a long cream-colored dress with embroidered flowers around the edge of the collar. The bodice had small pleats, meeting just below the bustline, which billowed out with a slightly gathered skirt. Over the dress was a sheer lace pinafore. Each lace motif had a sprinkle of beads. Mary showed Hester how, when removing the pinafore, the dress could be a special occasion or church dress. Laying on the shelf beside the dress was a matching hat. The brim was wide enough to hold the veil away from the face. However, the hat perfectly matched the dress with tiny rosettes and embroidered flowers matching the dress color when removing the pinafore. There were also mid-length ivory gloves with the same embroidered flowers around the cuff just below the elbow.

Holding the hat above her head to see how it would look

in the mirror, Hester's face softened as she turned to Belle and Mary.

"I said it before, this idea, the creation, is just beautiful and so practical. We should market this to the larger stores in San Francisco."

Not knowing what to say, Belle and Mary looked at each other.

"Aunt Hester, we have just started. I think you are getting ahead of what we are ready to do. Maybe tentatively in the future."

Putting her arms around both girls, Hester hugged them and then sat down at the table. "Don't mind me, you know how I am around the business of hats. I am so proud of you girls." As Mary served tea with fresh cookies, Hester looked at her niece, marveling at the changes she saw.

"Belle, Harry, and I have been thinking and talking about you a lot over the past few days. We need to talk about your future, this is not the time or place, but we thought we would try dinner again, maybe in a more relaxed setting now that you have settled down." She turned towards Mary. "I want Mary, Phillip, and the marshal person to join us for dessert." She winked at Belle. "Would that be all right?"

Looking at each other in agreement, they watched Hester as she motioned to Harry. He had been conversing with Phillip, and saw that she was ready to leave. The look in Hester's eyes told them that waiting for Harry to come into her life was well worth the wait. Looking at the bridal dress one last time, Hester and Harry left the store.

# CHAPTER 28

Looking out over his fields, Tomas watched his brother and his brother's wife pick produce to sell to the market. Tomas leaned on the fence post he was repairing and frowned. Thoughts of Belle slowed his ability to work. When he first saw her at the dance, he knew Belle was something special. Not like the other trollops he usually chased. Belle was a beauty, a real looker, clever, and brilliant. He wanted her. He continued planning for their future life together. He pictured himself working in the gardens and her fixing his meals when he came home. When children came along, Tomas would give her some time off before returning to work. When that didn't work, he tried to plan how to force her to be with him. She proved to be stubborn. That was a fact. Now she seemed to be hanging out with the marshal and that couple who owned the store. He had to get her away from them so he could talk her into coming with him. If that didn't work, he would have to kidnap her. Tomas was convinced of his charms and knew once he took her away from Mary and Phillip's influence, she would know he was the right man for her. He smirked. *Belle doesn't know what a good man I can be to a woman.*

The other girls in his life? They are just playthings. He wasn't serious about them. After all, a guy has needs. Gathering up his tools, he rode his horse from the work fields to the house. His sister had made the cabin pleasant. He looked around the room. *Any woman would be proud to live here.* There were Indian blankets on the walls of the log cabin. He had bought an iron cooking stove, the best one on the market according to the salesman, so she wouldn't have to cook on an open fire. The fireplace needed cleaning, but Belle could do that when she was fixing his dinner. The bed was over by the far wall. Since it was just him and her, he figured they didn't need that much privacy. Looking around, he thought, *maybe I should buy her a sewing machine.* There were plenty of things that needed mending. Tomas walked over to the sink along the wall, picked up the bucket, and went outside to the well.

Looking around, ensuring no one was near, Tomas pulled a long rope hooked to the side of the well. As he pulled the cord out of the well, a waterproof bag opened, and money fell to the ground. Picking it up, Tomas stuffed some of it in his pocket and lowered the full bag back into the well. He figured he should buy some new clothes for their wedding. Carrying a bucket of water into the cabin, he looked at the missing step to the porch. Someday, I will fix that step. When we have children, I wouldn't want them to fall. The rest of the porch was sagging and missing boards in places. He was careful where he stepped so he wouldn't fall through. After shaving and putting on his best shirt, he went around the cabin to hitch his horse. Since he only had one horse, he cleaned the buggy and prepared it for the ride into town later that evening.

~

Brett stayed away for most of the day, but early in the afternoon, he built up enough courage to face Mary and Phillip. Opening the store's door, Phillip was stocking supplies and Mary and Belle were working on their designs. There were no customers in the store. When Belle saw him, she walked towards him, took him by the hand and shyly led him into their break room. As he kissed her, he told her he was sorry for embarrassing her in front of her friends.

"Are you serious? Do you think they care? They want us to be together."

Belle pulled him closer. Reassuring him, she laughed.

"Are you sure you want to get married? I think we need to do it soon before I become a woman totally out of control."

Laughing happily, he told her, "I was so afraid that I let my wants ruin my desire for long-term. I never want to let you go. When do you want to tell everyone? Could we get married at my home?"

Bending on one knee, Brett took her hand. Kissing her fingers softly, he brought a small box out of his pocket. Belle gave a little gasp as he slipped the ring on her finger.

"It was my grandmother's. She felt the emerald was the bringer of good luck. When she died, she gave it to me for my bride. Do you like it, or do you want me to buy a different one for you?"

Clasping her hand close to her, Belle held her finger up to the light. Tiny glints of emerald green bounced off the ring, enhanced with diamonds on the side of the stone. She turned to him with tears in her eyes.

"It is perfect, Brett. I will never want anything else."

He drew her close.

"Belle, this is forever. I will never step in your way to stop you from being you. I just want to be near you and enjoy life with you."

At that time, Mary and Phillip entered the room.

"Sorry, we heard it all."

Hugging both and laughing at the joy of the moment, Mary, at last saw the happiness in the eyes of her friend. Phillip pulled a bottle of wine from behind him. Mary held the glasses.

"Guess we need to celebrate!" she exclaimed as he poured the wine.

The glasses clinked as they toasted the future. The two couples spent time discussing the upcoming wedding.

"When should we start planning?" asked Mary as she turned towards Belle.

Brett quickly stated, "Tomorrow."

Both women turned in unison.

"No, we need time to plan," said Mary. "Next week will be fine since you are in such a hurry."

"It's not me, although I thought it would be me. My wonderful bride wants to hurry. Of course, I risk death if we married before I told my mother," declared Brett when he saw the look on Mary's face.

# CHAPTER 29

Walking towards the hotel that evening, Belle and Brett looked at each other as if they were holding a secret. Their hands were intertwined and happiness surrounded them like a beacon. As they approached the dining room, Hester and Harry both rose to greet them. Belle again noticed how different Aunt Hester was now than when she had left home. Hester no longer had the pinch around her eyes. She seemed relaxed and not as critical as before she left to come to California.

"I hope you don't mind, but we already ordered for all of us."

"Before you start with your news, Aunt Hester, I know that you have just arrived, but I have some wonderful news about us." Looking at Brett and still holding his hands for support, he gently squeezed them, letting her know he was there for her. "Over the past few months, a lot has happened. I have known Brett for almost a year, and every day with him around has been joyful." Remembering the heartache when she left him on the ship and thought she had lost him, she added hesitatingly, "Well, almost." She started rushing her words. "I'm happy with Brett. We want to get married and would like it if you and Harry would stay for the wedding."

"Oh my!" exclaimed Hester. "That was some preparation, Belle, but you always did have a problem with smoothing the path before you ran down it. I'm so happy for the both of you. All I have ever wanted is for you to have a happy life." She looked at Harry. "If Harry agrees, of course, we will stay for the wedding."

Looking at the ring and seeing the emerald with the diamond settings, Hester hugged Belle. Harry reached across the table to shake Brett's hand.

As they sat down, Harry beamed with happiness towards the couple.

"This news is excellent. I am so happy for both of you. However, there are some things that you need to be aware of. Belle, I need to talk with you about your finances." He looked at Brett. "Do you mind leaving us for a little while so we can discuss this with Belle? We need to talk about her money and how to handle it."

Looking confused, Belle exclaimed, "Finances? I am working, Harry. So far, I have been able to pay my way and even save a little. I am doing just fine." She looked at Brett. "Whatever you have to say should be said in front of Brett."

"Belle, you don't understand what I am trying to tell you," Harry continued. "You are in a position that you do not have to worry about money. Your mother left you a sizable inheritance that I have been managing for a long time." Belle's face showed disbelief as Harry started again. "When your father died, he left a large estate, which was divided into three parts. Your brother took his part and left. The other two-thirds of the estate, combined with your mother's money was left for your care until you turned twenty-one. The bulk of the estate is yours. We are talking about a large sum of money, investments, and stocks."

Holding onto the table, Belle let out a sigh. Hearing this news was not what she was expecting. Belle was expecting them to tell her they didn't want her to marry Brett and to move home. Did she want to change her life? She looked at Brett, seeing his strong jawline and brown eyes looking back at her questioningly. No, she has all that she needs. She turned back to Harry.

"Harry, I am sure there are things that I will need in the future, but for now, I want you to continue managing the money as you have before. Money is not an essential thing in my life. I have friends, a job that I like, and most of all, I have Brett. I need to have time to think about the money." She looked down at the paper that Harry handed her across the table. Suddenly, she gasped. "This is a huge amount of money. Now I really need to think."

Reaching across the table, Hester held Belle's hand.

"I should have prepared you and told you about it a long time ago, but I never planned on you growing up this quick, nor did I ever expect that you would run away. I always thought we had plenty of time. When you left, I notified Harry. He was so concerned about you. He came to Maryville the same week. The best thing for me was finding his love. I know that this is all a surprise for you and that we sprung it on you suddenly, but you have been springing a lot on us as well. Let's enjoy our dinner for now. I am sure that you will have many questions later."

"Harry, over the last year, I have learned what it means to have friends, real friends. I have worked for a living, and have focused on my life. That is all I needed in my life. Since I haven't known about the money before, I am unsure what I want to do. Right now, my life is on track. I love my life and my future to be, and of course, my family and friends. Isn't that what life is about?"

As they ate their dinner, Tomas stood outside the hotel

window watching the couples' happiness, not knowing what was happening or being said. Following dinner, Mary and Phillip joined them for dessert. Watching the newly arrived couple join in on the celebration infuriated Tomas as he continued to spy on them. *Looks like my plan will have to change a little.* Seeing them raise their glasses in a toast, he watched as Brett pulled Belle close to him and kissed her on the cheek. The rest of them hugged the happy couple. As the couples sat down, Tomas glared through the window. *I'm not sure what they are celebrating, but it will soon be over. The marshal is stepping over the line. He will have to learn a lesson about touching Belle.* As he saw them ready to leave, he slunk back into the shadows.

Mary, Phillip, Brett, and Belle started back to the store. Tomas was in the shadows close behind. Chattering happily, the girls were walking in front, with the men ambling behind. As they opened the door to the store, the sound of a pistol cocked, putting both men on alert. Moving them along, the men pushed the girls to the ground as the sound of a gun went off.

The bullet hit the post beside them. Brett pulled Belle towards him. He looked carefully, trying to decide where the gun had fired from. Then bullets sounded around them as they hit the building. As one hit Brett in the leg, he fell to the ground, moaning. Mary screamed. Lights went on up and down the street, with men running out the front doors. Brett dragged his leg and pushed Belle through the door as he tried to reach his pistol. Mary and Phillip reached out and pulled Brett through the door.

Tomas yelled through the door.

"Belle, come out, and I will not kill the others."

Mary had ripped Brett's trouser leg to see the wound.

"Phillip, carry him into the back. I will grab my sewing kit. Are you okay, Belle?"

Phillip looked at Belle worriedly. "I will be right back. Stay away from the door. I won't leave you alone." Phillip grabbed Brett under his arms and helped him to the back of the store.

Tomas, having reloaded, started shooting at the windows, moving closer to the store's door. Belle crept through the darkened store to her displays. Fumbling under the counter, Belle pulled out her gun, ensuring the weapon was loaded and hid it under her skirt.

"Tomas, is that you? What do you want? Why are you doing this?" Belle called out as she moved closer to the door, trying to delay his actions.

"Belle, I know that you love me. You are just using the marshal to make me jealous and pay me back for the other women. I want it to be the way I planned. I won't go back to the other women. Just come with me quietly, and we will forget all of this. You don't have to be jealous anymore. I only want you."

Slowly he entered the store. Then he saw her, standing quietly by her displays.

"Tomas, I have no intention of going anywhere with you. If you leave right now, then I will forget all of this." Still moving towards her, she saw the pistol in one hand and the rope in the other. "Tomas, I do not want anyone to get hurt. Please leave. We can talk more about this after you have calmed down."

"Belle, do you think you can talk me out of this? By rights, you are mine. I have worked all my life, and as a reward, I deserve to have you. Why are you fighting this? Come with me and I will see that you are not hurt."

With each movement, she watched him move closer and closer.

At that moment, Phillip came through the back door with his rifle. When Tomas turned to shoot him, Belle ran to the other side and started up the staircase. He took a shot at Phillip but missed as Phillip ducked behind the door. Tomas heard people outside the door.

"What is going on in there? Phillip, are you okay?"

Seeing the blood on the door frame leading into the store, several men came through the door. Seeing Tomas throwing a rope towards Belle on the staircase and seeing the gun in Tomas's hands, they stopped.

Belle pleaded with him as the rope dropped around her shoulders.

"Don't do this, Tomas. I do not want to go with you."

Tomas slowly climbed the stairs, reeling in the rope at the same time. Each step caused alarm for the men at the door.

"If any of you men shoot towards me, I will kill her, and I mean it." From a few steps away he said, "Belle, I am tired of all of this foolishness. Tell them to go away, that we argued, it's over, and that we are leaving."

Looking straight into his eyes, he saw she was not afraid, which puzzled him.

"Tomas, this is your last chance. Back away and leave."

"No, Belle, I have come for what is mine. This is the end of your little game. We both know that you love me and that we have this already settled."

Tightening the rope, he started to pull her towards him.

"Last chance, Tomas."

When he didn't give in and as he continued to pull her forward, she moved the gun from behind her skirts and pulled the trigger, feeling the recoil. A surprised look crossed his face as he fell, the rope tightened, pulling her down the stairs with him. When they landed at the bottom of the steps, he dropped the rope and the gun. As she moved off of him, his blood covered the front of her dress and she cried. Tears of frustration and anger caused her to start shaking.

241

"What have I done? I have just killed a man," she whispered.

Phillip ran to Belle. He saw that the blood was not hers, and he gently took the gun away from her. Phillip held her tightly.

"You are one helluva woman, Belle Stoval."

He saw the shocked look on her face and her shaking. Still holding the weapon, Phillip led her to the back room with Brett. Setting her on the bench near Brett, she dropped her head into her hands. Brett enclosed her into his arms, murmuring only words they could hear. Phillip ran back to the store's doorway, where several men had started moving Tomas's body out of the store. When they found out what happened, one of the men helped load Tomas's body in his buggy to be taken back to his farm. Another man ran for the doctor for Brett.

As the townsmen were carrying Tomas's body out, Hester and Harry ran into the store.

"We heard the shooting while we were walking. Is everyone all right?" Seeing the blood on the floor, Hester grabbed Phillip's arm. "Where's Belle?"

Belle, hearing her aunt's voice, rushed out of the room into her arms, tears rolling down her face.

"I'm fine, but Brett is hurt."

As Belle returned to the back room, she saw Brett lying on the floor with Mary putting bandages on his leg.

"Oh, Brett, I am so sorry this has happened."

"Don't fret, little one. I am going to be fine. But as usual, I never get to rescue you. Could you just once let me take care of it?"

Laughing, she held him tightly. "Next time, maybe."

# CHAPTER 30

As Belle and Mary sat by the window, they looked out over the fields of citrus trees. It was late spring, and the trees were in full blossom. As they heard the bees' faint buzzing, they breathed in the sweet fragrances of the lemon and orange trees. Even though lemon trees sometimes bloom four times a year, spring is the only time both the lemons and oranges bloom at the same time. Early that morning, Brett's sister and her children had cut some of the blossoms to put into a bouquet along with the mustard greens, early roses, and clover. Through the window, Belle could hear the merriment in the courtyard. The children were running and laughing, while the adults were talking quietly. *This would be the life she wanted. Family, happiness, and love all around her.*

Mary was putting small sprigs of rosemary and orange blossom in Belle's hair as she arranged it up off her neck. They had worked all week on her dress. It was pale blue silk with a matching ice-blue lace pinafore. Small orange and dark blue flowers edged the dress's collar, around the sleeve hem, and on her hat's silk brim. Hester designed the unique hat working many hours to have it ready on time. The ice-blue lace veil hung from the band of the hat, falling softly past her shoulders. Her bright hair peeked out at the edging of her hat, framing her face. Mary stood back holding Belle's hands.

"Believe me. You do not look like that scruffy boy that I first traveled with from Maryville. You are a vision."

Brett's mother came through the door with her bouquet, stopping to look at Belle.

"My son is a fortunate man." She hugged Belle and asked if she was ready to go.

As she reached the courtyard, Belle was amazed at the decorations. Small lanterns hung from a streamer across the covered patio. Brett's family, Hester, Harry, Mary, and Phillip smiled as she walked to the altar. Giggling, only Mary knew that Belle was wearing her brother's boots for the "something old." Brett was leaning on a cane, watching every step that she was taking. His heart felt like it had stopped, looking at her beauty. As Belle reached him, she took his arm.

Leaning into him, she whispered.

"This is the beginning of our ever after. I love you more than you will ever know."

Brett, unable to control his grin, answered, "Never shall we part, and my love is only yours. I love you, Belle."

As the minister began the ceremony, the past disappeared in Belle's mind as she looked to the future.

# ACKNOWLEDGMENTS

I want to thank my beta readers, Cindy McGary, Ruth Reese, and Brenda Parker; my developmental editor, Victoria Griffin; my cover artist, Charlene Raddon; and my copy editor, Rachel Santino.

# ABOUT THE AUTHOR

Jo Donahue was born in Vinita, Oklahoma, and spent a lot of time on her grandmother's farm in Afton, Oklahoma. Jo lived and attended schools in Tulsa. Her love of horses, cows, and camping led her to write after retiring from a registered nursing career. Early in life, Jo decided to become a Western cowgirl. She is living that dream through her writings about women in the Old West. I hope you enjoyed this book. There is more to come.

To be notified of upcoming projects, please subscribe at:

jodonahueauthor@gmail.com

https://gardengatereflection.com

*Thank you for reading my book. I've got a favor to ask. Authors always need reviews, and the best ones come from book lovers like you. Would you post a review on Amazon while the book is still fresh in your mind? It would mean a lot to me.*

# COMING SOON

Look for the first book in my Lady Pinkerton Agent series:

*Dolly Greene: Pinkerton Agent*

Dolly is an agent working with the famed Kate Warne. Having lost her father, she is hired for the famed Pinkerton Agency. Her first assignment leads her to the famed Dalton Gang and the Younger Brothers. Will she be able to solve the case of the missing money and how they hid their loot? Is the sheriff on to her disguise? Perry, another agent, is trying to beat her to solve the case. Will he beat Dolly and claim the reward himself? This book promises plenty of action, history, with romance thrown in.